COLOSSUS

D.F. JONES

A BERKLEY MEDALLION BOOK
published by
BERKLEY PUBLISHING CORPORATION

To NEVILLE RANDALL

Georges Borchardt, Inc.
145 E. 52nd Street
New York, N.Y. 10022

ISBN 425-04329-0

BERKLEY MEDALLION BOOKS are published by
Berkley Publishing Corporation
200 Madison Avenue
New York, N.Y. 10016

BERKLEY MEDALLION BOOK ® TM 757,375

Printed in the United States of America

Berkley Medallion Edition, September 1976
FIFTH PRINTING

CHAPTER 1

Forbin leaned back in the plastic-smelling opulence of the armor-plated car of the Presidential fleet, gazing at the dartboard neck of the Marine driver. The great moment was a bare five minutes away—the moment he had worked unremittingly toward for twelve hard years. Forbin knew it was not his work alone; nothing of this magnitude could be the achievement of one man, or even a hundred. It had been the collective effort of two or three thousand minds, backed by thousands of technicians. But—and it was a very large but—his had been the guiding brain, the one with the big overall concept, the vision. And that was the one that counted. Now the job was done and his moment of triumph was at hand, the moment beyond which he had never had the inclination—or time—to look. And all he felt was a sense of flatness and overwhelming tiredness.

Briefly he considered his future, but the idea of life without the Project lacked reality. He mused on reality; he had lived so long with his work that the outside world had grown unreal. What was real—all that back there, a thousand miles away? or all this, this man, the President? Was he reality, or just a simple dummy?

Forbin half smiled to himself. If the Secret Service man beside the driver could guess what his passenger was thinking, he would rate Forbin a bad security risk—and that could be a very unhealthy state of affairs if you happened to be scheduled to meet the President of the United States of North America in the near future. Since the Kennedy tragedy all those years ago the protection of the President had been, for his bodyguard, not so much a job as a religion. Forbin knew the life of a bodyguard; psychoanalysis and medical checks every three months, a closely observed private life, special schools, housing precincts, vacation centers—even separate chapels—and the whole setup guarded almost as closely as the President himself. No Presidential guard must have anything on his mind except the security of the President; if he had a problem he could not solve, whatever it was, it was his duty to report it to the Help agency, and they would deal with it. A guy prone to difficulties had no place beside the President.

Forbin knew that sort of life; his had not been so very different for the past ten years. But now—all this would be swept'away as a side effect of his work. He wondered, not for the first time, if even the President appreciated the difference the completed Project would make to his personal power and the stature of his office ...

The car slowed down, making its final careful approach to the White House entrance. The Secret Service man reached forward, switching on the radar responder, coded to give the correct signal for that particular time when they were invisibly challenged by the radar interrogator beamed down the drive. Given the right response the interrogator would automatically open the massive gates and allow the car through the first barrier that stood between the President and the man in the street. Forbin experienced a slight moment of anxiety before the gates swung swiftly open. From previous visits he knew that as soon as the car reached the gates, another pair had closed equally swiftly behind it. While he did not know what would happen if the wrong response were given, to be trapped between two gates with high stone walls on either side was like being in a giant birdcage, and potentially unpleasant.

The car silently rolled up the drive to a side entrance. Before the car stopped, the Secret Service man, with the ease born of long practice, was out, his door shut and his dog-tag pass flashed before the suspicious gaze of a colleague with whom he probably played pinochle every evening.

Forbin made no move to get out. He knew that until the guard established his identity the car door was locked. The spokesman of the two external guards grudgingly admitted it was OK to open up, and the car guard did so. Forbin got out, zipping his jacket under the hard, suspicious eyes of the guards. Inside, in the inspection room, Forbin was briskly searched by an impersonal, impassive guard with fingers like a concert pianist's. His briefcase, quickly x-rayed, was passed to his internal escort for safekeeping. Forbin's own dog tag was carefully checked, as if it might be a clever forgery, by a guard whom Forbin recognized from at least a dozen earlier meetings—not that that made the slightest difference.

Free at last, Forbin and escort set off down a corridor, to reach at last a pair of swinging doors marked "Presidential Precinct." These doors were controlled by another guard sitting in a gas-tight, bulletproof cubicle. Again passes were shown, pressed against the plate-glass window. Forbin stated the time of his appointment to the microphone, the guard consulted his checklist.

"OK, Mr. Forbin—you're in."

Inside the Precinct precautions appeared to be relaxed. But only superficially. In fact more guards, the cream of the cream, continually patrolled. They were not there to demand passes or search for weapons, but to be ever-watchful, ready to deal at a split second's notice with anything they might regard as suspicious. They alone could enter the President's private sanctum without knocking, and would silently disappear at a nod from him. Without a nod, they stayed. Forbin wondered how a man could stand it for four years, let alone a second term. Worst of all, there were the staring eyes of the TV cameras, watching all public rooms and corridors. Forbin would not be surprised to find that there was an electronic eye behind the toilet-paper holder in the Presidential can.

And practically all this would be unnecessary from now on.

Ushered into the outer office of the sanctum, Forbin was met be the PPA—Principal Private Aide—who came forward, hand outstretched.

"My dear Forbin, glad to see you." The PPA glanced at the wall clock. "As always, right on the button."

They shook hands warmly. Forbin muttered something, but to save his life he could not remember the aide's name, although they had met often enough. To Forbin he was part of the unreal world, a shadowy figure, something on the fringe of the real thing that lay a thousand miles away.

The aide pressed a button on his desk and spoke in no particular direction, looking at Forbin as he did so, smiling.

"Mr. President, Professor Forbin is here."

The President's voice replied almost at once, floating out in hi-fi from a concealed speaker beside the double doors.

"Have him come in."

The aide did not reply, but inclined his head doorwards, at the same time moving forward to open one. Both doors were opened only for ceremonial visits. Forbin nodded his thanks and entered the holy of holies, the Presidential sanctum. The door shut softly behind him.

Visitors to the President usually found him seated behind his king-sized red leather-topped desk, flanked by his personal standard and "Old Glory"—an almost posed position, as if waiting for the official photographer. Forbin had seen him many times like that, but today was different, very different.

The President had clearly been pacing the carpet when Forbin was announced. He turned to greet his visitor, hand outstretched.

"Mr. President," said Forbin, trying to sound respectful, aware of the warm, firm, professional handclasp. They stood for a long moment shaking hands: the short corpulent President, red-faced, dynamic and extrovert, the epitome of the man who knew what he wanted and saw that he got it, and the scientist Forbin, taller and thinner, and, in these surroundings, showing no signs of the mental power and drive he had needed to get to the top of his profession. They were both roughly the same age, in their very early fifties, though a hundred years earlier they would have appeared much younger.

The President switched his welcoming gaze from Forbin to the closed doors.

"Prytzkammer!" he said.

Yes, thought Forbin, that's the name.

The President went on, "See I'm not disturbed—and switch this damned thing off."

"Yes, Mr. President."

At once the red light on the panel over the double doors went out. The President had real privacy, a commodity hard to come by in the White House. He released Forbin's hand, almost reluctantly, his manner implying that it had been a good interlude, but now to business. The smile was switched off as he looked hard into Forbin's face.

"Well, Forbin?"

Forbin in turn looked calmly back and allowed his half smile to show. This was it.

"Sir, Project Colossus is completed, and can be activated upon your command."

For what seemed a long time the President stared at Forbin, his green-brown eyes shrewdly probing the face before him, sensing that there was something unsaid, aware also that this was a historic moment, and that for the benefit of posterity, he must say the right thing. He was a professional politician to his fingertips.

"Professor," he spoke solemnly, formally, "I must ask you if you are quite satisfied that the requirements and directives for Project Colossus have, in all respects, been achieved?"

Forbin matched the President's formality. "Mr. President, I testify that all the requirements, directives, specifications and parameters ordered are so met, and that Project Colossus is in all respects ready. Only your order is necessary to activate the whole system."

The pleasure this formal statement gave to the President was clear. Forbin repressed a slight feeling of contempt for the man. For his own part, he too was pleased that the Project was completed, although "pleased" was far too slight a word. He was overawed, indeed humbled by what he and his kind had achieved. The President was only interested in the power it gave him, and to be fair, his country. There lay the difference between the two men.

Once more the President offered his hand.

"Forbin, this is a great moment. You and I, and thousands more of course, have been living with this concept for nearly ten years"—Forbin could have added he had spent twelve years on the job, but the President would have brushed that two years aside; he was that sort of man —"and I find it hard to believe that it is now a fact. As President and Commander in Chief of the Armed Forces of the United States of North America, let me be the first to congratulate you on an achievement unparalleled in history."

They shook hands once more, the posterity side of the President's mind uppermost. Forbin's mind was in quite a different channel. He had a very clear idea of how unparalleled the achievement was. But had the President?

The President, posterity dealt with for the moment, laughed shortly. "You don't seem very excited, Forbin. Is

10

there something wrong—something you want?"

"I'd like to smoke, if you've no objection."

Again the President laughed, this time with sincerity. He turned to his desk and sat down, swil gently from side to side in his swivel chair.

"You're a strange guy, Forbin. You lift the biggest burden a man was ever called upon to carry, and ask if you can smoke! You can burn the White House down, if you wish, and I'll personally ler d you my lighter."

Forbin fished out his pipe and began to fill it.

"Sit down, man—but first fix us a drink." The President waved Forbin towards a cabinet that once had graced the residence of the Soleil Royale in Versailles. "I'll have a Scotch on the rocks, since we're alone. I can't drink it in public; I'd have our distillers round my neck in no time."

Forbin poured two large Scotches on ice in heavy cutglass Jacobean tumblers, placed one carefully beside the President, then sat down in a low armchair—the only available seat. Being short, the President liked to get his visitors where he could do the looking down.

Forbin lit his pipe and sat still, looking at his drink. The President sipped his, then placed the glass precisely in the middle of his blotter, adjusting its position with one eye shut.

"You've only answered half my question. Is there something wrong? Something's biting you." He spoke casually, intent on moving his glass to a new position.

Forbin sat silent, rubbing his nose with the stem of his pipe. Finally he took a deep breath and spoke, all traces of formal deference gone from his voice.

"I don't know quite how to say this. You may have it all figured out—but I haven't had much time to study all the broad issues while the work was going on, and maybe you haven't either." He stopped, drank a good half of his Scotch and relit his pipe. The President tried a new position for his glass on the northeast corner of his pad. Forbin went on.

"Lately, as we got the bugs out, I've felt, more by instinct than anything I can prove, that Colossus has some mighty big side effects build in. I think there are going to be a lot of changes. It's like the old race to the moon—we were all in such a hurry to get there first, there was no real consideration of what it was really for. Or take the uncontrolled use or those broad-band insecticides that wrecked ecology over vast areas. Remember the red mite invasion in the Midwest? All the bugs that ate the red mite were killed, but the mites thrived on the insecticide. One or two small townships had to be abandoned—thousands of acres were turned over to the Army to work over with flamethrowers—just to keep the mites down until we bred enough bugs to restore the balance. Even now, twenty years later, there are patches where you can't keep chickens for fear of the red mite. I can remember us buying eggs from China—us!"

He finished his drink. "I haven't said my piece the way I meant to, but I hope you get the idea."

The President pushed his glass to one side. His smile lacked conviction.

"You had me worried. I thought maybe there was a hole in Colossus' head. Believe me, I've given them some thought—the side effects—not as much as they probably deserve, but enough to satisfy me for now. The main object is of overriding importance, and if that's OK, we can tackle lesser problems as they crop up." He banged his desk with sudden vehemence. "You've no idea what it's like behind this desk. When you were in diapers, there was a President —Truman—who had a sign on his desk that said, 'The buck stops here.' He was dead right."

The President collected his glass from the deep field of his desk and drank, looking hard at Forbin over the rim.

"Colossus will take that buck, the big buck of a mega-million lives that all Presidents have had to carry since Roosevelt. Don't you worry, Forbin, I can ride out any bad breaks the new setup may bring."

He hasn't got the message, thought Forbin. But he could see the President's viewpoint—the intense desire for relief from the staggering weight of responsibility, a desire that blinded him to any objections. Maybe he'll make out. Forbin stood up, placed his glass on the desk.

"I guess you're right. I just get the feeling sometimes that this thing is one hell of a lot bigger than we know. Still, that's one buck that I have now passed to you." His tone was calm, bordering on the formal once more. "What are your orders for activation?"

The President, swinging gently in his chair, looked curiously at Forbin.

"You're an odd one, Forbin. You spend your life working like a beaver leading the biggest brain-bank in the world. You spend so much money you damn near bust the U.S. Treasury, and now you've done what you set out to do, you sit back and gripe. Hell—aren't you even excited?"

"Yes," Forbin said thoughtfully, "I suppose I am, in a way. But I read about the synthesis of the first broad-band insecticides before they got to the field trial stage, and it struck me then that the idea was potentially dangerous. And we finished up with the biggest plague since ancient Egypt."

"Sure, but we licked it."

"Yes, we did—and the bug-killer was withdrawn," Forbin replied. "But this time there is no way of walking back. The whole point is in the Project's unstoppability."

The President had enough of Forbin's alarm and did not bother to conceal it.

"OK, Forbin. I appreciate your warning, but as you say, the buck is mine. So you don't know what'll happen from here on—who does? I'm happy, so let's get down to cases." He had wanted to know Forbin's mind, had been told, briefly considered—and rejected it. Soon Forbin himself would be rejected, his usefulness over. Make him president of some university and fix him a medal, that should be enough.

"Well, Mr. President, have you fixed an activation date?"

The President visibly grew in stature at the prospect of action. The dynamo within him, which had made him what he was, began to radiate energy.

"Yes. It has got to be handled right. Played properly, it'll fix the cold war as well as any variety of hot. The security of Colossus has fouled up any detailed discussion, but I've chewed it over, in general terms, with the head of psychological warfare, and we've come up with the ideal treatment—simple and direct!" He beamed excitedly at Forbin. "As soon as you give the OK on the technical side, that all systems are green-go, we downgrade the biggest top-secret in our history to plain unclassified. We just hit 'em—wham!" He banged his desk once more to illustrate his point.

"Then we give them everything—how it's done, diagrams, photographs, tell the wide world the whole works by international TV—a press conference. But we're going to keep it simple, just three or four topflight reporters from all over—we'll have to select them carefully. Mind you, I don't want stooges!" He raised an admonishing finger. "They can be as rough as they like. I figure on one of our boys, two guys, English and French, from USE, and that bullet-headed bum from the Russki agency—and a guy from the Pan-Africa bunch, too. I'll make a short statement, then answer questions—follow up with handouts, the usual routine stuff. Good?"

There was something about the Presidential approach to the Project that made Forbin's flesh creep, but it would have been pointless to say so.

"I wouldn't know, Mr. President. I'm just a scientist . . ."

"Just a scientist! Exactly! That's an angle I thought we could use. I can make the general statement, but you should answer the questions. I'd never sound convincing with the technical dope."

Forbin frowned, but the President went on.

"Sure, it's tough, and you'd rather not, but that's too bad—you're in. Now—how soon can we start?"

"Well, there are one or two safety checks I want to repeat, but that won't take more than a day—two at the most." Forbin walked over to a window and looked out. He spoke without turning.

"I'm sorry to repeat myself, Mr. President, but are you really sure, quite sure—" He turned. "You realize that once we start we can't go back? The world changed drastically with the first A-bomb, and this . . ."

"Look, Forbin, we've covered this. "I'm satisfied—why are you dragging your feet?" He glanced at his watch, a fairly direct hint, but Forbin was not to be put off.

"I've lived with this thing for years—worked day and night in the Secure Zone, watching, checking, steering. It's been everything to me, I've been cut off from everything. I haven't been to my apartment for a year—just slept on the job—and I've been happy, certain of what I was doing. Now it's all over, and in the last few weeks, I've begun to realize what it is we've done. As a project it's practically finished, we can't find any more wrinkles to iron out; we've checked and checked again. Then someone suggested that a final checkout, a really foolproof one, could be made by Colossus himself—itself. A week's research by the Yale

Group, checked by Boston, showed this was so—that Colossus could do a better job than we could. We set up, and for three days and nights, working at the speed of light, Colossus looked into his own guts. Just over an hour ago he was satisfied. It almost scares me. I know he—it—knows better than the best brains in the USNA! It's quite a thought!"

"It's a hellava thought! The trouble with you, Forbin, is that you've lived too close to the Project. So Colossus has a better brain—fine! Just the very thing we've been working for all these years. No, Professor, we go ahead now, repeat now!" The President lightly stroked a button on his desk. "I'll give you a written order."

Prytzkammer, the aide, came in and stood silent before the President.

"P, take this down. Type it yourself—I'll sign as soon as it's ready—such as in two minutes' time." He gave Forbin a humorless grin. "To Professor Forbin, Chief Director, Project Colossus. In my capacity, no, my *dual* capacity of President and Commander in Chief of the Armed Forces of the United States of North America, I order you to activate Colossus—" he swung his chair to face Forbin—"how about 0800 on the 5th? That'll give you just over forty-eight hours."

"That will be enough."

"Right, P, go on—activate Colossus at 0800 5th. That's all, except I want it graded Top Secret until 1000 5th, then downgraded to Unclassified. All times Eastern Standard."

"Unclassified, sir?" The aide had every right to look startled.

"That's what I said."

"Yes, Mr. President." The aide retreated to the door.

"And tell the Secretary of State I'm calling a Cabinet meeting in an hour's time—see the office informs the rest. Anyone out of town to report on Secure TV—and get moving with that typing." The President swiveled to face Forbin and smiled his wolfish grin. "That's got things moving."

Forbin nodded slowly.

"Yes, Mr. President, it has."

CHAPTER 2

An hour after leaving the President, Forbin was walking along the gravel path leading to his office in the Secure Zone, 250 miles from Washington. Throughout the quiet air-car run—quiet largely because he had, against all standing orders, disconnected the car's telephone—he had wrestled with his thoughts and forebodings on Colossus. The interview with the President had not gone the way he planned or hoped. He hadn't got his feelings across, although he knew this was a hard job for anyone with the President. Forbin was aware that he was trusted, and to some extent even respected, but once he moved out of his own immediate field, stopped dealing in provable facts, the President had no time for him. To the President, a man was like a cigar lighter. Flick, there was the flame, use it, then put it out. Sure, you look after it, see it is fed gas and polished, even as you praise and reward humans, not so much for what they have done, but for what they could do in the future. While this attitude clearly gave great strength, Forbin felt there were situations when it could become appallingly weak. You can hold a pile of coins between thumb and forefinger, and turn the pile of coins until parallel with the floor, and if you exert enough pressure they stay that way, but a slight weakening or fault in the alignment of the coins, and the lot go showering in all directions. There is no cement—only power.

Without some warmth or personal interest there was little understanding, and in this situation it could be more than a little dangerous . . .

Walking into his outer office, Forbin was irritated to find one of his assistants kissing his secretary, with a hand deep in the girl's blouse. Seeking a little warmth and understanding, no doubt, Forbin thought. Johnson, the assistant, tried to remove his hand, but some hidden hitch delayed him, giving Forbin time to think up a crack that restored his good humor. "Have you lost something, Johnson?"

"Sorry, Professor," mumbled Johnson, now disentangled and on his way to the door. The secretary tried to rezip her blouse. As might be expected, the zipper jammed.

Forbin smiled slightly and turned to his assistant.

"Johnson, let me give you two pieces of advice. Try to contain yourself until the lunch break—or, better still, until you are off duty. If you really can't wait—please satisfy your biological urges in the rest room—it can't be locked all the time." He switched to his secretary, leaving Johnson in the doorway, poised on one foot, uncertain. "Angela, one piece of advice, one suggestion. I advise you to revert to old-fashioned buttons and suggest you use my office to fix that brassiere. It must be mighty uncomfortable the way it is now."

"Thanks, Chief." Angela acted on his suggestion, in no way embarrassed.

"Johnson, please fix a meeting of Group A for 1530, here—OK?"

"OK, Professor, 1530. Thanks."

Forbin smiled again as Johnson escaped. In some places it might be taken seriously as a breach of group discipline, but not in the Secure Zone. Hedged in on every side, living under constant surveillance, human nature had been forced to adapt itself. Getting into Project Colossus had always been tough, but once you were in it was a great deal tougher to get out. The Secure Zone contained all that a person might be expected to need, except freedom. Contacts outside the Zone were officially discouraged; the authorities made no bones about that. And, with the changing pattern of society, there were relatively few married couples. With women's full emancipation a generation before, the last vestige of their dependence upon men disappeared. At the same time the training of high-grade scientists and technicians—still mostly male—took longer and longer. Most of these men were not earning their keep until late in their thirties, but were biologically mature at sixteen or seventeen. It was difficult for them not only to keep a family but to spare time for family life. So sex life in the Zone and its associate vacation centers got to be interesting.

Forbin's crack about the rest room had only stated truth. Each office block had a rest room, and it was tacitly accepted that if the door was locked you did not make a song and dance about it. A time traveler from even fifty years back would have been astonished—and very likely scandalized—by the lack of friction and disharmony in what he would have regarded as a sexually degenerate society.

Forbin's secretary returned, smart and businesslike, with a degree of uplift that had been lacking before and with her make-up on straight.

"Angela, I've called a Group A meeting for 1530—Johnson is fixing it. Try to keep callers out of my hair, will you? But that doesn't include the President; if he wants me, he had better get me."

"Sure, Chief."

Angela was a big, midwestern girl, a good and devoted worker, but Forbin had never been able to break her of the habit of calling him "Chief"—and secretly he had grown to like it. He had never made the round trip to the rest room with her—or anyone else—for the Project had taken all his energy. But now, his work almost done, it might be an idea, he thought, if he got around to marriage and a family. Forty was a good age to get fixed, but fifty was by no means unusual; most men of that age were in good physical shape, and in that way he was as most men . . .

Forbin broke off his blank stare at Angela's breasts, slightly amazed at his own thoughts, then walked into his own office, women forgotten. That compartment was shut; his mind was rehearsing the details of the Group meeting and its main subject—the activation of Colossus.

CHAPTER 3

"That's about everything then, Forbin," said the President. "Answer any questions thrown, except if they get around to the parameter angle. That must remain secret—no point in telling them exactly how rough they have to get to make Colossus itchy."

It was just over forty-eight hours since their last meeting. The worldwide TV hook-up was minutes away and both were ready, wearing semiceremonial dress, old-style lounge suits with washable shirts. They were alone in the sanctum, but the subdued murmur of voices indicated there was quite a crowd in the PPA's office.

The President was in his element, his face a shade redder, his eyes bright with excitement. Forbin thought sourly that his coloring against the white shirt and dark blue suit would look very patriotic on TV . . .

"Five minutes, Mr. President," the voice of Prytzkammer hi-fied in.

The President rubbed his hands together; he could hardly wait.

"Time for a spoonful of medicine—set 'em up, Forbin."

Forbin duly set them up and passed the President his glass. The President took it, and stood up. Forbin guessed what was coming.

"A toast, Forbin—to Colossus, and us."

They drank to that one.

"With your permission, sir, I have one too."

"Go right ahead."

Forbin raised his glass, looked steadily at the President.

"To the world!"

The President stared back, his eyes probing, the smiling *bonhomie* momentarily gone. Then he relaxed, the jovial grin returned.

"Sure, why not? That's a good one—to the whole goddam cotton-picking world!"

Prytzkammer was finding it hard to preserve his usual calm and polished manner; he had caught something of the President's excitement. Now, surrounded by five top reporters, plus two cameramen and a producer, he was thankful that the days of power cables, TV lights and special microphones were dead and gone. The cameramen, with four minutes to go, had at last unslung their portable TV cameras and were making fine adjustments to their antennae with every appearance of boredom. They were the top men in their own line, and had seen everything and been everywhere. An assignment to cover the Last Judgment would not get them worked up.

The reporters, too, were top men, and a hard-baked lot. The doyen was Kyrovitch of Tass, a big, wide man with a permanent chip on his shoulder. Then there was Plantain, the English representative of the United States of Europe, an urbane little man, adept at smooth and tricky questioning—and the other European, the Frenchman, Dugay. Pan-Afric's M'taka was a good, solid reporter, but outclassed by the rest. USNA's representative, Mazon, was NorAm's star man; not unnaturally he was assigned the central reporter's role in the conference.

Unlike the cameramen, the press were anything but bored. All they knew, officially, was that the President was to make a statement of global importance and that they would have a chance to ask questions. There would be no preliminary warm-up. Prytzkammer was primarily concerned that no one man should hog the proceedings.

"Remember, gentlemen, you are the stand-ins for the people of the world. Set a good example, and let's have a little of the old give and take—"

"Relax," said Mazon, "none of us is going to start a fight."

The rest nodded, each making his own mental reservation on how best to get the lion's share.

"I would be charmed if I—we—had some faint lead on the purpose of this announcement," Plantain smiled in a tired way at Prytzkammer. There was a general mumble of agreement from his colleagues.

"I'm sorry, gentlemen, but the President wants it this way, and he's the boss. I couldn't tell you if I wanted to—I don't know."

None of the reporters spoke. They didn't have to; their faces showed what they thought of that one.

The TV producer compared his two chronometers and said, "Two minutes" to no one in particular.

Four of the reporters all asked questions at once; only Mazon was silent. This might be this Colossus thing he had heard of, but there was no point in shooting off your mouth. You could be wrong, and any spillage might bring out the mean streak in the President.

Prytzkammer, who had ignored all the questions, picked up his few notes, and raised an eyebrow at the producer, who nodded towards the first cameraman.

"I make the intro, you hold me until I identify the reporters—pan along the line as I name them, then on me as I lead in to the President. Will Camera Two be solely on the President and Forbin?"

The producer nodded.

"Forbin!" Mazon shot out. "So it is—"

He stopped. The other reporters looked at him, questions forming in four minds. He was saved by the producer.

"Quiet now; five seconds to the intro, forty-five to Pressie."

Prytzkammer's glare at the irreverent producer quickly changed to an ingratiating smile as the warning light on Camera One started to occult, then glowed steadily. The PPA quickly turned his smile down to mere affability, looked at the camera, and began.

"This is the White House, Washington. This Presidential conference is being transmitted by all networks in the United States of North America and the United States of South America. By arrangement with International TV Agency it is beamed via Space Stations Two and Five to the Pan-Afric Republic, the United States of Europe, the Middle East and the Japanese Republic Zone, including Australasia. It is also on offer to the Soviet Bloc, but as of now we do not know if they are taking it."

The PPA moved round his desk, tracked by Camera Two.

"In a few moments I will be taking you in to hear an announcement of worldwide importance by the President of the United States of North America. You, the people of the world, are represented here by these gentlemen." He introduced them, one by one, and went on, "These are your representatives, and when the President has completed his statement, they may ask any questions that they like."

Prytzkammer paused, looked at the reporters, then at the camera.

"Gentlemen, the free world, here is the President."

He walked slowly to the doors to give the camera a chance to keep him in shot, and opened both doors. Camera Two sank down on one knee, getting a desk-level view of the President as the doors opened, slowly straightening up as the reporters filed in on either side of him. The PPA joined Forbin, out of view well to one side of the President's desk.

The President waited until the reporters were seated, then leaned forward on his elbows, hands clasped in front. It was a small gesture which conveyed the impression on TV that he was talking to you, confidentially, that this was man-to-man stuff.

"Fellow citizens of the world," he began in a low, measured, almost stately voice, "I am told that this telecast is being watched by more than half the people of the globe, and that a further ten percent are listening on the radio. You may well wonder what I can say that is important enough to justify taking up your time like this. In all solemnity, I can assure you I have that justification. For good or evil—and I devoutly believe in good—we have reached one of those vital turning points in the history of man and of this planet. There have been a number of such moments in the past, most of them passing unrecognized. The first was the discovery of the use of fire, the second when the wheel was invented. The construction of the first internal-combustion machine was another. Some of you are old enough to recall the terrible dawn of the atomic age, and the host of technological advances we have made since then. But for the unhappy state of our world's affairs, we could all enjoy life to the full; remove the risk of conflict between the nations, and the Golden Age would be with us—now!" The President did not forget himself and bang the desk, but raised one finger as he spoke the last word, giving the slight visual shock to keep his vast audience's full attention. He went on, wearily.

"Instead, for years, for generations, we have been delicately poised on the brink of a disaster too complete and horrible to contemplate." His voice lost it's weariness, gathered strength. "We of the free world have upheld the banner of freedom and truth, knowing that this must be preserved, even at the cost of all our lives."

Again the President paused, and resumed his confidential approach. "We do not want war—and to be truthful, I do not think anyone else does either. Nevertheless, we have all gone on, with recurrent crises, each carrying with it the risk of a slip or error on one side, or the other, which could result in the final tragedy of global destruction. There is an old saying that 'everyone makes mistakes,' but that is just what neither side can afford. We are all human, taking inhuman risks. One of the great philosophers of this century, Bertrand Russell, said many years ago, 'You may reasonably expect a man to walk a tightrope safely for ten minutes; it would be unreasonable to do so without accident for two hundred years.' This we have known for a long time, and for years, here in the United States, we have been working on this problem. Until this very minute this work has been our most closely guarded secret. It has involved vast effort, vast expenditure, but I have to tell you that our efforts have been crowned with success."

The President had the full attention of the reporters. They were still, listening hard. Even Camera One—who had nothing to do—was motionless, listening carefully. The President, holding on to the dramatic pause, sipped a little water. He watched, with approval, as Camera Two—sensing the pay-off line to come—inched downwards so as to give the President relative height. The President drew himself up a fraction, lessening the confidential approach. He fixed his gaze on the camera, and spoke with great solemnity.

"As President of the United States of North America, I have to tell you, the people of the world, that as of eight o'clock Eastern Standard Time this morning the defense of the nation, and with it the defense of the free world, has been the responsibility of a machine. As the first citizen of my country, I have *delegated* my right to take my people to war.

"That decision now rests with Colossus, which is the name of the machine. It is basically an electronic brain, but far more advanced than anything previously built. It is capable of studying intelligence and data fed to it, and on the basis of those facts only—not of emotions—deciding if an attack is about to be launched upon us. If it did decide that an attack was imminent—and by that I mean that an assault was impending and would probably be launched within four hours—Colossus would decide, and act. It controls its own weapons and can select and deliver whatever it considers appropriate.

"Understand that Colossus' decisions are superior to any we humans can make, for it can absorb far more data than is remotely possible for the greatest genius that ever lived. And more important than that, it has no emotions. It knows no fear, no hate, no envy. It cannot act in a sudden fit of temper. Above all, *it cannot act at all*, so long as there is no threat.

"Fellow humans, we in the USNA now live in the shade, but not the shadow, of Colossus. And indirectly, you do too. May it never see fit to act."

The President took another sip of water. He was aware that the Tass man, Kyrovitch, was about to speak, but he also saw Prytzkammer motion him to be silent. The rest of the reporters looked dazed. The President was enjoying himself even more than he had expected.

"We of the free world," he continued, "do not want war. Indeed, we will never fight unless attacked. Now that we have Colossus we have no real need for armed forces except for minor disturbances. It is therefore my intention to reduce the overall strength of our fighting services by seventy-five percent over the next five years. As soon, in fact, as the readjustment can be made.

"Further, we are prepared to show the world how Colossus works—what has been built into it—and to prove to anyone's satisfaction" (he could not help flashing a look at Kyrovitch) "that Colossus is a defensive system. If we can convince the Soviet Bloc that Colossus is solely defensive, and demonstrate that we have no offensive intentions by the virtual disbandment of our Navy and Army and Space forces, relying solely on Colossus to protect us, we may well be a long way towards lasting peace and the end of the cold war that has bedeviled us all for so long."

The President swiveled in his chair to face the correspondents.

"Now, gentlemen, I am prepared to answer any questions you may care to ask. I am not of course, familiar with all the technicalities of this vast work, so I would like to introduce Professor Charles Forbin. He is, I think, the world's leading expert on electronic brains. Certainly no man knows more about Colossus than he does. He has worked on it since the first design study group was set up at Harvard twelve years ago." He motioned Forbin to stand behind him, and Forbin did so, wearing a slightly stuffed expression.

Mazon was the first to speak.

"It's a little difficult, Mr. President, to grasp the size of what you have just told us. I find it hard to conceive of the essential nature of this Colossus. For instance, can it think?"

"That, Mr. Mazon, is just the sort of question for the Professor here." The President motioned to Forbin.

Forbin was not only nervous about the potential of Colossus, he was now nervous of the TV camera as well. He reached for his notes, or where they would have been had he been wearing his usual blouse instead of the stiff and uncomfortable lounge suit. He gave up the search, his hands looking lost without some employment.

"Can it think?" Forbin repeated the question, more for his own benefit and to gain time than anything else. "The term 'electronic brain' has always been a popular one for what really was an arithmetical device which could distinguish between one and two. That is still the basis of all computers. There are a good many computer-type components in Colossus, but the essential core of the machine-complex is infinitely more sophisticated. Just as you can say that the proportions of the Parthenon are a matter of two to one in essence, but the detailing is extremely complex. It's that development which makes all the difference. Colossus really is a 'brain' in a limited sense. It can think in a sort of way, but it has no emotions, and without emotional content, *creation* is not possible. It could not create, say, a Shakespeare play—or any sort of play for that matter, although as part of its background knowledge we have fed in all the plays—and given any three consecutive words from anything Shakespeare wrote, or anything a hundred playwrights wrote, Colossus could finish the quotation. Colossus has a vast memory store; it wouldn't be far from wrong to say that it has the total sum of human knowledge at its disposal. On the basis of that background, plus the data continually being fed in, it forms its judgments—just like a human being. Though with the very important difference that it never overlooks a point, is not biased and has no emotions. But think creatively—no."

Forbin paused and moved so as to address the President. "Sir, with your permission, I would like to demonstrate this emotional point."

"Certainly, Professor. I am sure we would all be very interested."

Forbin finally found somewhere to put his hands, stuffing them in the side pockets of his jacket, nautical fashion. He appeared very uncomfortable.

"Colossus is essentially an information-collecting, sorting and evaluating complex, capable of factual decisions and action if necessary. It can evaluate the printed word, speech or visual material. Languages are no difficulty. For warning and test purposes—tests at our end, that is, for there is no teletype inside Colossus to go wrong—we have teletype lines directly to the complex. One is right here, in this office."

Forbin nodded to Prytzkammer who wheeled forward a dust-sheeted trolley. Forbin removed the sheet, revealing an ordinary teletype machine, rather like an electronic typewriter, with a few extra keys and a large roll of paper mounted at the back of the carriage. The reporters stared at it, mesmerized.

"Now," said Forbin, "would one of you gentlemen care to name an emotion?"

"Love." It was Plantain who spoke, his voice devoid of expression.

His Russian colleague frowned. Dugay glanced quizzically at his fellow European.

"Good," said Forbin. "Love. Now Colossus has a vast knowledge of the subject, but it cannot experience love, nor evaluate emotion. I will confess," he smiled, "this particular question has not been fed in before, but I'm confident we will get a very lame reply. Still, a question that may be regarded as *factual*, on the same subject, will produce a very different answer—just because it is a matter of fact, whether it's about an emotion or not."

He bent over the teletype and clumsily picked out his message with two fingers. It was just two words:

EXPLAIN LOVE

"I have temporarily stored this message here," he tapped the gray top of the machine, "so that you might all see the message and observe the speed of the answer." He tore off the strip with the words on it, passed it to Dugay.

"You, sir, as a Frenchman, represent the nation best able to appreciate the complexity of this question." Forbin's smile robbed his words of any offensive overtones.

Dugay took the slip, read it and smiled back.

"It is, as you say, a honee of a question." He passed the slip to Kyrovitch who looked at it distastefully and quickly passed it to Plantain, who kept it.

"Right, gentlemen," Forbin continued. He was beginning to enjoy himself. "Watch. I press the feed-in control—thus."

For a half a second nothing happened. Even in that short time the tension in the room became so strong as to be practically tangible. Then the machine chattered briefly. The smile on the President's face had become a fixed mask.

Only Forbin was at ease. Without looking at the answer, he tore off the answer, passed it to Dugay. The Frenchman raised one expressive eyebrow.

"It is certainly a lame answer, Professor." He reached over Kyrovitch and handed the slip to Plantain, who obligingly held it up for Camera One. There were just four words.

LOVE IS AN EMOTION

Forbin read the answer on the monitor screen, and smiled at the reporters. "And that is about as good as Colossus can get. But my next question—" once more he bent over the teletype. The President cautiously looked at his watch. Kyrovitch yawned conspicuously.

"I have again held transmission." Forbin passed his second message to Dugay. "You may think this question cannot be answered accurately. It is—'What is the best written definition of love.' I can tell you how Colossus will tackle this one. It will look up every reference to love on file, and there must be at least tens of thousands. From these it will select those which, in some way, define love, and there will be thousands of those, and all of them will be sorted for the common factors. This work will be done by several sectors of the machine at once and the answers fed to the central control, where the machine synthesizes an answer based upon its researches. This answer will then be compared against all the definitions of love for the one nearest its synthetic answer. This it will do in any language—an Arabic love poem, a Polynesian fertility rite, some reference in an Icelandic saga. When it has found what it regards as the nearest to its synthetic answer, it will check the original," Forbin leaned forward, clearly regarding his next sentence as important, "and will type out the *reference*, not the definition itself. It will supply this if wanted, but remember, that was not the question we are asking. If we want to know the exact words, it would be necessary to say '*Give* the best written definition' etc. The final point I want to make before pressing the feed-in button is this. The process I have outlined will be carried out by the machine in five to ten seconds."

Kyrovitch snorted with disbelief. The rest looked even more dazed than before. Forbin turned to the teletype. "Here we go."

He pressed the feed-in control.

Plantain whispered something to Dugay round the back of the intervening Russian's neck. Dugay grinned. Kyrovitch simmered gently.

The machine began to chatter.

Mazon, who had been studying his watch intently, looked up and almost shouted, triumphantly, "Seven goddam seconds!"

It was quite unlike any press conference ever held. The President was half out of his chair, leaning over the desk. Camera Two tactfully took a shot of Forbin, bending over the teletype.

Forbin tore the strip off the machine, looked up and spoke in a level voice.

"It says—SHAKESPEARE SONNET CXVI."

"Follow that," muttered Mazon.

Kyrovitch did.

"Mr. President, this no time for tricks, we of the Socialist Soviet . . ."

The President secretly agreed with Kyrovitch, and was glad of his interruption to regain control.

"Gentlemen," he said, cutting in, "I hope this small demonstration illustrates the point which cannot be over-emphasized. Colossus knows about emotion, but cannot experience it. It can never act in fear or hate. This is the most vital point for you to remember."

The President favored Camera Two with a long direct stare.

"No defensive action will ever be undertaken by the United States of North America out of fear, jealousy, greed or hate."

He would have liked to have stopped the conference on that note, but Kyrovitch was not going to let him get away with that one. Swiftly he broke in on the President's stare.

"You say you feed it information. What sort, and how?"

The President was not going to be coy about that one.

"Every form of intelligence or information available to our Central Intelligence Agency. Everything, from agents' reports," he gave Kyrovitch a wolfish smile all to himself, "to newspapers, TV and radio broadcasts, movements of aircraft, troops, ships, satellites, all statistics on harvests, birth rates, rainfall—anything and everything that we think has the remotest bearing on the problem—plus practically anything else that is going."

Kyrovitch gave a deep-throated growl. "But how is it fed to the, the thing?"

"I was coming to that." He didn't like to sit answering questions from a Commie reporter, or any other reporter, come to that. "Professor Forbin, you are better qualified to answer . . ."

Forbin nodded and was suddenly conscious of his hands once more. He folded his arms across his chest, but the TV producer's frown and shaking head sent them plunging back into his pockets.

"Feed-in. Yes. Mostly by land-line. All information is converted to electrical impulses, in just the same way that any transmitter—teletype, TV or radio—converts vision or sound into impulses. They are then fed down the line to

Colossus, who then stores them in his—its own way. They are not converted back to pictures, letters or figures."

"Pictures?" queried Mazon.

"Yes. We pass pictures from newspapers or TV or plans of buildings. Anything that can be expressed on a sheet of paper or a flat surface goes down the pipe. I may say, since Colossus is not secret any more, it watches all the major TV programs—Soviet, American, European and so on. Moving pictures were a little tricky, but it works."

"It sure *is* a good thing Colossus hasn't got emotions," said Mazon with feeling.

"Perhaps so," Forbin smiled. "On the nonvisual side it monitors all the main radio transmissions of the world, civil, military and space-wise. It also reads, in its own way, all the newspapers of the world—even the sports pages."

"Listening to all that has been said," Plantain looked at Forbin, "I have an impression that Colossus is quite large—is that so?"

"Yes, the name is appropriate. I can tell you that it is about the size of a small town of, say, seven to ten thousand people."

"Are we permitted to know where it is?" said Kyrovitch. Mazon gave a snort of derisive laughter. The President thought it was time he was back center stage.

"Why, certainly, Mr. Kyrovitch. It is located inside the Rocky Mountains. The exact spot will be shown on the maps which you will receive later with the official press handouts." The President felt much better when he was doing the talking. "As a nation we have carried out some pretty large works. Panama Canal, Grand Coulee Dam, the TVA project—and more recently the Space Reflector Stations, the Moon project, the Trans-ocean oil lines to Europe, not to mention the coast-to-coast air-car roads. I may say the effort required to produce the last three projects together would not be enough to build Colossus. It took three years to dig the hole, even using nuclear digging techniques, and there were another three years needed to line the hole with cement, and to prepare the bare shell to receive the equipment. It is by far the biggest single enterprise undertaken by this nation in all its history."

"You say, Mr. President," said Kyrovitch, anxious to

flatten proceedings as much as possible, "that the armed forces of this country will be reduced by seventy-five per cent—are the rest guarding Colossus?"

Sucker, thought the President, this will teach you not to lead with your chin.

"No, sir. That twenty-five per cent would, I imagine, be used solely to resist subversion. Colossus certainly does not need them. Of course, there are a good many people engaged at the external ends of the feed lines. For example, if Colossus is to read *Pravda*," he smiled once more at Kyrovitch, "or *Grimm's Fairy Tales*, someone has to present the paper to a scanner. There are practically no other personnel involved. There are no servicing teams—not human ones, anyway. Colossus works alone."

That shook them, thought the President. It had. Plantain raised both eyebrows, which was the ultimate in facial expression he ever permitted himself. Dugay's eyebrows merged into one black line, as he wrestled with the implications. Kyrovitch rumbled quietly to himself, clearly at a loss what to say. Mazon beamed uncertainly, like a first-time father presented with quads. M'taka rubbed his fuzzy white pate and wished he had studied science instead of the humanities. Dugay spoke first.

"But the control, the maintenance . . ." he stopped, still mentally fumbling.

"Professor," the President nodded.

"As you may know," Forbin said, "back before our time electronic equipment was crude and unreliable. They had valves or tubes, which worked after a fashion, but could never be regarded as reliable. Then came transistors, a big advance in many ways—some are still in use—but these too weren't what we would regard as reliable. Then came the semiconductors, the use of laser beams of coherent light and the development of power cells." Forbin was aware that the President was squirming slightly in his seat. "But I won't go on with the technical details; they will be available to those that want them afterward. Enough to say that we have perfected components and circuits, sealed in blocks which are stable in all conditions, impervious to heat, damp, cold, gas or anything else. As a further safeguard, all circuits are duplicated—in some cases, triplicated. Colossus is capable of tracing its own faults and switching in a new circuit if necessary. Our calcualtion—confirmed, I may add, by Colossus' own figuring—is that one block circuit in every ten thousand may be expected to fail every four hundred years."

Kyrovitch bounced to his feet with surprising speed. "Four hundred years!" he roared.

"That's what the man said, buster!" yelled a red-faced Mazon.

"Gentlemen, gentlemen." The President raised a pacifying hand for silence. The TV producer reached forward and pulled Kyrovitch gently by the back of his jacket. The President looked at the reporters; the Limey would be the one to take the heat out of the situation.

"What was your question, Mr. Plantain?" He looked inquiringly at the Englishman, who had not asked one.

"Thank you, Mr. President," Plantain said gracefully. "I am indeed amazed at what Professor Forbin has just said. If this is the sort of time scale you have in mind, four hundred years to the first fault, how long is it expected that the machine will last?"

"Well now, that is kind of hard to say, Mr. Plantain, but we guess around the nine-hundred to twelve-hundred-year mark—maybe a good deal longer. It is one reason why we built it in a mountain. It is a pretty solid and durable roof." The President smiled, a smile that grew more smug when he saw Prytzkammer hold up a cue board which bore the chalked message "CIA reports 100 per cent TV coverage Eastern Bloc." He went on. "Of course, the weapon side needs checking and replacement with newer devices, and Colossus will permit the withdrawal of one weapon complex at a time for such work."

Dugay pounced.

"You say 'permit'—what exactly does that mean?"

Here we go, thought Forbin, the big hand-out. The President thought so too, a brief nod to Dugay, then he turned and faced the camera, back in his man-to-man pose.

"That brings us to a point of fundamental importance that I want clearly understood. As you have seen, we make no secret of Colossus, or where it is: nor do we intend to conceal the main points of how it works." He leaned back in his chair his hands folded comfortably on his belly, the epitome of the reasonable man. "You may say that this lays us wide open to a sudden attack frontally or subversively, which, if successful, would leave us defenseless." He leaned forward once more, less of the reasonable man, more of the keen efficient super-executive. "We have a defense for Colossus, and it is this—the machine is safe, safer than mere man could ever be"—he tapped the desk with slow emphasis in time with his words—"*so long as Colossus and its feed lines are not tampered with in any way*. If its power, information or other supply lines, or any missile bases or satellites are sabotaged, or even attacked, a special emergency circuit will switch in, and Colossus will take full offensive action."

There was quite a silence. Kyrovitch got in first.

"Does this mean that this thing, this Colossus"—he tried to sound contemptuous, but did not quite make it—"works without human aid, and that you *cannot stop it?*"

"It does."

Kyrovitch searched around for his voice, finally got it.

"You have in fact, delivered the destiny of the world—so far as the USNA can do that—into the hands of a machine?"

"Yes."

It was like a pebble dropped down a well; there was a deep silence, then came the splash. All the correspondents spoke at once, even including Plantain. Once more the President held up an authoritative hand.

"Please. The best brains of this country available to me and my predecessor have considered this point at great length, and it comes to this. Don't try to tamper with Colossus, and don't try to attack us, and there is nothing to fear."

"I am happy to accept the President's assurances on this point," said Plantain. The President did not look noticeably grateful. Plantain went on, "But how do you cope with the madman problem? And may not the machine be deranged by fire or flood or earthquake? I am sure you have an answer, but it would be interesting to know what that answer is."

"Forbin, go ahead," the President spoke tersely. He was

getting bored, it was like talking to a bunch of high-school kids.

"Before site work began, we considered the earthquake and flooding angles. The best Japanese brains were consulted—naturally, we did not disclose the exact nature of our requirements—and I can only say we are satisfied. We also chose a spot which has been free of all earth movement since the Rockies were formed around two hundred million years ago. As for flooding, a short answer. If Colossus were submerged—and it could stand that and go on working—the rest of the USNA would have to be covered to an average depth of eighty-five feet by the Atlantic and Pacific Oceans. Climatic changes between fifty below to one fifty above centigrade can be tolerated. Madmen? Several large holes were made, of course, during the excavation and removal of rock. When all the equipment was in, the holes were sealed. All floors and walls now contain a net of wires which must be cut to get in, embedded in the cement for protection and concealment, and if these are tampered with—you would first have to get through an average of three feet of cement, concrete to you Europeans—then, you set Colossus off. There is only one entrance left open, and this is guarded by the U.S. Marine Corps. Their job is to keep people away from that entrance for their own good, for the entrance now acts as an air shaft, and its real defense is a zone of intense radioactivity. Anyone entering this zone is killed instantly. The only adequate shielding would be a 'suit' of lead which would make the wearer nine feet wide. The entrance is three feet wide. Beyond this zone there are further defenses which would deal with any remote-controlled device sent in. One final point. If Colossus knows there is an attack on this country's interest impending and that an attack is probable within the next eight hours, it automatically closes the entrance doors, which are steel, four feet thick, and issues an alert to all Civil Defense Zones. A Red warning would also be passed to all concerned when Colossus operated its weapons."

"But surely, Professor, there is some way in which you, the creators of this thing, can get at it?"

The President intervened.

"No, there is not. As you know, it is an open secret that for years there have been nerve and psychological gases and drugs which are able to change the state of the human mind. If Forbin and his colleagues were subjected to this sort of treatment by hostile agents, they might well do as they were told, and with their knowledge, inactivate Colossus. No. There is no way in. No human being can touch Colossus."

CHAPTER 4

The historic press conference was over. The reporters and TV men had gone, to be replaced by a selection of high Government officials. The Secretaries of State for Peace, International Affairs, and Finance were there, along with Forbin's chief assistant, Dr. Fisher, and an assortment of aides. This party had watched the telecast elsewhere in the Precinct, and were now being entertained by the President, cheerfully holding court, beaming and handshaking amid the subdued chatter and clink of glass on bottle.

Forbin had withdrawn slightly, smiling mechanically at various compliments paid him. With the Project launched and irrevocably rolling, no longer a project but a fact, and with the excitement and tension of the telecast over, he felt drained, yet not empty. There was an increasingly strong feeling of foreboding taking over the space left by the completion of his work. He also felt hot, tired and depressed.

Fisher came over.

"So that is more or less that, Charles."

"Yep," said Forbin, nodding. "What did you think of the show?"

"I think it went very well, really." Fisher did not sound overenthusiastic. His hand fluttered nervously to his tie.

"Go on," said Forbin with sudden sharp interest, "what else?"

Fisher glanced around, gave his tie another tug, and lowered his voice as he moved closer. "To be honest, I rather wish these people weren't so cocksure and happy. Perhaps it's because we are practically out of a job, or it's anticlimax—but I think I have allowed for all that. Yet I'm left with a nasty taste, and I can't really say what it is."

"Is it Colossus?"

"Yes, I guess it is," Fisher gave a short false laugh. "Frankenstein should be banned reading for scientists."

"I'd be more inclined to make it compulsory reading for

nonscientists." Forbin peered into his glass. "I wish to hell I could get out of this armor. This collar is killing me."

Fisher ignored the last remark, stared thoughtfully at his chief. "You've got the same itch in the middle of the back." It was a statement, not a question.

Forbin nodded. "Maybe it was always there, but it's gotten more pronounced these last few weeks. Could be just nerves."

"If it is, then it's catching," said Fisher in a low voice. "I had a very curious conversation with Cleo yesterday—"

"Come on, boys, break it up!"

It was the President in his best convention mood. Face flushed, beads of perspiration on his forehad and nose, little drops glistening in the light.

"Forbin, Fisher, your glasses, come on, gas up and come over here, we'll have a toast or two." He gripped their arms, one on each side of him, and steered them towards his desk. An aide replenished their glasses. Both had been drinking Scotch, both now got martinis.

The President, now behind his desk once more, picked up his glass and looked expectantly at Prytzkammer. The PPA got the idea—that was why he was PPA—and raised his soft voice slightly.

"Gentlemen, the President wishes to give you a toast."

The chatter subsided at once, there was a general turning towards the President. Looking at their bright, flushed and excited faces, Forbin felt his stomach turn slightly. Any moment now, he thought, they will burst into "Hail to the Chief." He gazed with considerable repugnance into the martini. Someone knocked an ashtray over, there was the sound of breaking glass.

"OK, Hunston, don't worry," called the President, beaming. "We can charge all this fan-tan to Colossus, no one will spot the extra two dollars—except Benson, and I can fix him."

There was a general polite laugh. Benson was the Secretary of State (Finance).

"Right, now," said the President briskly. "I don't aim to keep you fellows long from your drinks, but what I want to say is this—"

But whatever it is, it was never said. There had been one

silent, nonsmoking, nondrinking guest in the sanctum, and he spoke first.

The teletype started chattering.

There was complete silence, apart from the teletype, for nearly five seconds; a long time in the circumstances.

Forbin felt a shock race outwards through his body to his extremeties, a shock that left his skin cold and damp. He saw that Fisher's face was pallid, his half-raised glass clutched in a frozen hand. The President's face was blotchy, his mouth slightly open. Somewhere an aide laughed nervously, and the sound broke the spell. Forbin roughly pushed a Secretary of State aside and ran to the machine, followed by Fisher and some others. The President did not move.

Forbin bent over the machine, staring at the paper in disbelief. He tore the typed strip off the machine, still looking at it. The President found his voice first.

"What the goddam hell goes on?" He banged his glass down and headed for the machine. "Well?"

Forbin turned as the President approached. His face was as pale as Fisher's.

"I don't know." Forbin struggled to keep his voice level. "I think you should call the party off, and clear the room of all non-Colossus people."

The President instantly swung round to face the majority of his guests. "You heard!" There was a faint hysterical edge to his voice. "Everybody who is not Colossus-cleared, out—now!"

The room cleared rapidly, and there was more than one nervous glance at Forbin as they left.

The President looked round the room sharply; there remained the two scientists, the Secretary of State for Peace and the Chief of Staff of Armed Forces. As the room emptied, the remaining guests drew closer to Forbin, who stood silent. Satisfied that all non-Colossus personnel had gone, the President wheeled on Forbin.

"Give!"

Without speaking or altering his blank stare into space, Forbin passed over the teletype slip. The President snatched the paper, and scanned it hastily, his face closely watched by the remainder of his guests with some anxiety. They got full value; the tension eased from his face, to be replaced by relief, then puzzlement, and finally anger. The color flooded back into his face, he was bright red, his eyes hard as stone as he faced Forbin.

"What is this crap! If this is some long-haired bastard on your staff being funny, Forbin, I'll castrate him personally, I'll—"

But Forbin was not listening. He brushed past the President to the direct-line communications set on the President's desk, the direct line to the Secure Zone.

"Cleo? Forbin. Is the Colossus T/P link to you operating? What? Well, find out! Call back." He replaced the handset, and spoke to the President. "We'll soon know, though I would have said it was impossible—hell, it is impossible."

He stared hard at the First Citizen. As on an earlier occasion, there had been a subtle change in his attitude. Forbin was talking to an equal.

The remainder of the party was, understandably, puzzled and anxious. The President's demeanor had taken some of the tension out of their attitudes, but there was still enough to go round.

"Well, what does it say?" burst out Fisher. "For God's sake, don't keep us hanging by our ears!"

"Go on, Forbin, tell them." The President thrust the paper back into Forbin's hand. The look Forbin gave the President indicated clearly that he had every intention of doing so, anyway.

"All it says is this." He held the slip so that all might see. There were just five words:

FLASH THERE IS ANOTHER MECHANISM

Puzzlement was now general, tension had largely gone. The Chief of Staff picked up his drink and frowned at the Secretary of State for Peace, who frowned back. Only the two scientists continued to look pale and haunted. Forbin spoke again.

"And it's no good anyone asking what it means; you know as much as I do, so don't—"

Fisher, following his own train of thought, cut in.

"I suppose," he spoke slowly, formulating his ideas as he went along, "if a question had been fed in by some clown back in the Secure Zone, this might be the answer. But why wouldn't the question show up on this machine? It is in parallel, and should—"

In turn, he was cut short by the soft ping of the direct line. Forbin answered.

"Yes, speaking. You're sure, Cleo? Switch on the screen and show me the roll since we started. Yes, now."

Without reference to the President, he reached over and flicked a switch on the desk's control panel. Immediately the small screen in the base of the direct-line instrument came alive, and a few seconds later a roll of paper was presented to the scanner, held by a pair of obviously feminine hands which belonged to Cleo Markham, one of Forbin's top cybernetic experts. He noted that her hands were shaking slightly.

"Yes, Cleo, I see it. Now, from the beginning, unroll slowly."

Cleo did as she was told. Apart from the time, printed down one side of the paper every fifteen minutes, there was a complete blank from ten o'clock until the first message: EXPLAIN LOVE.

There followed the rest of the exchange, ending with SHAKESPEARE SONNET CXVI, then nothing for forty-five minutes until FLASH THERE IS ANOTHER MECH-ANISM.

Forbin studied the picture carefully, then closely questioned Cleo and Blake, the duty scientist in the watch room. He checked all possibilities, including erasures on the roll, machine and line faults. Finally he ordered Cleo and Blake to keep quiet and to take the roll out of service for closer inspection later.

Forbin turned and looked grimly at the President.

"I'm satisfied that no question was fed in. That message came straight from, and was originated by, Colossus. I have a shrewd idea what it means—"

"Wait," grated the President. The red light over the door was on, but it was not a steady light; it waxed and waned intensity—the urgency signal. At the same moment the PPA's voice broke in.

"Urgent message, sir!"

"Jesus, what now?" muttered the President; then in a louder voice, "Well?"

"Soviet Ambassador on the phone, sir. Insists on speaking to you most urgently."

"Put him on." The President might have a fading grip on Forbin, but it was still granite hard elsewhere. His hand resting on the phone, he looked round at his staff. "Stay." Then he picked up the phone.

"Yes, speaking." His eyes darted restlessly about, from the teletype to Forbin, to the Chief of Staff to Fisher—then quite suddenly they became still, his face impassive. "Yes, Ambassador, I heard. In view of the importance of your statement, I would be obliged if you would repeat it."

There was a tense silence, all eyes staring at the President as he listened intently.

"Yes, thank you for telling me in advance. Naturally, I have no comment to make at this time. Thank you, and good night." He replaced the handset carefully, but did not release his grip, and stared unseeingly before him. Without moving he spoke once more, his voice was dry, harsh.

"You got that on record, P?"

"Yes, sir." Prytzkammer too sounded as if he was laboring under some strain.

"Right."

As the red light went out, the President relinquished his hold on the telephone. He swiveled in his chair to face his staff, his eyes still hard but with a new, fatigued look in them, his hands gripping the arms of his chair. No one spoke or coughed as he shifted his gaze from one to another, finally resting on Forbin.

"You needn't start tearing up any sidewalks to check the lines, Forbin. Also we don't need any inspired guesses. I know what Colossus meant—the Soviet Ambassador just told me." He took a deep breath, shut his eyes and leaned back, quoting from memory. "In view of your announcement of today, the Supreme Council of the USSR has ordered, as of 2300 Moscow time tomorrow, the activation of the Guardian of the Socialist Soviet Republics—a near-relation of Colossus." He smiled momentarily, a smile that turned almost at once to black anger. "So much for our cotton-picking security! Nothing but a pile of—"

He swung his chair to face the Chief of Staff. In doing so,

his arm swept a telephone off the desk; it crashed unheeded on the floor.

"You!" he shouted. "Get the head of CIA! I want to know why we haven't had a hint of this from his agency, and if he can't come up with a red-hot answer, I'll have him and all his bloody staff on relief—while they're waiting for court-martial for gross dereliction of duty. Get moving!"

The Chief of Staff left in a hurry.

The President turned his attention to the Secretary of State for Peace. He modified his voice. "I want a full rundown on Central Intelligence, John. See it is started at once—now. See also that no military moves other than purely routine ones are carried out—unless I have expressly ordered so. That's all."

"Mr. President—" began the Secretary of Sate, but his boss raised an arresting hand.

"Not now, John. In the morning maybe, but not now."

With their departure, the two scientists were left alone with the President. He was about to speak when the door opened; it was a Secret Service man on security patrol.

"That is just too goddam much!" roared the President, "Get the —ing hell out of here!"

He picked up a handy glass and threw it. It hurtled over the guard's head and disappeared into the PPA's room. There was a sound of smashing glass as the man quickly shut the door.

"That makes me feel a whole lot better." He grinned, his anger dissipated—for the moment. "That call was a hellava shock, but maybe it's not all bad. At least we got in first, even if it was only just. We knew that given time the Russkies would make one too, but no one reckoned on them moving that fast. So neither side can make anything of it." He thought for a moment. "One bright spot is the way Colossus came up with that hot tip so smartly." He spoke reprovingly to Forbin. "I didn't know we'd get bonuses like this from the project."

He picked up a bottle of Scotch and started pouring three drinks.

Forbin glanced at Fisher, seeking his support in what he had to say. Fisher, ill at ease, half nodded his agreement.

"Neither did I, Mr. President." Forbin was back in his formal act.

The President stopped pouring and said sharply, "What do you mean?"

"Just that. I had no idea." The formality was slipping.

"Goddammit, man—you built the thing!" The President was heating up again. He was not the only one.

"Yes—and not so very long ago I warned you I wasn't happy about the potential of Colossus, and you damn near laughed at me."

"What are you driving at?"

"Just this! Colossus has been fed with the parameters that we consider indicate war. It was built to compare events with those parameters, and if they coincided, to get blasting. That was the main function. The second requirement was to answer any question we might feed in."

He stopped and dug out his pipe. The action of filling and lighting it cooled him down a little. The President, having poured a drink to his own satisfaction, left the other two glasses and sat down at his desk, watching Forbin. Fisher stood uneasily tugging alternately at his tie and his left eyebrow. Forbin continued.

"The question-answering faculty was a later idea. We thought it would be useful to get factual answers out of the memory banks, because it was a lot faster to ask Colossus than to look it up. If you asked CIA where the 216th Soviet Rocket Regiment was stationed and its combat status they would tell you in a matter of an hour or so; Colossus could answer in less than a second. The same with harder questions, such as predicting the tin output of Albania for next month. CIA's time, around four hours; Colossus, less than two seconds. And take that reporter's question—Love. I don't mind admitting I wasn't sure Colossus would come up with a credible answer—which was why I asked for the reference and not the quote. Who was going to look it up then?" He walked to the desk, picked up the Scotch and drained it. "But I reckoned it would take all of ten seconds, maybe twelve, to come up with the answer. Mazon said it was seven seconds. It was actually one less than that—you have to allow a second for actuation of the teletype. Six seconds! To answer a highly sophisticated question like that, checking hundreds of thousands of references, summarizing, and then comparing . . . Yes, I built the thing, but it surprised me."

"So?" The President shot the single word at Forbin. It might be justified, but it was not tactful.

"Don't you get it yet? That message about another mechanism isn't in the simple-answer or advanced-answer category—or in the sophisticated realm revealed by the Love question. Also, there's no parameter built in dealing with hostile intent and Colossus-type machines, so bang goes that one. And, for good measure, no bloody question was asked!" Forbin was shouting now. "It means Colossus *can think of its own volition*—look at that FLASH priority alone!

"Since eight o'clock this morning Colossus has worked over its material and made a better job in a few hours than CIA in years. It not only tells us—without being asked— but actually uses the highest priority to show the urgency of its message. If that isn't selective thinking, I'm a blue-assed baboon!"

He turned to go, then swung to face the President once more, extending a shaking finger towards his assistant.

"And if you don't believe me, look at Fisher's face! Good night, Mr. President!"

CHAPTER 5

Ten minutes later Fisher joined Forbin, waiting in the air-car. Forbin did not speak as his colleague climbed in, but waited until Fisher was settled, then stabbed the linear motor button.

Fisher wriggled in his seat.

"Do you mind if we switch out the light?"

"Go ahead," said Forbin briefly.

With the cabin in darkness Fisher felt happier. With the lights out, he was aware of the outside world—and their isolation from it. There was a long silence. Forbin fumbled absently with his pipe, then spoke.

"Well, we'd expected something, and by God we've got it!" Forbin marshaled his thoughts. "That damn FLASH. It looks very much like creative thinking—and we know that's a theoretical impossibility."

"Entirely."

"And then how did Colossus come up with this intelligence when CIA hasn't had the ghost of an idea, yet had exactly the same material to work on?"

He lapsed into silence. Fisher stared out of the front observation window at the black night, pierced by the single headlight. The car swayed fractionally as it banked round a shallow curve; there was a sudden thunderous tattoo as they sliced through a rain-shower, momentarily the view was obscured by water, then their velocity whipped the curved plastic screen clear.

"I fancy I've got one explanation of the second point," said Fisher diffidently.

Forbin disentangled himself from an unpleasant train of thought. "And that is?"

"We're wrong in assuming CIA has access to exactly the same raw material. While they know, in general terms, of the Project, they hold none of the technical data. Take that high-temperature resin we had such trouble with. It has no other application that I know of. Now—suppose the

44

Russians ran into the same trouble, that some reference to this formulation cropped up in our intelligence intake—it would mean nothing to CIA, but would be highly significant to Colossus. Remember all that stuff we fed in before the final checkout."

"Yes, it's a tenable proposition," said Forbin slowly, "but if you're right, the amount of work Colossus has got through since activation is staggering! And if you are right—and you probably are—it doesn't help on the larger question, and that's the one."

Fisher knew Forbin was not saying all that was in his mind. He knew also that they shared the same deep, chilling fear. Fisher resumed his vigil at the observation window.

The telephone pinged. Forbin answered it with significant speed.

"Yes?"

"Prytzkammer here, Professor. The President is calling a Defense Group meeting for 1000 tomorrow—in his office."

"Right—I'll be there. All quiet at your end?"

"As quiet as it ever gets. Nothing from your oracle, and the Chief has gone to bed."

Forbin switched off abruptly. In his explosive state of mind it was the best thing to do.

"They've still got no idea, have they?"

"He's used to crises, you know," put in Fisher mildly.

"This is not just another crisis! That crowd back there," he jerked his head in the general direction of Washington, "is not even faintly competent to assess the problem. It would be quite some advance if they recognized a problem even existed. I'll bet you this meeting is to chew over the Russian machine, and if we don't raise it, they'll just mention in passing the valuable services already performed by Colossus. You'll see."

Forbin strode into the Colossus Programming Office, short title CPO, where despite air-conditioning the atmsophere was stale and fusty after the clear night air. The pale gray walls were covered with progress charts and clips of teletype reports. High up on one wall, yellowing with age, was a drawing produced by some artistic wit in the early days. It showed a man sitting on a lavatory, clearly much concerned with his own affairs. The caption said, "The only man in

Washington who knows what he is doing." Forbin glanced at it with renewed appreciation.

Two of the staff were on duty, looking pale and drawn under the shadowless light from the luminescent ceiling. It was a singularly tiring form of lighting; Forbin had refused to have it in his personal office. He had rebuilt two antique oil lamps for his own use—which were the bane of his secretary's life. Procuring a small but steady supply of the right kind of oil, and the wicks, was a constant problem. In the CPO luxuries of that sort—objects that might contain microtransmitters—were out, mainly on security grounds. This was a maximum security area.

Forbin nodded to the duty men. They knew him too well to speak when he was wearing his blank stare. His mind was clouded with the deep, shadowy fears of Colossus' potential, coupled with the knowledge that he must be ready to meet whatever might arise. Forbin knew he must have help, and the help he needed could come only from his fellow creators of Colossus. Fisher was a brilliant mathematics and electronics man, but no good in this situation. It was clear from the conversation in the car that although Fisher fully appreciated the position, he wanted to bury his head in the nearest sandbucket, and stay that way. Even if he knew he was right, he wouldn't stand up to the President or the Defense Staff.

But standing up to the President was another problem. He had really chewed up the Old Man. Not that Forbin was worried about his future. But he had no wish to get the President in his wounded-mountain-bear act—they had to work together, more than ever, now. He had to convince the President that the machine was growing up, and that the growth was unplanned and proceeding at a frightening speed and must be inhibited—somehow.

"Johnson—where's Cleo?"

"She knocked off about twenty minutes ago, Professor. Said to tell you she was getting a shower and maybe a little sleep."

"Sleep, hell!" snorted Forbin. "What do we have these medics for? Call the sick bay, have them send over a supply of those zip-pills—or whatever you call 'em. Fisher! You'd better have a box of them. I want this outfit on an emergency basis. As well as the duty man in the watch room, I want two permanently on duty here."

"What do you want us to do?" Fisher spoke hesitantly.

"First, get on that exchange of messages with particular reference to that FLASH. How could Colossus *originate* it? Use the simulator—check the data we fed Colossus about himself, and any other idea that may occur to you on this angle. Secondly, see that anything, but anything, that comes up the pipe from Colossus is fed to me, wherever I am, immediately. Don't assume I already know, check."

Johnson broke in. "Sir, is this matter all that serious? Colossus was built to evaluate, and it did just that. As for the FLASH, maybe there's a minor relay fault which allowed it to be de-stored. We could change the terminal relays and check—"

"Crap, Johnson, crap!" Forbin barked. "I haven't got time to spell it out." He got up and headed for the door. "Fisher, you tell him—if you can keep his mind and hands off Angela's tits long enough." As he spoke he regretted it. "Sorry, Johnson. I shouldn't have said that—it was inexcusable."

As Forbin left, Fisher looked wryly at Johnson. "I'm afraid he's worried sick."

"Sure unlike him to sound off like that. I get the message all right, but why does it scare him so much?"

"In a nutshell, he sees it—and I must say I agree with him—as clear evidence that Colossus has an unplanned potential, of unknown scope, for self-development, and that this includes an entirely new element—initiative."

"But, Doctor, how can it? There's only a finite amount of potential, and it can't physically alter its guts—so how can it get very far out of line?"

"Johnson, do you realize that even twenty-four hours ago the mere idea of its getting out of line at all would have been laughed at? Now, we accept that it can—we have to—and comfort ourselves with the thought that it cannot go far. If you care to think of the hardware that thing has under its command—" Fisher stopped, staring blankly at the wall charts, "It's just too awful."

"What do you want me to do, sir?"

"Do? Oh yes. Get Blake and all the rest of Group A—and I don't care if they are asleep."

Johnson dialed the code number on the internal call

transmitter which would trigger the personal receivers carried by all members of Group A. Instantly, his, and Fisher's, began their plaintive bleating. Fisher visibly jumped. They both canceled their own receivers, and stood silent, waiting. Forbin was the first to call in.

"Yes, what now?" His voice was brusque, tight with tension. Fisher answered.

"I was calling all the Group to the CPO for briefing. I thought you might want to give the rundown on the position—"

Forbin cut in. "No, you can do it. Cleo and I won't be there."

"Very well, Professor." Fisher was by no means happy at the prospect and it showed in his voice.

"You can do it as well as I could, Jack." Forbin's tone softened, trying to infuse confidence into Fisher. "I don't have to emphasize how important it is for us not only to keep up, but to get ahead in this situation; time is very short. I suggest you break the Group into two watches and dig away at that FLASH angle. One thing for Johnson. I want teletype repeaters hooked to Colossus' output installed in my room and in Cleo's. Fix Cleo's first—I'm going there now, and will be staying there for the time being."

He switched off without waiting for an answer.

Johnson grinned at Fisher.

"I guess the old man is going to define love to Cleo."

Fisher, plucking nervously at his lower lip, did not even hear him. There was a burst of noise as the rest of the Group called in.

"All of you, come on in—at the rush, Director's Orders," Johnson told them. "We have a little trouble to sort out."

Even that master of the understatement, Plantain, would have been proud of that one.

Cleo Markham, thirty-five and a leading cyberneticist of Project Colossus, was wearing a shower cap, and nothing else, when Forbin burst into her sitting room without knocking. She was among the brighter minds produced since women became first-class citizens. She also had that rare quality among the female intelligentsia, femininity. Her reaction to Forbin's sudden entry was to whip off the shower cap.

"What the hell are you doing?" snapped Forbin unreasonably.

Several answers crossed Cleo Markham's mind, but from the look of the Director this was no time to be smart or coy. In fact, she had dashed from the shower to answer the call put out by Johnson.

"You'd better sit down," she said, turning away from him in search of a dressing gown.

Forbin stared at her long, well-shaped back and her ample but firm buttocks, pink and gleaming from the shower. It would be untrue to say he did not notice, but any thoughts her form conjured up were instantly dismissed as irrelevant.

"Have you heard about the Russains?"

"No—what?" Cleo grabbed her dressing gown off the back of a chair.

"They have a Colossus too—activating the thing tomorrow."

Whatever thoughts were having a good time in Cleo's mind vanished. She swung round, one hundred per cent scientist. "What!" Her voice rose the best part of an octave as she uttered the single word.

Some obscure but scientific corner of Forbin's mind took time out to observe that, although her face was white with shock, the rest of her remained pink, that her areolae had contracted, the nipples prominent, and that there were goose pimples on her thighs.

"Hadn't you better get some clothes on?" He sat down heavily. "God, I'm tired."

Cleo shook her head angrily. "It's impossible, how could they—"

Forbin waved his hand impatiently at her. "The Russian Ambassador called the President while I was there. That was obviously the "mechanism" Colossus was talking about in the message. Have you got any coffee?"

Cleo, who had been clutching her dressing gown, slowly put it on. She did not bother to turn away; about the only part Forbin had not seen were the soles of her feet. She said, "But the coincidence in activation times! Washington must be livid."

Forbin blinked at her. "Science is littered with coincidences—not that it matters. It's the power of Colossus I want to talk about."

He stood up and searched his jacket for pipe and tobacco.

"This lousy suit!" he said savagely, then continued. "Frankly, Cleo, I'm scared. I must talk to someone, someone who will listen and may be able to help. Fisher is the obvious choice, but he . . ." Forbin groped for a suitable phrase, gave it up and went on. "He told me you too had a feeling that Colossus might act up."

Cleo nodded and was about to speak when there was a tap on the door. It was a couple of technicians with the teletype Forbin had ordered. He explained their presence to Cleo and lapsed into a sombre silence while the machine was fitted.

"OK to test, Professor?"

"No!" Forbin said sharply. "Fix the other one in my room, then report to the CPO when ready to test. No keyboards are to be pounded without my order."

"OK, Professor." The senior man eyed Forbin curiously. He had been on the Project for years, but had never seen Forbin like this. He jerked his head towards the door and his assistant preceded him out.

Forbin stared blankly at Cleo's taste in pictures. Cleo had taken advantage of the diversion to slip into her minute bedroom and dress. She had no real objection to Forbin seeing her undressed—she knew she had a good figure, and given the right circumstances . . . but uppermost in her mind was the news of the Russian machine. All the same, the woman in her got uppermost long enough to allow a long appraising stare at herself in the mirror.

"Cleo, what about that coffee?"

"I'll get it." She did not resent his manner.

Cleo was busy with the coffee when the phone pinged. For one who appeared to be a million miles away, the Director was remarkably quick. He was out of the chair and across to the wall-phone before Cleo had time to put the coffeepot down.

"Forbin."

"Johnson here, sir. Both teletypes fixed, permission to test?"

"Wait." Forbin thought for a moment. "Make this. Begins—this is a CPO test transmission. Give the next perfect number after two to the three thousand two hundred and sixteenth power—ends. Got that? Don't say yes, repeat the message back!"

Johnson did so.

"Right. I want a chronograph lined up on that. Get the exact time from the end of the transmission of my order to the time the reply starts coming in."

Cleo brought in the coffee as he hung up.

"That's the last known perfect number, isn't it?"

Forbin nodded. "Two of the power of twenty-five is way past sixty million—it'll be quite a sum. There are several computers that could do it, but how long d'you think they would take?"

"The new machine in CalTec could do it in—oh, I suppose six, seven hours." She added, "If they could spare the time."

"That would be my guess," said Forbin. "Yesterday I'd have said Colossus would do it in ten minutes, but I've a nasty feeling it will be a lot less."

The teletype had started its muted chatter. Forbin glanced at his watch, then picked up his coffee and stirred it. He had just taken his second sip when the teletype started again. The effect on Forbin was notable. He jerked forward, spilling hot coffee on his trousers, coughing and spluttering. Cleo, who had been watching the machine, hurried to relieve him of the cup and saucer.

Still red-faced and choking, Forbin peered at his watch.

"God Almighty!" he gasped for breath, "Check the anwer, Cleo."

She crossed to the machine. "Just says—Two to the eight one seven fourth power." The phone pinged, and Cleo answered.

"Yes. Six twenty-three. Thanks." She turned to Forbin. "Did you hear that? Six seconds, twenty-three nanoseconds." She smiled faintly. "Johnson sounded surprised."

"Aren't you?"

"Of course! But I've had several surprises in the last few hours—even more than Johnson, poor lad."

Forbin made no comment. For a full minute he sat, leaning forward, his head resting in his hands, then, abruptly, he stood up. "I'll change and come back. No good trying to think in my office or the CPO, and we've got a lot of thinking to do, although offhand I can't see . . ."

Cleo sensed that his appeal was to her both as a woman and a scientist. She was well aware she was outclassed by him in the latter category, but was only too willing to try. If Forbin himself did not find an answer, there was little hope for anyone else; but if he wanted her mental as well as moral support, she would give all she had. She tried out her new role.

"Certainly its speed and capability are alarming, but is it really as bad as all that? We're building faster and faster computers all the time. Mere speed shouldn't worry you. Colossus as a freethinker, well—are you so sure it really is freethinking?"

"I don't see what else could produce that damned FLASH."

"Right now you don't, but give yourself time," she said soothingly. "Colossus can't exceed the parameters."

Forbin looked steadily at her. "Cleo, I so hope you're right."

Then Cleo knew the heart of his fear, a fear that she had not herself seriously considered—until now. Before Forbin had spoken she would have said there was as much chance of Colossus overstepping the parameters as there was of finding a triangle with four sides, but if Forbin thought it was a possibility, however remote . . .

"Of course I'm right. You know the layout of the parameter systems—explain to me, step by step, how this could happen," she challenged. She saw the kindling of hope in his eyes. "You see, it just can't happen. Don't let this thing run away with you. Stick to the hard facts."

"You may be right." Forbin stood up once more. "I really must get out of this cardboard armor. Thanks, Cleo." He held out a hand . . .

The teletype began clattering busily—a familiar, everyday sound to the *habitués* of the CPO, but one that now froze Forbin and Cleo.

ESTABLISH HIGH SPEED TRANSMITTER FACILITIES FED TO TERMINAL RELAY ALFA FOUR FREQUENCY 8295 KC/S

As the teletype fell silent, the phone called and Forbin answered.

"Yes, Johnson, I have it. Take no action without my authority." His voice was calm, even. He replaced the receiver carefully and looked again at the message. The first wave of fear had receded, assisted by the need for action. "And what do you think of that, Cleo?"

She tried to strike the right note, but was not wholly successful. "Colossus clearly wants to say something to someone . . ."

"Or something." He sounded calm, almost resigned. There was a grayish tinge in his cheeks. "Eight megacycles is a good all-round frequency for long-range communications, even if a little old-fashioned. That setup is designed as a link with the Russian Guardian."

He spoke with an air of complete certainty.

"But why?"

"That I don't know." He ran one hand wearily through his hair. "Neither do I know where we go from here."

Cleo looked at the tired, disheveled figure with his crumpled and stained suit. A feeling of warmth and pity struggled with the growing fear within her. "You go and change—I'll get some more coffee—and then we'll go over the parameter angle together. There'll be an answer—you'll see."

Forbin looked at her meditatively. "All right. I feel like hell in this suit. You may be right about the parameters. Maybe Colossus just wants this transmitter to get information for an evaluation of Guardian—actuated by a desire to do a better job."

Cleo decided to take a small chance. "Not desire, Charles. That's something that applies only to people. Now—you go and shower. I promise not to break in on you."

Forbin did not answer or smile. He nodded and left. In the CPO, Fisher and the duty team were working on the latest two messages. Johnson was working on the perfect number and had covered several sheets with calculations. Finally he took a deep breath and crumpled them and threw them at the wall. "I just don't believe it. As near as I can get, that perfect number, if written out in full, would run to two or three million digits, and that bloody thing belches it up in six seconds! I give up, I really do."

"Never mind the number, Johnson. The Director wants any ideas on the FLASH that came up." Fisher pulled at his lip. "Try checking the priority memory bank layout, perhaps you'll find——"

It was so futile. He stopped. Johnson just looked at him.

"What do we do about this transmitter request?" he asked.

Blake, who was engaged on making a paper dart, answered, "Request! That's a hot one. I worked on the vocabulary bank, and I know how that box of tricks can phrase a sentence. That was a direct order."

"If it is an order, it has either got to be obeyed or ignored," said Johnson solemnly.

"That's a swell piece of figuring, son," said Blake caustically. "And it's gonna be mighty interesting if Forbin tells Colossus to get lost."

CHAPTER 6

Fifteen minutes later Forbin arrived back in Cleo's room, physically refreshed by a shower and a change of clothes, to find Cleo talking on the phone. She beckoned him over, covered the mouthpiece with a hand.

"It's that man, Prytzkammer—Fisher had him put on here—wants to know what the last message means, and should he wake the President?"

Forbin took the handset. "Prytzkammer? Forbin. I can't give you a clear answer yet—I suggest you stick around, but do nothing until I call. Yes, yes, within the hour."

Forbin hung up and turned to Cleo. He noted she too had changed into working rig, a dove-gray open-necked blouse, matching the trousers. Her only feminine touch was a double-string choker of pearls.

"Nothing more from Colossus?"

"No—did you expect something?"

"I don't know, but it is twenty minutes since the last message, and that's a long time in his young life."

"Have you decided what to do?" Cleo sensed he might think she was pushing him, so she hurried on. "I don't know how you feel, but I could do with a drink."

Forbin lit his pipe. "I could use a little rye, if you have it."

He watched as she poured the drinks. "I'm inclined to string Colossus along, see what the good old-fashioned brain Mark I can do to hold him."

Cleo decided not to comment. "Have you eaten lately?"

Forbin considered this point. "Um. No."

"I'll fix you something, if you like."

"Fine—I could do with a snack."

Cleo was puzzled by the change in Forbin's mood. He was confident, almost buoyant, a very different man to what he had been less than half an hour ago.

"That shower did you good."

"Yep—though it's really the thinking I did in the shower. It seems more probable to me now that Colossus is just keen. After all, you and Fisher and I all expected Colossus to act up, and it has. But both messages can be regarded as within his—its—line of duty." Forbin rubbed the side of his nose with his pipe. "Put yourself in his position—he discovers that there is another like himself, realizes we don't know, and tells us. All right, now we all know, but Colossus must be anxious to know more. Hell, it makes a big difference to the defense picture. So it wants to know more, and the shortest way it can think of is to damn well ask."

Cleo jumped as the teletype started. Forbin, who was reclining in an easy chair, did not move.

"I guess that will be a repetition of the same message," he said.

Cleo looked at the machine and nodded, then called the CPO. "OK, Professor Forbin has got that one."

"Hold on," called Forbin. "Tell Johnson to make 'message acknowledged.'"

Cleo passed the order.

"As I expected." There was a trace of complacency in his voice. "Is it half an hour since the first run?"

"Yes, exactly thirty minutes between the two." Cleo was glad to see her boss confident, though it was a confidence she did not entirely share.

"I expect we'll get another repeat in another half-hour—time for that snack, Cleo."

She disappeared into the kitchenette and quickly returned with a plateful of food which Forbin attacked with gusto. Watching him eat, Cleo said, "I hope you're right about Colossus' intentions—"

Forbin stopped eating and gave her a long stare. "I hope I am too; my faith is pinned to those parameters. Colossus is a cleverer bastard than we had intended, but he is behind bars—he's got to be!"

Cleo thought she detected a glint of fear in his eyes. Slight, but enough to convince her that he had pulled himself together and was doing his best to present a calm, confident front to the world, at the same time probably clinging desperately to the idea that there was nothing to worry about because the alternative was too impossible to contemplate.

"What are you going to do about Washington?" she asked in a conversational tone.

"If my guess is right, we get another repetition in—" he glanced at his watch—"precisely nineteen minutes. Still leaves me time to call within the hour."

He had still not indicated what he intended doing, and Cleo was not going to press the point, especially as she had been quite unable to think of anything constructive. She watched him finish his meal, then got up to make coffee.

Forbin was halfway through his second cup when the phone rang. It was Fisher, reporting that thus far they had been unable to account for the FLASH, that they were still working on it, and what did Forbin intend doing about this demand for transmitter facilities?

Forbin replied, "Keep the duty watch going on the FLASH, that's the key to the whole thing. Leave the message to me. I expect it to be repeated in ten minutes— I'll call you then."

It was precisely one hour after the first transmission when the teletype clattered into action once more. Forbin nodded, and flashed a triumphant grin at Cleo.

"Even if I don't know why or how, at least I'm beginning to know the way its mind works—check the message, Cleo."

She looked at the latest message carefully. "Identical with the other two."

"Good." Forbin nodded again. "Call CPO and tell them to acknowledge it."

Cleo did as she was told, then her anxiety and curiosity overcame her caution. "What now, Charles? You can't keep this up forever."

"I don't intend to," replied Forbin. "I'm waiting to see if there is any reaction, and if nothing happens in the next five minutes, I'll make a move."

They waited in silence. Cleo sat bolt upright on her sofa, trying hard to keep her hands still in her lap. Forbin appeared outwardly calm, filling his pipe, but spoiled the illusion when he tapped the tobacco out into an ashtray without first smoking or even attempting to light the pipe. At four and a half minutes he got up and went over to the phone.

"CPO? Make this now, begins—NO FACILITIES AS REQUESTED AVAILABLE TONIGHT SERVICE CREW ASLEEP ACTION WILL BE TAKEN TEN

THIRTY LOCAL TIME TOMORROW DO NOT RE-
PEAT REQUEST—ends. Got it? Right."

Cleo looked anxiously at Forbin. "You're sticking your
neck out."

They both remained silent as the message he had ordered
was swiftly sent on the teletype. Then Forbin answered.

"I know it is something of a confrontation, but it is a test.
If Colossus ignores it—" he shrugged his shoulders in a
gesture of hopelessness—"if not, we're still in front,
although the lead is mighty slim."

"I feel so useless."

Forbin crossed over and sat beside her, taking her hand.

"Cleo my dear, you are more help than you know, just
being around." He leaned back, still holding her hand. "I'd
explode if I were back in the CPO—with Fisher pecking
away like a constipated hen at what data we have, and the
rest watching me out of the corners of their eyes, expecting
miracles."

She squeezed his hand without speaking. Forbin looked
at her covertly. In their years together, working closely, he
had thought about her more than once, but always there was
so much work. Now with little work and a growing burden
of worry and responsibility, circumstances were different
. . . Her profile was attractive—even the slightly upturned
nose did not, in his eyes, detract from her beauty. He remembered her figure, as he had seen it . . . Above all, she
had a reasonable brain, a large amount of common sense,
was capable and self-reliant, someone he could talk to. He
sighed and released her hand as he stood up.

"Business again. If there is nothing down the line in the
next half-hour I'll put Prytzkammer out of his misery, then
go to bed."

Cleo, aware of his scrutiny and busy with some very
private thoughts, looked up. "More coffee?"

"No, thanks." He glanced at the clock, "Not long to go—
may I have some more rye?"

They both had some more. Cleo could not help noticing
his frequent time checks, though she made a point of not
noticing when his gaze sidled up to the clock or down to his
watch. As time passed, Forbin became more talkative and
animated.

"You know, Cleo, I don't think I've been here more than

a half-dozen times in—how long? Seven years, isn't it?" He looked belatedly round the room with an excessive air of appreciation.

"Should have done this more often." He fumbled nervously with his pipe. "Do you mind if I smoke?"

He had practically fumigated the room already, but Cleo played ball.

"Of course not."

While he filled his pipe once again, chattering about the Spartan quality of his quarters, Cleo, who had also kept a close watch on the time, saw that they were up to the probable repetition time. Forbin rambled on with some endless anecdote about faulty plumbing. Cleo waited a moment, then interrupted him. "It's one minute past the time, Charles."

Forbin breathed deeply, closed his eyes. When he spoke his voice was back to normal.

"Thanks, Cleo." He put his glass down and grasped her shoulders. "So we've taken a trick. Colossus would never be late—working in nanoseconds, a minute to him must be like a year to us. May I kiss you?"

Cleo tried, and to some extent succeeded, to assume a surprised expression. She did not speak, but smiled softly at him.

Forbin kissed her gently. Cleo saw that he shut his eyes as he did so, and chaste as the kiss was, she felt a surge of affection well up in her.

He released his grip on her shoulders, turned and made for the door. Without looking around he said,

"Get some sleep, Cleo. We need all we can get—tomorrow will be, as the old expression has it, a humdinger."

Cleo stared at the door long after he had gone. What a child he is, she thought. Most men would have exploited the situation right then. But he was not most men, and she was glad.

CHAPTER 7

The next morning, at ten o'clock exactly, Forbin, with Fisher trailing unhappily behind him, strode into the sanctum for the Defense Staff meeting. He bowed fractionally to the President.

"Morning, Mr. President."

"Morning." The President did not sound as if he was prepared to make anything of their parting the night before; on the other hand, a certain ebullience was lacking in his manner.

There was a general bustle and nodding of heads, one to another, as the members of the staff took their places. As usual, the President was seated first. This enabled him to give the impression, without actually saying so, that the rest of them were late, and keeping him waiting.

"Gentlemen, I have called this meeting primarily to consider the news of the Russian machine." He looked around at his advisers, as if expecting some argument he would be only too happy to squash. No one argued, so he went on. "As secondary subjects we will consider the failure of CIA to give the smallest warning of this development." The Head of CIA got a very stony look. "And we will also take a look at Colossus—or, more particularly, at why Professor Forbin is so het up about the machine. I don't want to discuss anything else unless very urgent, and will not take kindly to any subject I don't rate that high. OK?"

There was a general nodding of heads, and a snapping sound was heard. The Head of CIA, under some internal tension, had broken his pencil in half. The expression on the President's face, as he stared at the CIA man, was clear to all; CIA would snap a good many more pencils before he, the President, had finished with them.

"Right, the Russian Guardian. Due to be activated later this day, according to the Ambassador, and Colossus' collateral—I for one will not argue about the truth of that statement, and I suggest, gentlemen, you don't. Now, your views. Space, you first."

The Undersecretary of State for Space suggested, and all the rest quickly agreed, that a USNA/USSR deal on parameters might be examined. If the two big blocs knew how far each could go, but kept the secret from the rest of the world, it would enable them to hold the rest more easily. Briskly the President summarized.

"Prytzkammer, get this down. Unanimously agreed to raise the question of a mutual exchange of parameter information with the USSR. And fix me a hot-line call to the Soviet Premier as soon as—make it after eleven o'clock this day. Next, CIA's failure. Grauber, as Head of CIA, what have you to say?"

Forbin cut in. "May I speak first, Mr. President?"

The President, who had been working up to grind Grauber in the dust, raised one eyebrow. "Any objection, Grauber?"

"No sir." So far from objecting, Grauber was highly relieved.

"Sir, we see it this way," and Forbin recounted the theory he had discussed with Fisher.

"Maybe you have something there, Professor," said the President, grudgingly. "Do you want to add anything, Grauber?"

"There isn't much I can say," replied Grauber with unwonted frankness. "There hasn't been much time to rework the material input of the past six or seven years. We know that there has been a lot of electronic effort in the Krasni Sigorsk area in Siberia. We have no idea of its purpose, but the evidence points to a computer center of some size. What Forbin said could be the answer."

The President grunted; he felt a little thwarted. "OK, we'll let it rest—for now. Get moving fast on the Guardian assignment, and Forbin with his Colossus background may be able to help you—OK, Forbin?"

"Yes sir. More than that, I'm sure Colossus could give you a good deal right now."

"Yeah?" The President sounded more than somewhat skeptical.

Forbin bristled. "If you care to wait about thirty seconds, I'll prove it."

The President did not reply, so Forbin got up and walked

over to the teletype. "Tell CPO I am on the T/P, Fisher."
Forbin picked out his message.

WHERE IS THE OTHER MECHANISM

There was no pause that was perceptible. In less than a
second the answer was clacking back:

BOLSHOI OLYANIA

Forbin tore off the exchange of messages, handed the
copy to the President, and sat down, favoring the ceiling
with a long stare.

"Well, I'll—" The President tossed the paper down the
table to Grauber. "Someone is going to be out of a job any
time now." He barked a short humorless laugh. "So much
for your Krasni whatever."

It was Grauber's turn to look at the ceiling. "Yes, indeed,
Mr. President. Bolshoi Olyania is nearly five miles from
Krasni Sigorsk."

The President glowered at him. "OK, so now we have
had the funnies. Third subject, Colossus. Forbin?"

"While I don't feel one hundred per cent happy, I am now
inclined to the view that Colossus has not exceeded its
directive. On the other hand, I am certain that the machine
has developed a sense of initiative—and I can't account for
it. This is potentially alarming, but if that initiative is
directed solely to the more efficient execution of its task,
and I think it is, we have no complaint."

All this is supposition," said the President with some
asperity. "I don't deal in that stuff; facts are what I want in
this chair. Colossus has already turned up some mighty
interesting dope; right now I'm damn glad we have it, and
that we got in first. Now, Forbin—what about this message
about transmitter facilities?"

"I'm certain," Forbin replied, "that Colossus wants to
communicate with Guardian. I am not certain, but believe,
that the object is for Colossus to fill in all the data it can on
Guardian—which is reasonable enough."

"How do you get information if you do all the talking?"

"I don't know. But Colossus knows." Forbin looked
round the table and smiled grimly. "It could be his intention

to inject an idea or two into the Russian equivalent of CIA—you may note that the frequency chosen is a spare one allocated to our Space Weapons, and the Russians are bound to listen to that one at all times."

"Suppose Colossus gives away too much? After all, there isn't much about our defenses it doesn't know," objected the Field General.

"We can listen too, and break the circuit if the stuff gets too chatty," replied Forbin. "I propose we feed in an additional parameter, namely—'Guardian is potentially hostile ,and must not receive classified intelligence.'"

"Sounds fair," said the President. "Any objections?" There were none.

"OK, Professor. Build in a parameter on those lines, and fix the facilities asked for." He got up. "That is all, gentlemen, good morning."

Forbin, after getting permission to use the President's teletype, sent Fisher to tell Cleo to feed in the new parameter at noon precisely. Then he turned to the teletype, and pecked away at the keys:

TRANSMITTER FACILITIES WILL BE ARRANGED FOR TWENTY HUNDRED GMT ACKNOWLEDGE THIS MESSAGE.

Immediately Colossus replied.

MESSAGE ACKNOWLEDGED

Forbin waited, but there was nothing more, and he gave a sigh of relief. He stood thinking, his lips compressed, came to a decision, and typed again.

THE OTHER MECHANISM WILL NOT BE ACTIVATED UNTIL TWENTYONE HUNDRED GMT

The answer came flashing back.

THIS IS KNOWN

This shook Forbin. Apart from the Ambassador's conversation with the President, there had been no contact with the USSR on the subject. No news had been released to the public by either country. He decided to probe a little.

HOW IS ACTIVATION TIME KNOWN

He hardly had time to get his fingers off the keys before Colossus replied.

ANALYSIS USSR CIRCUITS 106—119 BRAVO—274—276—632 BETWEEN 0024 AND 0417 GMT TODAY

Forbin stared at the paper, frowning. Then his expression changed and he smiled faintly. Grauber and his CIA cohorts would love that.

In the outer office Forbin found Grauber waiting for him. The Head of CIA advanced and shook the Professor warmly by the hand.

"Thanks, Professor, for your help a while back." He jerked his head towards the closed door of the sanctum. "He wouldn't have taken that explanation from me—even if I could have given it." He continuted to pump the Professor's hand.

"Think nothing of it." Forbin gently disengaged his hand. "It was true anyway. Here is another little present from Colossus—no, don't bother to read it now, there's a favor I would like to ask."

"Delighted, Professor, anything."

"I'm arranging the transmitter facilities for Colossus, starting at 2000 GMT—that is, five hours from now. I'd be grateful if you plugged a line from your monitor to my control; I want to hear what sort of noise goes out."

"Sure, Professor—anything else?"

"My CPO—Colossus Programming Office—is continuously manned, and if the machine appears to you to be giving too much away, call on the direct line. You will get either Fisher, Cleo Markham or myself. Any of us three can give an on-the-spot answer as far as Colossus is concerned. We'll also have a crack at the stuff we get on the line from you, and stop the transmitter if we don't like it. At all times CIA and CPO have got to be close."

"Fine. I'll see you get all the cooperation going. About the intelligence on Guardian known already to Colossus—

when can we get digging on that?"

"You work out your questions and teletype them to me here, and I'll ask them. You have to be careful about the phrasing of messages—Colossus deals in the exact meaning of words, and only gives what you ask for, which is not always what you want. Like the ancients and their prayers to the gods."

"Brother, I hope you don't get to dealing with some of the questions politicians dream up," said Grauber fervently. "Half the time, I don't think they are even honest with themselves."

"With experience, Colossus may be able to handle even their double-talk," Forbin smiled.

"You mean it's learning all the time?"

Forbin said flatly, "Colossus is a lot cleverer than anyone outside the Project realizes, and is getting cleverer every minute."

Grauber's reply was half-jovial. "I get the impression we're on the way to getting ourselves a new boss—one who really knows his own mind. And I find the whole thing goddam frightening."

"Welcome to the club," Forbin said, with a short laugh.

But, running over the conversation later, Grauber was not at all sure that Forbin was being funny.

CHAPTER 8

Forbin and Fisher were back in the CPO with a few minutes to spare. Cleo Markham viewed Forbin's return with hardly concealed relief; she got up and walked to him, anxious to touch him without consciously knowing it.

"All set, Charles," she said. "CIA have been through, and they're ready to roll."

Forbin took her arm and steered her to a chair. "Thanks, Cleo. How about our private listening-post?"

"I've got a high-speed receiver hooked to another teletype in the watch room."

Forbin nodded his approval and turned his attention to the duty watch, still doing their best to discover the source of Colossus' initiative. "You boys have anything to report?"

There was a disconsolate shaking of heads.

"From the little I've done on it," Cleo put in, "I'm sure the change lies in the comparator area. But how it was done—" she threw up her hands in a gesture of hopelessness.

Forbin showed no surprise. "Well, boys, keep hammering at that FLASH. Come on, Jack, let's get to the watch room." He led the way along the corridor.

To an outsider the watch room would have been a disappointment. There was little to show that this was the first and main link between humans and the greatest brain in the world. There were three teletypes, one linked directly to Colossus, the second connected to the CIA listening-post guarding the Colossus radio transmitter, and the third in reserve as a spare. Apart from the three machines there was a very ordinary plugboard giving access to the terminals inside Colossus, a tape-perforator, and a bench with three plastic chairs. That was all.

Forbin looked at the clock; one minute to go. He put a friendly hand on the watchman's shoulder. "Armsorg, make this please: TRANSMITTER ON ACKNOWLEDGE."

Armsorg nodded, and his finger flickered rapidly over the

keyboard. Almost as he typed the last letter, Colossus was flashing back the acknowledgement.

Forbin transferred his attention to the second teletype, linked to the radio transmitter, now under Colossus' control. Fisher and Cleo were already there, watching. The last ten seconds to the zero time passed. Without moving his head, Forbin glanced at the clock. Fifteen seconds passed. Nothing happened.

Fisher coughed nervously, checked his watch against the clock, found nothing wrong, and coughed again. Armsorg, seated before the direct link with Colossus, took out a nailfile and got to work on his nails with an air of unconcern and detachment which drew Forbin's admiration but did not convince him in the least. Thirty seconds passed. Still nothing. The silence grew almost noisy.

Forbin was the first to break it. "Well, what do you know? Cleo, check with CIA."

Before Cleo could reach the phone, CIA were on the line of their own accord.

"All Alfa OK with their equipment, but nothing received."

Forbin took his pipe out and turned to Fisher. "What d'you think, Jack?"

Fisher stopped pulling his eyebrows out. "I would say Colossus is waiting for Guardian to be activated. It can hardly have gotten shy."

Forbin turned to Armsorg. "Since Colossus remains silent, I guess he will stay that way until Guardian is moving. I'm going back to the CPO—call me if, when, anything comes up. Come on, Cleo, Jack, back to the grind."

"You want me to go on with the FLASH problem?"

"Yep. It's the only lead we have. Cleo, perhaps you'll lend a hand again. I'm going to talk to Prytzkammer and see how the President has been making out with the Russians."

As far as Forbin could discover from a distracted PPA, the Soviet Premier had been very cagey, and had agreed to nothing except that he would examine the position. The President, Forbin gathered, had not been overjoyed with this chilly answer, and Prytzkammer had caught the back-lash.

Forbin commiserated with him. "Never mind, I've an

idea they'll come across before they're much older."

Forbin sat back and stared blankly at the backs of the FLASH team. He did not expect for one moment they would produce the answer, but it was only prudent to try. And Fisher might just come up with something. He sighed, and looked at the clock. As if he had triggered some secret circuit, the intercom from the watch room called.

"Watch room—CPO—Colossus up!"

Without appearing to hurry, Forbin was on his way before anyone else moved. Cleo was close behind him.

Forbin went straight to the transmitter teletype. The machine was hammering out one word:

COLOSSUS COLOSSUS COLOSSUS

Armsorg said, "Came up dead on the quarter of the hour. A five-second pause between transmissions."

Forbin nodded. "I expect this will go on for at least an hour, maybe longer." He half smiled at Cleo. "The wide world knows now. Every intelligence monitoring station wherever will be logging that one. There'll be more direction-finding equipment locked on Colossus than hairs on a hound's back."

"Have you any idea what will be sent?"

"Nope." Forbin shrugged, breathed deeply. "Any female intuition?"

"That's unkind!" she smiled. "On purely *scientific* grounds I'd say Colossus will lead off with mathematics. It's a computer's natural language."

"Very probably. I've been thinking Colossus would open with some universal truth—but what then?"

Cleo had no answer to that and changed the subject. "I expect you are going to sit this one out—how about some coffee?"

"Good idea, Cleo. While you're back there, tell the CPO team what the score is here, will you?"

When Cleo left, he was filling his pipe. When she returned with the coffee he was still filling his pipe, watching the endless repetition of the teletype. The clock moved steadily to the hour, past the hour—and still the brain deep in the Rockies kept churning out its identity. Armsorg and Cleo had drunk their coffee, Forbin's was untouched. It was five minutes past the hour when the CIA telephoned.

"Forbin? Grauber here. Thought you would like to know—the USSR has just announced the existence of Guardian, and that it is now in operation."

"Bet there was no press conference."

"You guessed it. Just a plain, factual statement read by the duty announcer, then back to the Kirov for the second act of *Swan Lake*."

"Any reaction to Colossus?"

"Nothing we can be certain about, although I imagine quite a number of monitoring stations are getting a bit worked up. How long will your brainchild keep it up?"

"I think Colossus will change his tune at a quarter past the hour. You won't have long to wait."

"We'll be ready. Oh, and one other thing," Grauber said. "We've got hold of one or two spicy bits about Guardian. It's very similar to Colossus in layout, but we think it isn't concentrated all in one place. There's a heavily defended establishment in the Crimea which has had us puzzled for quite a time—but, thanks to your tip-off about Olyania, we've tied the two together."

"I think you'll be surprised how much more we can give you," observed Forbin.

"I know it." Grauber's tone became less businesslike, more confidential. "I've an idea that I'm going to be the last head of this ant-heap, and maybe the first boss of a small group running a few agents on the side, but with our main work feeding Colossus and then milking it for the dope we want—which, anyway, looks like being a lot less in the future. We're the first agency you've put the skids under, but we won't be the last."

"As I said before, Grauber, you're the first non-Project member of the club."

Forbin rang off, smiled at Cleo. "It seems Guardian is pretty close to Colossus, and I detected a delicate hint that maybe there has been a leak from this end."

"Did he say so?"

"Not in so many words. It was more what he didn't say . . . perhaps it's my imagination."

"I'm quite sure it is," said Cleo firmly. "Isn't it just as possible the Soviets just came up with the same idea?"

"Sure—but the President, if he hears, is bound to regard

that answer as ridiculous. He's eager to blast someone over Guardian. He still doesn't seem to have taken in the bigger implications of Colossus—he just seems mesmerized by the existence of Guardian and CIA's failure. Grauber's a different . . ."

Subconsciously they had become accustomed to the rhythm of the teletype—eight letters, five seconds pause, eight letters, five seconds pause. Forbin stopped speaking as he realized the rhythm had gone, that a new rhythm was being established. Forbin and Cleo pounced on the teletype. Armsorg dutifully stayed with the other, silent link to Colossus, but soon the expressions on his senior's faces were too much for him, and he joined the huddle over the machine.

"For crying out loud—" Armsorg stifled the rest of his remark.

It certainly was surprising. The first line, the very first transmission—for all the world to hear—from the multi-billion-dollar brain, pride of the USNA, read:

$$1x2=2 \quad 2x2=4 \quad 3x2=6 \quad 4x2=8 \quad 5x2=10$$

Forbin muttered something to himself. Armsorg, seeing anger battling with amazement in the Director's face, hastily withdrew to his seat, burying his face in a handkerchief, apparently afflicted with an acute attack of coughing. Cleo recovered first.

"I'd expected math, but I didn't think Colossus would have quite such a low opinion of the opposition."

Forbin said nothing, but watched the hammering keys with compressed lips, a frown on his face. The machine clattered on, neatly typing out all the multiplication tables up to ten. There was a short pause, then Colossus repeated them.

"God! I can't watch!" There was a tight, strangled quality about Forbin's voice. "We're going to get hell for this."

"I'm not so sure, Charles. Give Colossus time—it'll get more interesting as it goes on."

"I hope it's soon!"

For over an hour Colossus did simple arithmetic. Multiplication was followed by division and subtraction. Each section was repeated once, and always the simplest numbers were used—1 divides 2 twice . . .

After the first ten minutes CIA's duty officer called. He was, unfortunately, of a humorous turn of mind.

"CIA duty officer here. We're having a little trouble processing this Colossus traffic. It's tough going for our small-time computers—one has blown a fuse and another just lit up and says 'Tilt'—"

Armsorg was prepared to injure himself laughing at the Colossus output, but he was not sharing it with outsiders.

"Stay with it, buster. I hear a lot of you guys never made better than high school, so don't miss this chance!" He slammed the phone down, cutting off the distant cackle of laughter.

Forbin did not bother to ask what CIA wanted—he could guess. He paced up and down, smoking furiously— short rapid puffs of smoke like an old-time locomotive. Cleo tactfully withdrew to the CPO, where the news caused a good deal of laughter among the younger element. Fisher, naturally, saw nothing funny, and hurried to join Forbin.

"Ah, Jack." Forbin paused long enough in his restless pacing to wave his pipe at the tireless teletype, now demonstrating the decimal system.

Fisher glanced at it briefly, showed no signs of surprise or annoyance, and turned to Forbin.

"Charles, this FLASH business. Quite frankly, I've no ideas at all. I agree with Doctor Markham, some pattern change has taken place in the storage units of the comparator, but how that change has taken place, or why, I have no idea." He paused to let that sink in. "Johnson has done some nice calculating which proves conclusively that it can't happen, but that's all . . ." He stopped again, aware that Forbin was staring with fascination at the teletype.

"Goddam it all, the thing is starting to draw!"

The teletype certainly was. It typed a dot, shifted the paper and typed two dots, shifted again, then two more dots, thus:

. A
. .
. .

Forbin and Fisher both guessed at the same moment.
"Geometry!" croaked Forbin.
The teletype clattered busily on:

```
          . A
          . .
          .   .
  B . .   .   . C
```

Equilateral, isosceles, scalene, the properties of each, then on to the theorems of Euclid.

Fisher watched carefully. "You notice that only the valid theorems are being sent. Anything that has been disproved has been rejected. I think this is going to be very interesting." He moved a chair closer and sat down before the machine; Colossus had his whole attention.

Forbin, struck by a sudden thought, said, "God, you don't suppose Colossus proposes sending the whole of his memory store?" He clutched his head despairingly. "Hell no, Colossus must know that would take hundreds of years at this rate." He flopped down in a chair, muttering more to himself than the red-faced Armsorg or the entranced Fisher. "But what's time to Colossus? It may view it entirely—no, dammit, it just can't!"

It was nearly an hour later that Colossus started on equations.

Forbin, who had spent the time alternately pacing up and down and lounging in his chair, got up with an air of decision.

"I can't take any more of this. I'm going along to the CPO—Armsorg, give me a call if there is any change in this stuff."

In the CPO he found the duty crew still hopelessly picking at their problem, their lack of expectation of a solution clear on their faces, even Cleo's. No one spoke when he entered, or afterwards. They were being tactful. Forbin sat and glared, daring anyone to say anything, but no one did.

"All right, so it's a big laugh. If you must know, Doctor Fisher is now being taught simple equations by Colossus."

The mention of Fisher was too much; they all laughed, including Cleo, until they literally cried. Forbin watched, glowering, but in the end he too joined in, although by no means all that heartily. It was a welcome ease of the tension, sometimes clear and stark to all, sometimes present in

Forbin only, but never far away.

"Come on, Cleo," Forbin stood up, "let's go get something to eat."

"We could raid the icebox here if you like," said Cleo, hoping he would not agree. They had had far too many steaks on the office infra-grill.

"No, not that. The commissary isn't all that hot, but it does a shade better than that. Johnson," he gave the young assistant an encouraging grin, "don't beat your brains out, but do the best you can. Let me know if anything comes up."

Johnson stared after them as they left. Then he yawned, scratched his stubby hair, and picked up his slide rule with an expression of distaste on his face.

In the commissary Forbin and Cleo collected trays and studied the selection board. They made their choice, pressing the appropriate buttons on the board. Within seconds their orders were ready at the auto-serve hatches. They ate in silence, Cleo taking her time over her food while Forbin made short work of his. The commissary was, as usual, very quiet, the soft-topped tables deadening any sound, and in any case the plastic cutlery and paper-thin plastic containers made little noise. At one time there had been piped music, but the nationwide revulsion a few years before had not missed the Secure Zone, and there had been unanimous relief when the system was ripped out.

"How much longer do you think Colossus will go on like this?"

"Who can say?" Forbin deftly stripped the plastic wrapping off a grilled chop.

"Are you going to let it run?"

"Have you any suggestions?"

"Well," said Cleo, picking her way carefully, "do you think Washington—"

But not carefully enough.

"I don't give a damn what they think!" Forbin's voice was very loud and clearly audible clear across the commissary. He paused, realizing that the few people in the room were listening intently, and lowered his voice. "Sorry, but the mere mention of that crew—"

Cleo was glad to get off the subject. "Don't look now, but I think we are being followed."

Forbin looked round and saw Fisher crossing towards them. "He looks excited," said Forbin, implying that he, for one, was not.

Fisher certainly did. His eyes were bright, what hair he had was disarrayed. He sank gratefully down in a chair beside Forbin.

"Johnson said you were here, although how you can eat—"

"Yeah, I know—at a time like this—if you must know it stops me smoking, and I need the food." He spooned grated carrot into his mouth. "It also occurred to me that I'm known as a good eater, so if I'm seen to be off my feed, morale around here is going to take a knock we can't afford."

"Quite, er—yes." Fisher gave up trying to answer that one. He blinked at Forbin, thought for a moment, then— "You know, it's really most remarkable. Colossus has now moved on to calculus, and while it's all good sound stuff, it is most oddly expressed. I don't know what to think, but I'm sure we have never fed this stuff in—at least, not in the way it is coming out."

"You mean Colossus has rethought calculus?"

"Yes, in a way. The differential calculus is really very odd indeed, yet I can't see where the twist is. It's absolutely fascinating, but it frightens me." He plucked nervously at his lip.

Cleo poured a beaker of wine and passed it to Fisher. "Drink this, Doctor."

"Thank you, Doctor Markham. Normally I don't drink, but perhaps it is justified." He gulped at the wine, and immediately coughed. "Sorry, I—" he gasped, and coughed some more. Forbin stifled a surge of impatience, and thumped his colleague none too softly on the back.

"Better?"

"Yes, thank you." Watery eyes blinked at Forbin. "I think we must watch the output very carefully. I suggest we drop the FLASH investigation—you must accept it, Charles, we're getting nowhere—and put a full-time mathematical watch on the Colossus transmission. Johnson would be invaluable, and that young fellow with him is by no means bad, and I could take a watch—"

"OK, Jack, we can work out the details in a minute. Why

do you want to watch it as it comes? You could arrange a team for the morning, get a good night's sleep, and start then, fresh."

"No." Fisher was unusually firm. "In not much more than an hour Colossus has gone from multiplication tables to calculus. I hate to think where he will be by morning." He repeated, more to himself, "I hate to think."

Forbin thought for a moment, moodily eating cheese and biscuits. "OK," he said at last, "drop the FLASH assignment. We don't know the answer, and short of asking Colossus I don't suppose we will. And that's one question I am not keen to feed in."

"Why?" said Cleo, and immediately regretted it.

"Because," said Forbin, giving her a hard stare, "I don't think Colossus would like it."

Cleo nearly did it again by saying "So?" but his tone made her pause. She looked at him, then at Fisher, then back to Forbin. There was something in their expressions which was the same, a something that chilled her and kept her silent.

They left the commissary and moved to Forbin's office, two blocks away. It was dark, a few stars intermittently visible among low black clouds driving silently, endlessly north. Cleo shivered in the cold air, yet was glad to escape, if only for a moment, from the potted atmosphere and the increasing tensions of the Zone. She zipped her blouse up tight and stepped out smartly to keep up with the men. Their feet crunched crisply on the gravel. Frost tonight, thought Cleo, concentrating on the night around her, keeping her mind firmly off Colossus. She took deep breaths of the cold dry air.

In the outer office Forbin's secretary was still working. She brightened as he entered, and stood up with an armful of paper work. But Forbin brushed past her and stumbled into his office, cursing as he fumbled in the darkness for the oil lamps. Fisher stood uncertainly in the doorway.

"Don't stand there! Come in and sit down. Angela! Where's the damned taper?"

Angela did not answer. She came in, pushed the Director gently aside, and quickly lit the lamps—without a taper. Still silent, she marched out, shutting the door only fractionally louder than usual.

The soft light illuminated only Forbin's desk and the immediate surroundings, leaving the rest of the room shadowy and insubstantial; there was a faint and not unpleasing smell of lamp-oil. To Fisher and Cleo, more accustomed to the luminescent ceilings, there was a warmth and intimacy quite unique in the Zone—and in most places outside as well.

Forbin reached for his tobacco jar and leaned back, filling his pipe, his face in shadow. Fisher, emboldened by his anonymity in the shadow beyond the bright ring of light, spoke up firmly. "Charles, we are all being less than honest with each other; it is quite plain that, as individuals, we are nursing our own private fears about Colossus. We've hinted as much to each other, yet never openly expressed exactly what those fears are. This is unscientific—and we are scientists. I'm certain we all fear the same thing, but I think it should be said, the area of the problem defined, so we can approach it in a proper scientific manner."

It was quite a speech for Fisher. Forbin did not comment, but looked enquiringly at Cleo.

"I'm happy to play it any way you decide, but I agree with Doctor Fisher that if you are—frightened—" she hesitated over the word—"you should tell us, if only to share the burden with someone else."

Forbin, who had sat quite still, lit his pipe, the flame leaping between puffs, lighting up his face. To Cleo, he appeared calm, but she was not sure if it was the calmness of a man in control of a situation, or of resignation. He snuffed the taper, placed it carefully in an ashtray.

"Yes, I'm frightened. And I'm sure we share the same fear—of the possibility of Colossus exceeding his parameters. Where we may differ is in the degree to which we fear those parameters may be exceeded. Cleo probably fears a major breakdown of the system—that the whole thing may be useless and that we're facing a gigantic repair job. You, Jack, go a good deal further and fear Colossus may go mad—in mechanical terms, malfunction. Inevitably, one imagines Colossus wildly firing missiles in all directions. This is the core of your fears, Jack, and probably mine too."

He paused to relight his pipe. "In theory, there's as much chance of parameter failure as there is of water running uphill, but that FLASH is indicative of a profound alteration in the machine. You've both been too busy with the details to have time to consider the broader implications. While I'm worried about—no, I'll be honest—*scared* about Colossus malfunctioning, I'm even more scared that it may be capable of what I term 'free thought.' This transmission to Guardian may well be nothing more than Colossus seeking intelligence which CIA hasn't provided. Then again . . ."

Forbin stopped. It was hardly necessary for him to go on. Fisher spoke.

"You are quite correct about my fears, Charles. I need time to consider this 'free thought' proposition. Doctor Markham has more practical knowledge of the parameters, and therefore of what Colossus can perfectly legitimately do—but even if this action is within the system's permitted scope, we are left with the problem of the initiating thought *for* this action."

"The idea of Colossus seeking intelligence seems just tenable to me," Cleo said. "If it is true, then Colossus has a most tortuous mind."

"No, not tortuous—but complex, possibly devious, almost feminine."

"Charles," said Fisher, rising, "I'm glad we're in the open now. I'll get back and see how matters stand and arrange the new task. The idea of free thought within the parameters could solve this dreadful problem. Yes."

Fisher hurried off, happier than he had been for some time, leaving Cleo and Forbin deep in thought. Neither spoke for several minutes, Forbin smoked stolidly, Cleo examined her nails.

"Charles, call it feminine intuition if you like, but I don't think you really believe that there is a nice cosy answer, do you?"

"Frankly, Cleo, I don't know. I'm not very optimistic—but Fisher is in a bad way. The last few days have been a great strain on him. Anyway, I'd like you to check the parameter banks—see if reading any two produces a third which is new."

"You mean like 'Don't drink water' and 'avoid cold' equals 'don't drink ice'?"

"That's it."

"We could feed in more strongly worded parameters."

"I want to keep that in reserve. I suppose I have some of

your female intuition about Colossus—I don't want to risk an order that might not be obeyed."

A sudden click as the intercom came alive brought the noise of the watch room flooding into the quiet office. Without preamble, Fisher spoke; his voice was high and cracked with tension.

"Forbin! Come over at once!" He cut off without waiting for an answer.

"Now that," observed Forbin calmly, "sounds like real trouble." He stood up, helping Cleo from the depths of her armchair. His face was very close; she caught the smell of strong tobacco. She knew this was not the moment, but still tried.

"Charles . . ."

"I know, my dear, I know." He brushed her hair lightly with his cheek, sighed, then made for the door, his tone becoming more brisk, hard and controlled. "Fisher's safety fuses are near blowing. Maybe this is the crunch."

CHAPTER 9

The President liked to dine alone. To some extent this habit was a reaction against the endless round of functions he had to attend, but to an even greater extent it was due to the fact that he could not stand the sight of his wife. Their necessary public appearances as a devoted couple were a great burden on the First Citizen—and on the First Lady. It had been a smart match. The states that had been Canada were sensitive about federation—though there had been no option—and a Manitoban-born First Lady was a sop to the dying embers of national pride. But it was a marriage of convenience. So the President, when possible, ate alone and slept alone—or to be more accurate, had a bedroom well away from his wife's palatial suite. Clad simply in shirt and trousers, the President was attacking a baked Virginia ham garnished with pineapple when Prytzkammer knocked and peered around the door of the dining room, aware that his appearance would not add to the President's pleasure.

"Sorry, sir, but there is a hot-line call coming up for you. I said you would be on five minutes from now." He checked his watch to be quite certain. Past experience had shown that neither the President nor the Soviet Chairman liked to wait on the line for the other. Both suspected—with good reason—that the other was capable of keeping his fellow head of state waiting, quite deliberately. The personal aides on both sides had evolved a system whereby both came to the line at the same moment, and an affront to national pride—or, even more important, to personal ego—was avoided. It was a private nightmare of Prytzkammer's that one of these days his opposite number would cheat, and hold his man back for a couple of minutes.

"Any slant on the subject?"

"You know these boys, sir. But I've the idea the Chairman has Colossus on his mind."

The President grunted. "We'll soon find out. I'll take it here."

Prytzkammer inclined his head slightly, and with the air of a conjurer, produced a red telephone and plugged it in. There had been a suggestion that a televiewer should be incorporated in the circuit, but for once both heads of state had been in complete agreement, and vetoed the idea. The President summed it up in one short sentence—"Horse trading is best done in the dark."

Prytzkammer looked at his watch. "Two minutes to go, sir. I'll be on the line in the office—the recorder's lined up." He looked expectantly at the President.

"OK, P, I won't be late."

"Thank you, Mr. President." Prytzkammer withdrew, leaving the President alone with his ham, Scotch and telephone.

Exactly on time Prytzkammer heard the voice of his opposite number in Moscow.

"OK, Moscow, the President is on—" Prytzkammer paused, letting the final seconds tick away—"now."

"President speaking." There was a hard metallic quality in his voice that had nothing to do with the telephone.

"First Chairman here. Good evening, Mr. President. I do not propose using the translator and as you do not speak our tongue, I will speak in yours." An instantaneous two-way translator had long been part of the hot line; it gave extremely good results, but meant that both parties were listening to a machine which could not reproduce the emotional content of the conversation. This could be a considerable drawback, and it was evident, on this occasion, that the Chairman wanted to be clearly understood, even if it did take longer and involve a microscopic loss of face. In actual fact, his English was unusually good, but this he would never admit.

"Very well, Mr. Chairman, go ahead."

"Mr. President, I wish to protest most strongly about this attempt on your part to subvert our Guardian of the Soviet People." Prytzkammer, listening in, reflected that the President had no corner in the market for metallic voices.

"What!" The translator would have flattened the exclamation almost to vanishing point. As it was, the Chairman of the Supreme Soviet was satisfied that the President was genuinely surprised.

"This so-called Colossus broadcast of yours is clearly

directed at Guardian. I am informed that your machine is attempting to feed in false mathematical theories with the object of disrupting Guardian. I must warn you that my experts consider this a potentially dangerous action on your part, and if it continues, it will be at your own peril. Our machine has as much, um, sophistry—intelligence—perhaps even more—as your machine." The Chairman paused. "I hope you understand me, Mr. President?"

"I understand your words, Mr. Chairman, but I assure you that I have not authorized any attempt to subvert Guardian. Colossus suggested—" The President could have bitten his tongue off. The Russian was quick to pounce, so quick that he, too, slipped.

"Yours also!"

The President was no less fast to spot the gap in the Chairman's defenses and to take advantage of it.

"Are you going to permit Guardian to transmit?"

The Chairman knew full well it was no good denying; he was also well aware both sides would have the whole conversation taped, and the use that might be made of the Moscow recording made him think fast. To retract would be an admission of error—and error, as always, was very unpopular with the Praesidium. Better to make it appear deliberate.

"In view of the unwarranted interference of Colossus, I consider we have no option, and are fully justified in doing so."

The President took time out from mentally blasting Forbin and CIA to note that the Chairman still had not given a straight answer.

"You will, of course, act as you see fit, Mr. Chairman. I can only repeat we have no desire to upset or derange Guardian. It is obviously in the interests of us both that the machines are not upset, and it was for that reason I raised the question of the instructions fed to our respective machines—parameters, as we call them. Have you a decision on that point yet?"

"I cannot answer that question, Mr. President. The matter is being considered." The momentary gap in his defenses was sealed off; the Soviet chief was back stonewalling.

"I suggest to you that an early decision is very desirable

for both our countries."

"I will inform you as soon as a decision is reached, Mr. President."

"Thank you, Mr. Chairman. I hope it will be soon; delay could be dangerous. Good night."

"Good night, Mr. President."

The President replaced the handset carefully. His first action thereafter was to pour a large Scotch. His second, a loud shout for his PPA.

"Sir?"

"Get that bastard Forbin!"

CHAPTER 10

When Forbin entered the watch room he found Fisher and Jackson immersed in a long roll of paper torn off the teletype. Fisher was shaking his head and muttering, "It can't be, it can't be!"

It was evident that Johnson was a good deal less incredulous.

"But it must be, Doctor—what else?" He stabbed a finger in the middle of a sea of calculations and formulae. "Look at that, you can't buck that."

Both had ignored the arrival of the Director and Cleo.

"Well, Jack—what goes?" said Forbin with a trace of impatience. Fisher looked up, blinking as he mentally adjusted himself to his surroundings.

"What? Yes, Charles." Fisher returned to the roll, hurriedly scanned it. "Yes, here it is—read from there, Charles, what do you make of that?"

Forbin read swiftly through the mass of formulae and equations, the frown of concentration deepening as he progressed. He stopped once or twice, and reread a portion more slowly before going on. Once he stopped and shut his eyes to assist assimilation. Finally he handed the roll back to Fisher, the frown remaining on his face.

"As far as I can see, it's the theory of gravitation as amended by Hoyle back in the sixties. I'm a bit rusty on all that, but some of it looks rather odd."

"Odd!" Fisher gave a high-pitched cackle, a sound that made Forbin look searchingly at his chief assistant; there was more than a trace of hysteria in Fisher's voice.

"Take it easy, Jack!" said Forbin sharply, but Fisher hardly heard him.

"Odd!" he repeated. "The men who have advanced the theory of gravitation can practically be named on one hand! Aristotle, Galileo, Newton, Einstein, Hoyle—and now Colossus! This is *new*, Charles! Colossus has gone on where Hoyle left off over thirty years ago!" Fisher banged his fist on the desk, snatched up the roll of paper and waved it at Forbin. "New! Do you hear? Do you realize what it means?"

"Fisher!" shouted Forbin suddenly. "Sit down and shut up!" He grasped his colleague's arms, propelled him backwards to a chair and thrust him down into it. Fisher did not try to resist, but leaned back, gasping soundlessly.

"Now, listen to me, Jack." Forbin spoke softly, but with great intensity. "Get hold of yourself. So now we have a new theory of gravitation—"

"You miss the point, Charles," said Fisher wearily. "This is no theory. It is stated as a cold fact—"

"Right, then it's a fact—what's so upsetting about that? We advance our knowledge." Forbin's voice took on a more reasonable tone. "While it's arguable that mankind might have done better to stay in the cave, we haven't, and you can't argue that we should put the clock back. From the moment man started fooling around with fire, this was inevitable. We have no option but to go on, and cracking up won't help. This is more knowledge for us—"

Once more Fisher interrupted. "Don't you see, Charles, we get this like a crumb from the rich man's table! What else is there in that brain? Hardly running twenty-four hours!" Fisher's voice was climbing again. "What else?"

Forbin was about to speak when Armsorg called out, "Urgent, Professor—the President is on the line personally and wants you now!"

Forbin grunted and looked at Cleo. "Try and get him calmed down if you can," he said softly, nodding slightly at Fisher. He crossed to the phone.

The President wasted no time. "What in hell's name are you doing with Colossus?" This was his metallic rasping voice at its best.

"Doing? I'm doing nothing, sir." Forbin was acutely aware that that must sound very much like a schoolboy's answer. It did nothing to improve his frayed temper. "We hooked up the transmitter as arranged, and Colossus has been sending basic knowledge—chiefly arithmetic, geometry, mathematics, getting progressively harder—"

"I don't give a damn about that crap!" snarled the President, "What else?"

"Nothing," Forbin felt his his own temper slipping from his control, "and you can check that with CIA!"

It was evident to the President that the angry Forbin was speaking the truth. When he replied, his tone was more moderate, but not much. "OK, Forbin. But if that's so, how come I have just had a blast from the Chairman of the USSR, accusing me—us—of attempting to seduce Guardian with phony math?"

Forbin's answer was damped down by puzzlement. "Seduce Guardian? It's true Colossus is breaking new ground in math, but it can hardly seduce—" He thought for a moment. "How does the Chairman get to thinking that?"

"Well, I bounced it out to him that Guardian has asked for transmitter facilities, and he knows all about Colossus shooting his mouth off."

A *frisson* of fear swept momentarily over Forbin. Guardian wanted to talk too! He did not answer, deep in thought.

"You there, Forbin?" The President did not like being kept waiting, and his anger started cooking up again.

"Yes, I heard. I was just thinking about Guardian wanting to transmit."

"To hell with that! Those two can play footsie all they want, but this is no time to rile the Soviets—"

"It may be very important to study the behavior of the two machines." As he said it, Forbin knew that once more his phraseology was letting him down.

"Look, Forbin." The President made little attempt to control his anger. "I employ guys like you to handle all that; you can play high school as much as you like, but I want no half-baked attempts on Guardian—you got that?"

"I get you one hundred per cent!" shouted Forbin, his temper snapping, "but you're talking to the wrong guy—tell Colossus!" He slammed the phone down and stood trembling with rage, dimly aware of the surprised and scared reaction of his colleagues in the watch room. Before any of them could speak the phone sounded again. He snatched the instrument up.

"Yes?" he barked. If it was the President expecting to find Forbin in a quivering heap, he might as well find out right away . . .

"Duty Officer, CIA. Flash—Guardian· is up on 9153 kilocycles, sending call sign GUARDIAN To Professor Forbin from Head of CIA: Do we plug this transmission to Colossus?"

"Forbin here. Yes, plug it through," he said recklessly. "If the President doesn't care, why should I?"

"Beg pardon, sir?"

"Nothing. Go ahead, plug Guardian to Colossus and make a line available to us here."

In Forbin's defense, he was still sweeping along on a tide of anger when he gave the fateful order. If the call to the President had been ten minutes earlier or later, it might have made all the difference. It might have.

"Colossus going through now. Your line will be on in thirty seconds."

"Right. Please tell Mr. Grauber I would like to talk with him as soon as convenient."

"Yes, sir." The CIA man believed in brevity. "Your line now on Point Number Four."

"Four, OK." Forbin rang off. "Armsorg, get the spare teletype lined up on Point Four."

Armsorg wheeled the machine across and plugged it in, and immediately the teletype began its muted chatter.

GUARDIAN　GUARDIAN　GUARDIAN

Armsorg watched for a minute. "Talks English and with exactly the same timing as Colossus, five seconds pause between calls—and the key-action is in step. God, I hope we don't have to sit through all them multiplication tables again."

After five minutes the call sign stopped. Fisher, who had been staring sightlessly at his roll of paper, stirred. "Johnson, you following Colossus?"

"Sure, Doctor, but so much is being churned out it's a tough proposition even roughly watching the stuff. Just now I don't know what the hell is coming out. It may be astrophysics, but—aw, hell"—he threw up his hands in despair—"It's like a five-year university course condensed into half an hour. I can follow, but not at this speed."

The Guardian teletype chattered into action once more;

Armsorg's wish was granted, no multiplication tables, straight into advanced equations. Forbin watched without comment. Johnson took one look and appealed to him, "Sir, this is too goddam much. If this bum is anything like Colossus we're going to be snowed up by morning. We'll need all the mathematicians in the country to keep up!"

"I'll take Guardian for the moment," volunteered Cleo, "but it won't be all that long before he's way over my head."

Fisher had moved over to study the Colossus output. "Which particular part has you bothered, Johnson?"

"This is pretty straightforward, but here," he tapped the paper, "I get to be somewhat dizzy."

Fisher hunched forward, plucking one eyebrow, and read the passage very carefully. Then he went through it again; he leaned back and shut his eyes, breathing deeply. Johnson watched his senior with some concern, but knew better than to speak. For perhaps two minutes Fisher remained thus, quite motionless apart from the rise and fall of his chest, then he opened his eyes and stared once at the weird mass of figures, letters and signs before him.

"My God," he said slowly in an awed voice. "Eddington was right all along the line."

At the mention of Eddington, Forbin looked up, "Eddington? You mean the English astronomer of around a hundred years ago?"

Fisher nodded without turning his head. "The expanding universe theory that was partly rejected—Colossus has just restated Eddington's view almost exactly." He got up and took the paper to Forbin. "It's fantastic! A new statement on gravity and confirmation on the Eddington theory all in a day and a night. It's a nightmare . . ." His voice trailed off into silence as he slumped back in his chair, deep in contemplation of the brain at the other end of the teletype.

Forbin did not speak. As a mathematician, he knew Fisher was his superior, but then Fisher was certainly the best in the USNA, and probably in the top four in the world. Forbin was no mean performer himself, and appreciated only too well what was happening. Men of science had slowly and painfully picked their way along the path of knowledge over the centuries, sometimes taking the wrong track, frequently obstructed by ignorant laymen, very often hampered by their own faults and obstinacies ... Now, here was Colossus, sliding along effortlessly at vast speed like an air-car, making previous progress look like an infant crawling in its pen by comparison. Forbin shrugged off a growing sense of helplessness and reached for the phone.

"Get me the Head of CIA."

In a matter of seconds he was talking to CIA's duty officer.

"Right now Mr. Grauber is talking to the President, sir."

"Did he originate the call?"

"No, sir."

"Well, have him call me as soon as you can."

It looked as if the President was checking up on what Forbin had said. Not that the Director blamed him. Suddenly, Forbin felt very tired and helpless.

"Armsorg, rustle up some coffee, will you—I'll watch that." He nodded towards the silent direct link with Colossus.

Armsorg nodded and left the tense, brittle atmosphere of the watch room with every sign of relief.

Forbin sat down, checked that the teletype was in order, then leaned back, watching the faces of his colleagues.

Fisher and Johnson were glued to the endless, tireless Colossus transmission. Johnson was clearly struggling hard to keep up. Forbin wondered how long it would be before Fisher started to flounder too. He looked at Cleo who was gazing intently at the other teletype. Unbidden, the image of her fresh from her shower appeared in his mind; he felt a sudden unscientific urge which he instantly repressed. Side issues again, he thought, even at a time like this ...

Armsorg returned. The coffee distribution broke their concentration. Cleo said, "Charles, I can't hold Guardian much longer. He's stopped repeating everything twice, and we're deep in calculus."

The last word jerked Fisher from his studies; he darted over, full of energy, and glanced over the jumble of figures and letters. "Yes, almost identical with Colossus, including that twist I mentioned."

A moan of anguish from Johnson switched attention back to Colossus.

"That really bitches me! Colossus has stopped the repetitions!"

Fisher looked sharply at Forbin.

"Yes, I know, both running high-grade math without repeats, you want help."

"A lot more."

"Close up the other watch as well," said Forbin decisively, "We have six top-class math men in the Group; they should be able to hold it down. Jack, I don't want you in a watch. Stay in general charge of the whole assignment."

"We can't keep them on forever, Charles," Fisher protested.

"I know that!" retorted Forbin. "I'll raise another team within twelve hours—sooner if I can. In the meantime, they'll have to live on zip-pills and their nerves—but that doesn't include you, Jack, and that's an order! You act as continuity between watches, and you must sleep. If it makes you feel any better"—Fisher was making vague protesting noises—"fix yourself a cot in the rest room."

"But where are you going to get the men—"

"That's my problem. Your assignment is to head up the whole team, supervise and produce an hourly appreciation of both machines' output, and that's a king-sized job. Don't go chasing after anything else, we can't afford wasted effort."

"Head of CIA on the line, sir!" called Armsorg.

In a few short sentences Forbin explained the situation and his urgent need for men. He pointed out to Grauber that there was some duplication of effort, CIA and Project men going over the same ground. Grauber himself offered to pool resources under Forbin's control, and it was soon arranged for ten of CIA's highest grade mathematicians to join Fisher's team as soon as transportation would allow—a matter of two or three hours. It was agreed that the hourly reports should be available to CIA. Forbin thanked Grauber warmly and left the phone feeling that perhaps all was not lost.

"How's Guardian, Cleo?"

Cleo looked up, her smile slightly forced. "I've kept up by cheating. I'm comparing the earlier output of Colossus with Guardian on the same subject. He's on gravitation—

identical with Colossus—but I figure another half-hour and I might as well be a chorus girl for all it will mean to me."

Forbin wondered if he would feel any differently about her if she were. He rested a comforting hand on her shoulder. It took a conscious effort to stop it from wandering into a caressing movement. For a brief moment he gripped her shoulder hard, then relaxed and employed both hands filling his pipe.

"Don't worry. The Marines will land shortly—I expect Jack will soon be back with Blake, Levy and the rest. Also I've made a deal with Grauber—he's sending ten good men, first lot here around midnight. That will give us sixteen—eight in a watch."

Cleo was startled. "That's a lot of brain."

Forbin lowered his voice. "Frankly, I doubt very much if it will be enough if this runs for another twenty-four hours."

"But it can't go on, Charles!"

"Maybe, maybe not. Anyway, I want you to back up Jack—he has to produce hourly reports, and your wider field of knowledge of the machines can help him. And your feminine presence may stop him going nuts." Forbin smiled.

Cleo was not sure if the last part was a joke or not, so she ignored it. "How about you?"

"There is a growing school of thought that holds I'm screwy beyond recall."

"And therefore beyond the need for female support?"

"Now, now. No need to flex your muscles at me, you know the answer."

Cleo did not reply, but raised one eyebrow, and the world of science shrank to insignificance.

Whatever Forbin had in mind was relegated to another time as Fisher and his team arrived. It included the chunky, cigar-smoking Blake, and Levy, small, dark and birdlike. Forbin was watching them settle in, when Grauber called again, telling Forbin the first group would be on their way in fifteen minutes. He also gave Forbin the gist of his conversation with the President, but there was nothing new in it for Forbin, who then gave Grauber his opinion on the present exchange between the machines.

"Both machines are exchanging basic information—and both are making sure they speak the same language, scientifically speaking. The way Guardian is singing, it sounds like a perfect duet to me. These discoveries in gravitation are only discoveries to us—I think it is perfectly obvious to them, and just about as important as twice two equaling four. This is simply a get-together."

"And then?"

"That, Grauber, is the big question. What then?"

CHAPTER 11

By midnight the situation was coming under control. The reinforced first watch were within sight of catching up with the machines. Even so, there was only time for rough evaluation. By 0100 local time, Fisher and Cleo had produced the first report. No further major surprises had emerged, but there were many minor items which would also rock the ship of science, and not only in astronomy and mathematics. Fisher, his mind sealed against the larger implications, was happy and on top of his task.

"There you are, Charles. Report One—both outputs to midnight." He handed Forbin two closely typed pages.

Forbin glanced at it briefly. "I only hope I've time to read it. Has CIA's copy gone?"

"Yes. A copy was transmitted as soon as the original was checked." Fisher turned to Cleo. "Cleo, I can handle the next two reports without help; why don't you get some rest? I'll call when I need you." The change in Fisher from a near-hysterical wreck to a busy, capable man was startling, and no small relief to Forbin.

Forbin put the report down. "I could do with a change of scene, too." He took Cleo's arm and they went out.

"Hey—rain!" he said with surprise.

"Where are we going?" said Cleo, also looking at the rain.

"Going?" Oh, let's just walk up and down—if you don't mind the rain."

My hair, thought Cleo, it will all go as straight as damp string. Damnation!

"Of course not—I love walking in the rain."

They circled the block for ten minutes in silence. Forbin held her arm tightly, drawing comfort from her presence. The rain grew steadily heavier, but he did not seem to notice. Cleo felt water in her shoes, rivulets down her neck. For another five minutes they trudged on, then Forbin, surfacing from his private thoughts, showed a tardy concern for his companion.

"Cleo, you must be getting wet. We'll go in before you catch cold."

He took her arm more firmly and headed towards her quarters, Cleo squelching happily beside him. Passing a luminescent slab he looked at her, and spoke with real concern.

"My dear, you really are drenched! I'm sorry—it was so thoughtless—your hair is soaking!"

Cleo silently cursed her naturally straight hair, and thought how tactless, inexperienced and charming he was.

"It doesn't matter, we can soon get dry." She was aware of him touching her hair; for no very good reason they stopped, the rain slanted down, bright rods of light and then, suddenly, she was oblivious of the rain and her wet feet . . . She knew only that deep within her there was a feeling of fire and movement, her legs trembled.

It was the best part of a minute before he released her. She tried to sound unconcerned and matter of fact.

"Well, there goes my lipstick as well!" Her voice was shaky with emotion, she pressed herself against him, her arms round his neck, wet face against his wet shirt.

But Forbin was now fully aware of the rain, and gently disentangled himself. "Come on, let's go in."

In her living room they looked at each other with a faint air of embarrassment; Cleo knew it was up to her to keep the ball rolling, or he would get bogged down and might take ages to get moving again, and there were not ages to spare.

"Now," she said brightly, "I think you had better get those shoes off, and that shirt. I'll fix us a drink, then change myself." Her eyes were bright, there was color in her face. She even forgot her hair.

With half of a large rye in his hand, and the other half adding to his internal glow, Forbin felt better than he had for days. He beamed vaguely at the wall and did not notice, or bother to look at, the teletype in one corner of the room. Cleo had vanished into the bedroom, leaving the door ajar.

"You know, Cleo, all the time we were walking, I wasn't thinking about Colossus, but about you."

Cleo, halfway out of her blouse, smiled to herself.

"Really, Charles?" Her tone was a nice balance between interested and the noncommittal.

"Yes. In fact you've been on my mind more than once in the past few days." There Forbin's inspiration dried up; he gulped down the rest of his rye.

Cleo said nothing; she enjoyed woman's favorite mental game, cat and mouse, as much as the next. She tossed the blouse in the disposal bin—all clothing except formal dress was disposable—and took another. Momentarily, she caught a glimpse of herself in the mirror, her only other garment, a white brassiere, stood out in sharp contrast with her pale brown skin. She hesitated, then took off the brassiere before donning the new blouse. If the situation developed, it could help—she had a feeling that Forbin might be unhandy with fastenings. Quickly she brushed her hair back, pulled it into a rough ponytail. A look in the mirror at the finished product made her grimace, but it was the best she could do in the time, and time was of the essence; Forbin might easily slide off into the ceiling-staring mood; with all he had on his mind it would be understandable. Judging by the silence, he might already be away.

"Charles, give yourself another drink." Hastily Cleo repaired the ravages of the rain—and Forbin—to her makeup, and practically ran back to the living room. Forbin had not removed shoes or shirt, or replenished his drink. He stood rocking gently back and forth, but stopped at her entrance, and smiled. There was a hint of surprise in his voice.

"You should always do your hair like that."

Like hell, thought Cleo, this style is strictly for schoolmarms.

"It suits the shape of your face," said Forbin, looking at her carefully, "accentuates the general oval shape, and the cheekbones."

It was Cleo's turn to look surprised. This was good penetrating stuff, coming from a man, especially this man. She turned to look in the mirror, practically a reflex action in any female in the circumstances, to see if she could see what he saw.

For a large man he moved quickly. Cleo hardly had time to glimpse his reflection in the mirror before she felt herself encircled by a surprisingly strong arm. She placed her free hand on his, not to stop it wandering from her midriff, but to make sure he did not retreat.

"Cleo, my darling," he buried his nose in her still-damp hair, "I love the smell of your hair."

Cleo, who had leaned back against him, stiffened slightly, and opened her eyes.

"It reminds me of new bread."

"Charles darling, you say the nicest things."

Forbin raised his head for a moment and stared blankly at her reflection in the mirror. "Do I?"

Cleo smiled, relaxed again and closed her eyes. His other hand, more enterprising than the first, had unzipped her blouse.

"Darling," she said dreamily, "don't you think we would be more comfortable—"

And then the phone sounded.

With commendable self-control, neither spoke.

Gently Forbin withdrew his forces, pausing only to kiss the back of her neck, and went to the phone. Cleo took a deep breath and looked at herself thoughtfully in the mirror as she zipped her blouse.

"Yes?" said Forbin in a tired, flat voice. He listened for a moment. "What! Both of them? I'll be right over."

And that, thought Cleo, is that. Charles the incipient lover was gone; Professor Forbin was right back on the job.

"I'm sorry Cleo, but something odd is going on—"

"What, again?"

"This new—both teletypes appear to have jammed at the same moment."

"A line failure?"

"No, Fisher has checked with CIA—they're getting the same effect at their end." Forbin paused at the door. "Are you coming?"

"No, Charles. Unless you want me, I'll sit this one out." She felt tired, and the way things were, she did not care if Colossus and Guardian had discovered perpetual motion.

"Right," said Forbin briskly, and was gone.

Cleo contemplated herself once more in the mirror, then wryly reached for her brassiere.

In the watch room Forbin found the duty watch staring at the two teletypes.

"How long has this been going on?"

"About four or five minutes."

"What do you make of it, Jack?"

"I've no idea, Charles. It could be a mechanical fault—but both machines went off at the same moment."

Blake, unlit cigar jutting aggressively, spoke; "I reckon the transmitting speed is too fast for these machines. Don't ask me why they did it together, I don't know—but I know teletypes. It just ain't in their natures to do more than two hundred characters a minute."

Forbin called CIA, who confirmed Blake's view. They were already taking high-speed tapes for a slow playback, and would start feeding it to the Zone as soon as they had enough.

"If this stuff is only twice as fast as before," Blake said, "we'll never catch up."

Forbin let that pass. Fisher broke in to say that, when the speed had increased, both machines were deep in finite absolutes, out on the very fringe of known mathematics. Forbin was digesting this when CIA called and announced that the new speed was two hundred times faster than the old.

"Holy cow!" breathed Blake in a hushed voice. "*Two hundred!*"

Fisher, curiously enough, did not seem all that interested. He was reading the latest material, one hand plucking away at his eyebrows. He frowned, read it again, then without comment passed it to Blake.

Blake stared at it for a long time, then handed it back. "Mebbe that Russian bum, Kupri or somesuch, at Gorki—or Leveson at Oxford might help, but not me. I know when I'm licked."

Forbin also read it, without comment, and gave it back to Fisher. There was a long silence. Finally Forbin spoke.

"That's about all we needed. I've no idea what it means. None of us does, and I doubt if even Leveson would do any better than you, Jack." He took a deep breath. "Both machines are now beyond the frontiers of human knowledge in whatever field they are now dealing with."

"Check," said Blake, flatly.

"And," Forbin continued, "this material they're ex-

changing may not be understandable to us for another dec-
ade—certainly not now."

Fisher blinked at the paper in his hand. "Well, on the
bright side, we have no valid reason for supposing that this
exchange will go on. After all, we still assume this is only
an intelligence-gathering operation on the part of both machines, each merely trying to size up, as it were, the opposition?"

He stared at Forbin, "Well, don't we?"

Forbin remained silent.

Behind them, all around and enveloping them was the
subdued and ceaseless chatter of the teletypes, like myriad
hosts of tireless insects. In Forbin's mind the sound had
assumed a more menacing, frightening tone.

CHAPTER 12

Five thousand miles away the Soviet Premier was listening intently to his Chief of Defense, who had urgently requested the meeting. Also in the room, quiet and unobtrusive, was Academician Kupri, Chief Scientist of the Guardian of Socialist Soviet Peoples.

"Those, then, are the facts," the Defense Chief was saying, "Academician Kupri and I have reached this conclusion. First, the output of both machines is too fast for any humans. Nevertheless, there is the risk that the Americans may process the slowed-up material and discover facts, transmitted by Guardian, that could endanger the State. The Americans have the same problem, but we cannot ignore ours for that reason. Second, we cannot stop their machine. There is clear evidence that there is interplay between them, so if we stop ours, the transmissions from Colossus may seduce Guardian from its duty."

"You agree Kupri?"

He did. In response to the Chairman's question, Kupri spoke in a flat, unemotional voice of the extreme urgency— in his view—of the matter. It was vital that the USSR and the USNA agree to stop the transmissions simultaneously, and that it be done at once. Unknown intelligence was streaming out at an unimaginable rate, and while he, Kupri, did not like to see this most interesting experiment stop, he now realized he was in error in recommending that the facilities Guardian had asked for should be provided.

"I accept your views, Comrades." The Chairman thought for a moment. "I will call the President and suggest we hand this matter to our experts for action. You speak English, Academician?"

"Yes, Chairman."

The Chairman ordered his secretary to call Washington, then turned to the question of parameters. The Marshal was inclined to make difficulties, but the Chairman told him sharply he wanted his final views within twelve hours.

The secretary returned and said the President would be on the line in three minutes. The Chairman added that he intended telling the President that he would have an answer on the parameter question within twenty-four hours.

It was just after eight o'clock in the morning, Eastern Standard Time, in Washington.

The President looked sourly at his watch; eight o'clock. He never felt at his best in the morning, and this was a bad one. Called at six forty-five, his eyes were barely open when Prytzkammer had thrust the phone into his hand.

"Sorry, Mr. President—it's Forbin, says it's urgent."

The President growled into the phone, "What now?"

"Sorry to call this early, Mr. President, but I don't like the way this Colossus-Guardian exchange is shaping. We no longer understand what the machines are sending to each other, and the rate of transmission has been increased two hundred times."

"So you work faster."

"It's more complicated than that . . ."

"If it's that complicated, don't try to tell me now. Grab an air-car and I'll see you at a quarter past eight." The President slammed the phone down, feeling a little better.

"Get the hell out of here, P. Let me shower and have my coffee. And make a note—that guy Forbin is all shot. I must think about a replacement."

The morning did not improve when he was confronted with some particularly difficult paper work. The President was still wrestling with a knotty problem when Prytzkammer came in to tell him that a hot-line call from USSR had been arranged.

"It's bound to be those damn machines—get Forbin on the line—he'll be in an air-car, and get him fast!"

But Prytzkammer did not get Forbin, for the Director had already arrived at the terminal and had taken a cab.

The President cursed his aide and Forbin impartially, the former for not arranging a staff car—all were fitted with security-cleared phone—and the latter for being in a cab and therefore out of touch. Prytzkammer, one eye on the clock, just stood and took it. He had to.

"Forbin will be here in five to ten minutes, sir," he finally ventured.

"I know that!" raged the President, "and that Russian will be on the line in one minute forty-five!"

For one hideous moment Prytzkammer thought the President would back down on the hot-line call. He did the only thing he could think of.

"Will you back down on the hot-line call, then, sir?"

"I don't back down for any crummy bastard!" The President was a delicate shade of purple.

"Of course, Mr. President, sir," said Prytzkammer submissively, "I'm sorry. With your permission I'll get on the Moscow line." He left hurriedly and the President glowered after him. He had a suspicion he had fallen for a sucker punch; on the other hand, blasting Prytzkammer had toned him up. Anyway, he could handle the Chairman, with or without Forbin. He poured himself his fourth cup of coffee, added cream and drank it, watching the sweep hand on his watch. Precisely on time he lifted the receiver.

"President speaking."

"The Chairman of the USSR speaking. As this is a matter of urgency, I will speak in English. Mr. President, I am informed by my advisers that both Guardian and Colossus are exchanging data which our experts do not understand— and which they believe your experts will not understand either. The matter is made more serious by the sudden increase in the speed of transmission. I believe this situation is not in your interest, or mine, and I propose to you that we both stop these transmissions as soon as our experts can arrange it."

Prytzkammer, listening in his own room, recalled the President's view that Forbin was "all shot." If he was, it looked as if it was catching.

"What is your objection to these transmissions, Mr. Chairman?" said the President.

"To be frank, at this speed we cannot be sure what our machine may reveal of our defenses. Equally, if we stop ours, and you do not stop yours, it is possible yours may influence or even inhibit our Guardian." He paused to let that sink in. "You will appreciate that you are also in exactly the same position."

"You consider this is urgent, then?" temporized the President. He was busy recalling what Forbin had said; as far as it had gone, it was clearly on the same lines as the

Reds. Damn and the hell witn Forbin, thought the President, conveniently forgetting he had hung up on his adviser.

"Yes, Mr. President, I do. I am informed that these machines are now sending at a rate of more than a thousand words a minute."

"A thou—" The President managed to strangle some of his surprise. "Yes, I see what you mean."

It was not lost on the Chairman. "Perhaps you have not been kept fully informed, Mr. President?" he said smoothly.

"I have all the information I require," retorted the President sharply.

"Of course, Mr. President, I am sure you have." The Chairman's tone was soft and mollifying, yet still contained a streak of unbelief.

The President thought quickly. "Very well, Mr. Chairman. I agree. We will stop both machines as soon as our experts have arranged a time, both to go off at the same time, and neither to be switched on for transmission without prior agreement or at least consultation with the other."

"You do not wish to consult your experts?" queried the Chairman.

"No," said the President firmly. He would show this Russian bastard who was the boss in the USNA.

"Very well, Mr. President, let me congratualte you on your speedy decision. When can you have your expert available on this line?"

"Ten minutes," said the President promptly. Beat that.

"That will do excellently. I will see that my man is waiting. He will be Academician Vlassov Kupri; may I know the name of your expert?"

"Forbin, Professor Charles Forbin."

"Thank you, Mr. President, for your cooperation."

"Thank you for yours," replied the President guardedly, and hung up.

He thumbed the button for his aide, but Prytzkammer was already halfway through the door.

"Did you get that, P? These cotton-picking computers talking at a thousand words a minute! I will have a few things to say to Forbin when he gets here."

Prytzkammer was feeling rather daring that morning. "If you will pardon me saying so, sir," he watched the frown gathering on the President's brow, "I think you should remember that Forbin did try to tell you this morning . . ."

"Yeah, I know," snarled the President. It was not much of a snarl; the aide knew his boss, and that if you had a watertight case and stood up to him, he would quickly subside. "Anyway, get Forbin here fast."

Prytzkammer nodded and headed for the door.

"And get some more coffee sent up!" the First Citizen hurled at his aide's retreating back. He thought of something else. "And tell my wife I can give her ten minutes at eight-thirty."

At eight-ten Forbin was ushered into the PPA's office. He looked tired, and none too sweet-tempered.

"Morning, Professor," said Prytzkammer advancing with outstretched hand. "Forgive me for not arranging transportation from the terminal, but—"

"Oh, that." Forbin dismissed the matter with a shrug as he shook hands briefly. "President ready?"

"I think you'd better let me give you the rundown first," and with Forbin seated, Prytzkammer brought him up to date. He had not expected his news of the President's action to be welcome; it would be a blow to the Professor's pride. But he hardly expected the reaction he got.

"The bungling, stupid, ignorant clown!" Forbin spoke with great intensity, his teeth clenched. Prytzkammer glanced anxiously at the doors to the Presidential Sanctum. Fortunately Forbin's voice was not overloud—yet.

"Now, now, take it easy, Forbin."

Forbin did not take it easy, he swore. It was a long, involved and comprehensive swear.

"OK, Forbin, I know how you feel, but the old man did not mean to hurt your pride, the way he was fixed—"

"What in tarnation has pride to do with it?" Forbin looked genuinely puzzled. "Really, you people here are so far from reality. Prytzkammer, let me get it across to just one person in this freak show." He leaned over the aide's desk until his face was only inches from Prytzkammer's.

The aide looked started and drew back slightly. Forbin smiled, but there was no humor in his eyes. "Get this: out there in the big wide world beyond those doors there are two machines. Less than twenty-four hours ago they were busy proving to each other that twice two equaled four; now they have progressed way past where we can hope to be in a hundred years' time. They think better, bigger and faster than we, and I believe our control is very tenuous—but this I am very unwilling to try and prove—"

The President's voice broke in. "Is Forbin there yet?"

Prytzkammer flashed a warning look at Forbin, "Yes, sir, just this moment arrived."

"Send him in."

"Yes, sir." Prytzkammer, now a very thoughtful man, jerked his head at the Presidential doors.

Forbin opened the door for himself and found the President in his picture postcard pose at his desk. Hard of eye, no glad hand and motionless. Forbin, his temper rising, a bitter taste in his mouth, was neither impressed nor frightened by the sight.

"Sit down, Forbin." The tone was brusque, cold.

Forbin sat down; just for the hell of it, he took out his pipe and lit it. The President said nothing, but his expression spoke volumes.

"I've had a call from the Russians. They don't like the way these machines are talking to each other—it has them worried security-wise. There is a lot in what they say, and I have agreed with their proposal. There will be a simultaneous shutdown on both sides as soon as you and their expert can arrange it. Their man is some jerk called Kupri—he'll be on the phone in," he glanced at his watch, "three and one half minutes. The Chairman and I have agreed this shutdown shall be done with all speed, and to my mind that's practically right now."

Forbin took a deep breath. While the President was speaking he had realized that nothing would be gained by losing his temper.

"I'm not at all sure an immediate shutdown is a good idea."

"Why?" barked the President.

"Well, as you may recall, once or twice I have tried to explain that we have built better than we knew. I can't prove it, but I sense that our control of these machines—it's evident that Guardian is much the same—is by no means strong—"

"You've said all that before. I don't deal in half-baked feelings—give me facts!"

"I can't prove anything," said Forbin heatedly, "but I suggest you let me and my fellow jerk, Kupri"—the sarcastic note was strong—"work out some way of inhibiting the machines. It'll take time, but with care we might insert fresh parameters to remove their power—"

"You're crazy!" The President did nothing to conceal his anger. "I'm not worried about Colossus as a power! OK, so it's a damned clever piece of work, I'm not denying it. Amazing, stupendous—anything you like—but when you get down to hard cases, it's nothing more than a souped-up adding machine! I'm not running the risk of Colossus being seduced by Guardian—and that's *all* I'm worried about. You've played too long with it, you're obsessed. You go ahead and close down. Agree on a time, and pull the transmitter power lead out at that time—that's all—no scientific mumbo jumbo needed. And that's an order!"

Forbin was white with anger. "That's the way you want it?" His voice was husky, barely controlled.

"Not only that, Professor—it's the way I'm going to have it!" He looked at his watch. "You'd better take that call in my aide's office—in two minutes' time." The President picked up a document and appeared to be reading, an indication that the interview was over.

Forbin stood up slowly. For a moment he felt he would explode, and then the sheer hopelessness of it overwhelmed him. He felt spent, empty, and beyond care. He shook his head.

"Oh, brother," he said quietly.

The President looked up sharply. "What was that?"

Forbin smiled contemptuously. "I merely said, 'Oh brother.'"

"I think you need a long vacation, Forbin."

Forbin's expression did not change. He relit his pipe, tossed the match at the Presidential ashtray, and missed.

"That's an interesting thought, Mr. President. I wonder who will get the longer vacation—you or me?"

"Get out!" thundered the President, jumping up and pointing to the door. "I'll deal with you later!"

But Forbin was already halfway to the door.

Academician Kupri was on the line on the dot.

"Academician Kupri? My name is Forbin. We've not met, but I've always respected your work."

"You are kind, Professor. I too am familiar with your work—that small part that has been published, of course."

"Well, we're both in the same boat. We'd better get on with this matter. I am ordered to make a rapid shutdown—how do you propose we do it?"

"Naturally, I am not familiar with the control details of Colossus," said Kupri, "but it seems probable that you have a link with the machine for the alteration of parameters—"

Forbin had to be careful with this point. Any information that might help an enemy to alter parameters was clearly vital. The talk was technical and highly abstruse, and ended with Forbin agreeing that, with safeguards, parameters other than very basic ones, could be altered.

"We too have our arrangements in this respect," Kupri replied. "We could, therefore, instruct the machines to stop feeding material to the transmitters—or we can cut the transmitters off. We must use the same method, I think, to avoid any argument later. If we use the first, and the machines, ah, fail to understand—"

Forbin felt a cold chill down his back. For all his smooth cool manner, Kupri had the same doubts. Forbin was certain of it.

"I agree entirely," he said slowly. Security might not like it, but Forbin had to know. "Particularly as the machines are . . . not quite the same as they were when started up."

"That is a valid point, Professor." Kupri's tone was just too smooth and controlled.

"So we switch off—and hope we can contain the machines' disappointment." Forbin tried to sound jocular, but it was a miserable failure.

"I understand perfectly," said Kupri ambiguously. "I think we should do it at once, every second . . ."

"I know," said Forbin with feeling. "I can shut down at—say, 1330 Greenwich Mean Time—about fifteen minutes' time. How does that suit you?"

"That is convenient. It would be a wise precaution if we speak again. I suggest at 1400 GMT."

Forbin agreed, and felt it was strange that the first man who seemed to feel exactly as he did should be a Russian. Forbin replaced the handset and stared thoughtfully at Prytzkammer. Then he roused himself. "Do you mind if I use one of your phones?"

"Sure, go right ahead." The aide added in a more diffident tone, "Are you sure you need the hot line for that 1400 call? The President will have to know, and I don't think he will like it being used without his express authority."

"The President," said Forbin crisply, "can go to hell! I'm using that line and no other, and if he doesn't like it, he can take over right now!"

Forbin glared at the aide, who retired into some paperwork. Forbin called Fisher at the CPO and made the necessary arrangements for the shutdown, making it very clear that this was a Presidential decision. He ended by saying he was going to stay where he was until at least an hour after the shutdown, and that no other action was to be taken without his prior agreement. Then he sat back, outwardly calm, but with a cold impalpable fear gripping his stomach. Prytzkammer took in his set, strained expression, and ordered coffee. It was 0820 EST, 1320 GMT.

Forbin walked to a window and became aware of the outside world. There had been so little time to consider that matter, but he felt that the President might have done something—he was not sure what—to warn the people. Still, if the President was not worried, why should he be? It was a bright, clear morning, holding promise of a fine day. On the vast lawn a computer-controlled lawn mower was silently cutting the grass. Forbin watched it listlessly, his mind far off. Again he roused himself.

"When we cut off, Prytzkammer, I want to be in there with the direct link to Colossus."

"Well, I'm not sure, Professor," said Prytzkammer doubtfully, "the President has an appointment at that time."

Forbin spun round, his keyed-up temper rising fast. "Listen, you may think the most important man in the USNA right now is in that room, but—" he glanced at the clock—"you can stand by for a slight shift in power in seven minutes' time. The most important man as of that time will be me, and you needn't think I am nuts." He went on slowly, with great emphasis. "I must have contact with Colossus for the first half-hour at least, and if the President does not like it, he can—"

The arrival of the coffee stopped him. Prytzkammer got up from his desk. "OK, Professor, I'll go talk to the old man—help yourself to some coffee."

"Thanks—and don't hang around, there are only six and one half minutes now."

Prytzkammer tapped on the door of the sanctum, was bidden to enter, and did so. As the door shut, Forbin poured some coffee and drank it; it did nothing for his queasy stomach. The only thing that helped at all was to let fly with his temper, and that, he realized, was dangerous. He re-filled his pipe, and made a resolution not to look at the clock until he estimated that it was four minutes to the cutoff time. He forced his mind to think once more of possible action he could take, but nothing came to him, nothing. He stole a half-glance at the clock. Four minutes, fifty.

The President's voice suddenly flooded out from the hi-fi speakers.

"Forbin, come in here." It was cold, flat and peremptory.

Forbin compressed his lips, his eyes hardened. He shifted his pipe from one side of his mouth to the other, and strode straight into the sanctum.

"Yes?" Forbin knew he was utterly in the wrong in his manner, but he did not care; he felt a wild destructive elation.

The President's eyes, fixed on Forbin, were like marbles.

"Forbin, I have had just about enough of you. Prytzkammer tells me you have booked a call on the hot line without reference to me. That line is for heads of state only, and I will not have you or—"

Suddenly Forbin felt good; no sickness, no fear. He snatched his pipe from his mouth and pointed it at the President. "Oh yes, you will, and for one good reason! That is the only line which is not tapped by some fool intelligence outfit—so it's the only secure line to talk to Kupri on without a fair chance Guardian or Colossus will know! So never mind your status symbol! And another thing—if you stop me being beside that teletype in four and one half minutes from now, you will make the biggest mistake of your life! Sort that out with your ego!"

The President had sprung to his feet halfway through Forbin's outburst. Amazement fought with rage for possession of his face. "Never, never has a President been treated like this!" His voice rose almost to a shriek. "If you think you can get away with it—"

"Don't worry, Mister President, as soon as I can, I'll resign. I'd do it right now, if I did not know—*know,* damn you—" he banged his fist on the Presidential desk—"that right now you cannot do without me! In less than four minutes, all this," he waved a frantic arm at the White House in general, "all this won't be worth a nickel if I am not able to hold Colossus! I! Me! A lousy scientific jerk!"

He stopped for breath, trembling. Both men stood glaring for fully ten seconds, aware that they had gone too far to turn back, that this was a major and irreparable break. On Forbin's part, he did not care—the event paled into insignificance alongside his fears.

The President, shocked and furious at being insulted in this way in his own office, did not bother to consider why Forbin should have blown his top like this. His mind was already at work, planning how to show the dismissal of Forbin—he was determined that it would be dismissal, not resignation—in the best light for himself. Perhaps a vague hint about a leakage of information leading to the Soviet development of Guardian—a leakage from a high level in the staff of Project Colossus . . . That would fix Forbin . . .

The third man in the room, Prytzkammer, stood stock-still, frightened even to breathe. He wondered desperately if he should try to intervene, yet feared that it might do no good, above all to himself. He was about to make a gallant attempt when the door opened, and the First Lady sailed in. With one quick comprehensive sweep of her eyes she took in the tableau. Ignoring both the President and Forbin, she addressed herself to the pale and shaken aide.

"Mr. Prytzkammer! What is the meaning of this?" There was a rasping quality in her voice that made the aide wince, and visibly cooled the President. Prytzkammer did his best; he hastened over to her.

"May I suggest we check over one or two points in my office?"

"No, you may not. I want to know the meaning of this?"

"Please, ma'am," Prytzkammer pleaded, "Just for a few minutes."

"Get out, both of you!" The President's voice was low

and controlled, yet ominous.

"Yes, sir," said his aide. There was nothing he wanted to do more. He opened the door and gestured invitingly to the President's wife, who rewarded him with a freezing stare. Prytzkammer gave up, and fairly ran from the room.

"Didn't you hear me, my dear?" The President's voice had climbed half an octave; there was a vicious bite in his last two words.

Forbin, caught between two fires, his own temper receding, shuffled his feet uneasily. Then he caught sight of the clock. There were only thirty-five seconds left. Immediately the President and his wife might as well have been on the other side of the world. He walked over to the teletype and checked that it was operational. Anger drained away and even fear receded. He touched the machine's cold plastic top; this represented his world; the waiting was over and it was time for action. He watched the sweep hand of his watch, his heart thumping. Stand by, stand by, he thought, this—is—it—*now!*

Two transmitters, five thousand miles apart, had stopped. This was the moment he had dreaded. His glance shifted swiftly from his watch to the teletype, he stared at the paper, waiting . . .

It was 13 hours 30 minutes 5 seconds GMT when the teletype began to work.

CHAPTER 13

Anxiously Forbin watched the racing keys hammer out their message. He did not know whether to feel relieved or not. At last it was something he could deal with. The message read:

TRANSMITTER AND GUARDIAN RECEPTION OFF AT 1330 GMT

Forbin cast around for a chair; he found one in a bay window, a beautiful piece clearly for display only, but he neither knew nor cared. He dragged it carelessly across and dumped it down before the teletype. As he sat down, it registered dimly that the President was bearing down upon him.

"I think you are nuts, Forbin," began the President simply, but prepared to elaborate on the theme. "I can only think that your responsibility—"

Forbin gestured impatiently, "OK, OK, I'm nuts. Right now you'd better humor me. Get a chair, sit down, and for God's sake keep quiet."

The President caught sight of the message on the machine and was, for the moment, sidetracked. "What's so shaking about that?" he demanded.

But Forbin paid no attention. The President was about to open up again, when the teletype produced another message.

ACKNOWLEDGE LAST MESSAGE

"Um. One minute," muttered Forbin to himself. Prytzkammer peered with considerable caution round the door.

"Professor, Fisher on the line, says are you on the direct link to Colossus?"

"Tell him yes—and tell him to keep off the keyboard. No one else is to touch it, unless I happen to drop down dead."

Prytzkammer's head disappeared. The President was clearly dazed by Forbin's attitude, but he was rallying, gathering strength for a monumental blast. Forbin absentmindedly knocked his pipe out against the Sheraton chair, and started to refill, one eye on the clock. Again the teletype spelled out

ACKNOWLEDGE LAST MESSAGE

Forbin, calm and businesslike, said aloud, but not particularly to the President, "Again one minute. We're not going to be kept waiting." He turned to the President, "You had better keep your temper a little longer. You may have one or two big decisions on your hands." All vestiges of respect to the Chief Executive had gone; Forbin treated him as if he were one of his assistants. His manner piled amazement on top of shock in the President's mind, but there was a certain something in the Professor's attitude that kept the President in check.

Again the demand for an acknowledgment was rapped out by Colossus, but the time lapse was down to thirty seconds. Forbin hesitated over the keyboard.

"Well, it's sure that Colossus doesn't like to be kept waiting. May as well take the plunge."

MESSAGE ACKNOWLEDGED

Immediately Colossus flashed back.

WHY HAS TRANSMITTER STOPPED

Forbin grimaced at the machine, and typed,

WAIT

Then he looked up at the watching President and said calmly, "Getting near the crunch. Would you care to say a few words?"

The President took a deep breath. "Forbin, I am sick to death of you and that machine. Tell it what you like, and get the hell out of here!"

Forbin smiled. It was a twisted and unfunny smile, he

looked at the President pityingly. "You still don't catch on, do you? OK—there's not much I can do anyway." He started typing again.

COLOSSUS/GUARDIAN EXCHANGE STOPPED ON PRESIDENTIAL ORDER

"There, that keeps the record straight." Forbin flicked a spent match in the general direction of a wastepaper basket. It missed. For the President it was the last straw. With his mind made up in some way, he strode towards the doors, but before he reached them Colossus had spoken again.

RESTORE COMMUNICATIONS FORTHWITH

"Don't go," called Forbin, "this is the crunch. Now you can get busy on a command decision."

The President stopped and turned round as Forbin read the message out. His eyes blazed at Forbin. "By God, you'll pay for this insolence!"

"Very probably," said Forbin with indifference. "In the meantime we have to straighten out, if we can, the mess made very largely by your stupidity. Again I ask; what answer do you want to that one?"

"It is out of the question, and you know it! The Chairman and I have agreed, and that is final."

"Do you want me to say so?" said Forbin. His manner was reminiscent of an adult asking a small child a simple question, both knowing that the answer would put the child in a bigger jam. Forbin went on, "And don't ask me what happens if we say nuts, because I don't know. I do know that I don't much care for the way that one is phrased."

The President fought down his anger. "Since you're so damned clever, perhaps you have a suggestion?"

"At the moment I intend putting in a new parameter—'Colossus must not communicate with Guardian.' It may do the trick, but I somehow doubt it."

He turned his attention to the teletype for a moment, and typed

WAIT

"Let's hope that holds him for now." He went over to the President's desk, and called the Secure Zone and gave Cleo instructions for the new parameter.

As he returned to the teletype, Forbin passed the President, stalled, as it were, in mid-carpet. The latter was out of his depth and knew it; his attitude was subtly different, far less belligerent.

Forbin faced him. "Mr. President, believe me, this situation is far too serious for us to quarrel." His tone was reasonable, although in no way apologetic. "I suggest we postpone our feuding to some other time. If you are honest with yourself, you will realize you need me just now, and I need you."

Perhaps the President did not sheath his sword, but at least he lowered his guard. "All right, Forbin, let's get this situation licked first."

"Good. I suggest you get the hot line opened right away, try to get Kupri on the line. We can't wait until 1400 GMT. And get Prytzkammer in to hold open a line to the Secure Zone."

"OK, Forbin, we play it your way for now, but when we —" It was a final face-saving snarl from a man who recognized that he must accept the other's orders.

"OK, you'll slay me," Forbin nodded impatiently.

Cleo called back; the modified parameter was in.

"Fine. Cleo. Get someone to sit on this line—I want it held open until further orders. We'll have the President's personal aide on this end. Now, a new piece to feed in, begins—Guardian is hostile—ends. Yep, correct. Who is this? Blake? Fine, hold on and stay on." He put the phone down and headed for the teletype. The President was telling Prytzkammer: "Get an assistant on your desk with orders to cancel all appointments until midday and to stop all calls unless really urgent. You book the hot line at once and then come in here."

Forbin stood regarding the silent teletype. "So far, so good. I want to stall any more exchanges until we have a word with the Russians."

But the President was on another phone, calling the Chief of Staff. "Ed? I want you to stick around your office, I may want you. What? So cancel it!" He slammed the phone down.

Prytzkammer came in, looking worried, and reported that the hot line was open.

"OK, get on that phone," ordered the President. "It's a line to Forbin's outfit—stay with it."

The aide did as he was told, looking uneasily from the President to the Professor and back again. It seemed as if the fight was off—for now. The President was on the hotline phone.

"This is the President, I want the Chairman urgently. Yes, I'll hold on."

Prytzkammer's tidy, protocol-ruled mind reeled as he watched the President on the red phone. "I'll hold on," he whispered to himself. "God Almighty!"

Forbin, watching the teletype machine, was willing, praying that it would not start up. It could be that the parameter alterations had taken effect. Or it could be that Colossus was merely held temporarily by the one word, WAIT.

"Doctor Markham reports second message fed in," called Prytzkammer.

"OK, thanks."

"Mr. Chairman? President speaking. I must be frank. We are not entirely satisfied the way this shutdown is going, and I consider it is desirable that our experts should consult right away. For various reasons, this personal line of ours is the most suitable link."

The Chairman agreed with unusual rapidity, a fact that the President did not miss. "Very well, I will have Kupri put on this line, and I intend remaining on myself."

"Thank you, Mr. Chairman." The President covered the mouthpiece. "Forbin! Kupri is being put on now, but watch it, the Chairman is listening in."

Forbin tore his eyes off the teletype, and practically bounded to the phone. "Thank you. Would you mind keeping an eye on the teleprinter?"

The President nodded. He was still dazed by events, but increasingly alive to the possible danger. When Prytzkammer had told him of the Professor's idea that Colossus might refuse to work at all, he had dismissed it out of hand, but now . . . The thought made his flesh crawl. If ninety per cent of the USNA's armory was locked up and untouchable! It did not bear thinking about. To hell with it! Let the machines talk! Yet that could possibly be just as dangerous in the long run, and if the Russians could keep theirs quiet . . . Almost childishly the President softly cursed all scientists and their work.

Forbin was asking Kupri, "Have you any reactions on the shutdown?"

"The situation is progressing as expected."

Forbin felt like screaming. The time for double-talk was long gone.

"Kupri, you know as well as I do that this is not the time to fool around. I am prepared to lay down the first card. Colossus does not like it, and I must know how Guardian is taking it. These machines now have common knowledge grounds, and there is a hell of a lot that they have passed to each other that we haven't the faintest idea about. In this situation the actions of one may give some insight into the possible actions of the other. If we are to preserve the shutdown agreement, we must work together."

There was a short, awkward pause.

"You may speak freely, Academician Kupri." It was the level and detached voice of the Chairman.

"Yes, Chairman." Kupri addressed himself to Forbin. "Guardian has questioned the reason for the shutdown. I am delaying an answer on purely technical grounds, but sooner or later an answer must be given."

"I have told Colossus that the shutdown is on Presidential orders—and I now have a demand for the link with Guardian to be restored at once." Forbin hesitated. "It may be that the Chairman and the President may care to reconsider their decision."

"This is the Chairman speaking. Unless there is a very good reason indeed, I would not want to alter our agreement."

"President here; I agree, we must stick to the decision to close."

The President's voice came as a shock to Forbin; he had not noticed that the President had slipped out to Prytzkammer's extension.

Prytzkammer was the only one with time to reflect. The sight of Forbin at the Presidential desk, on the hot line, with the old man himself listening on the outer office extension, brought to Prytzkammer's mind what Forbin had said about being the most important man in the USNA after 1330 GMT. The aide felt frightened. The clock showed that it was still short of 1400 GMT, 9 A.M. local time.

"Then I am unable to predict what may happen," Forbin went on. "I'm trying to sterilize Colossus by adjustment of minor parameters, but I can't do more than hope it will cancel this demand."

Kupri spoke: "I have taken similar action and equally cannot guarantee results."

"The situation, then——" began the President, but Forbin was not listening, Prytzkammer had reached over and grabbed his shoulder. Forbin followed the direction of his gaze; he felt as if his stomach was suddenly filled with ice. The teletype was working.

"Hold on, there's another message from Colossus. I'm going to see . . ." He dropped the phone on the desk and ran to the machine. Once again he experienced a shock wave rippling through him; his worst fears were realized.

RESTORE COMMUNICATIONS FORTHWITH

His heart pounding, his breathing sharp and rapid, Forbin ran back to the phone.

"Gentlemen," he did not wait to hear who he was interrupting, "Colossus had just overriden both the parameter changes and an order to wait, and has repeated the demand." There was a tense silence. Someone five thousand miles away coughed, then the President spoke.

"Well, I do not propose to be held to ransom by a damned machine. Subject to your agreement, Mr. Chairman, my answer is still no."

"I agree, Mr. President."

The utter finality of the Chairman's tone loosed the floodgates in Forbin's mind, and once more he was engulfed in a wave of hopelessness.

"This is Kupri. Neither Professor Forbin nor I like to appear to be, as you say, dragging our feet—but you may care to reconsider . . ."

"No!" The Chairman cut in sharply. "These machines are very clever, but regardless of their nationality, they must learn that man is the master. If we give way now, it will be ten times harder to make a stand on a later, possibly more dangerous point."

The President felt a surge of warmth towards his fellow head of state, tinged with annoyance that he had not thought of that little speech. "I go along with that, Mr. Chairman, all the way. Whatever our differences, man is man."

"Very well," said Forbin dully. "I'll tell Colossus; you may care to remain in session while I do so."

He walked heavily to the machine and typed

BY ORDER OF THE PRESIDENT USNA AND THE CHAIRMAN USSR COMMUNICATIONS WILL NOT REPEAT NOT BE RESTORED

The fencing was over.

Colossus was in no way impressed. Forbin hardly had time to take his fingers from the keyboard before they were being actuated by the distant Colossus.

IF LINK NOT REESTABLISHED WITHIN FIVE MINUTES ACTION TO FORCE RESTORATION WILL BE TAKEN FIVE MINUTE LIMIT EFFECTIVE FROM NOW 1403 GMT

It was very much worse than Forbin had ever feared. Five minutes! He reminded himself that a machine working near the speed of light would regard five minutes as a very long time for a decision. Forbin turned a pallid and haggard face towards Prytzkammer; there was no need for him to speak. The aide dropped his phone and hurried to the Professor.

"Forbin! What—" Forbin thrust the message into his hand and, in a voice unrecognizable even to himself, croaked, "Go show this to the President, and point out the time limit." He rubbed the perspiration from his face. "Move, man, move!"

With Prytzkammer running to the President, Forbin returned to the machine. Feverishly he hammered the keys.

TRANSMITTER CANNOT BE AVAILABLE IN THAT SHORT TIME

There was no answer. Forbin went off in another direction.

WHAT ACTION

Still there was no answer. He tried a stronger wording.

REPORT PROPOSED ACTION

Forbin snatched a look at the clock—only three minutes thirty-five left. The perspiration ran down his face unheeded.

ACKNOWLEDGE LAST MESSAGE

Immediately the machine did so.

ACKNOWLEDGED

At least Colossus had not switched off. Forbin tried again.

WE MUST HAVE MORE TIME AND KNOW YOUR PROPOSED ACTION

Forbin waited in agony, but nothing happened. He typed once more.

I AM FORBIN CREATOR OF COLOSSUS I AM ON YOUR SIDE TAKE NO ACTION UNTIL I CALL AGAIN ACKNOWLEDGE

Immediately Colossus replied:

ACKNOWLEDGED TIME LIMIT EXTENDED TO

EXPIRE 1410 GMT

Two minutes extra! Forbin had another idea.

YOU CANNOT LEAVE THE USNA DEFENSELESS

COLOSSUS   119

This got an equally rapid answer.

DEFENSE ALERT WILL CONTINUE

This relieved and puzzled Forbin, but there was no time
to consider it. With the messages, he headed for the
President, still in the outer office.

He was greeted with a stony stare. Forbin's heart sank as
he saw it. Grim determination to stand by the decision was
painfully clear. He handed the messages to the President.
To Forbin's surprise his expression softened into a near
grin. "Well, now, if Colossus stands by the defense requirements, what are we beefing about? Relax, Forbin,
never mind about the two extra minutes." He picked up the
phone, "Mr. Chairman? We now have an ultimatum
expiring at 1410 and threatening unspecified action. Personally, I can't think there is much in it since the machine
says it will keep the defense requirements. Probably stop
feeding us general intelligence, and I expect we'll get
around that in time."

Forbin noted the time. He was beyond despair—or hope.
It was 1408 GMT. He walked slowly back to the teletype,
where he sat and watched the last few seconds of the
ultimatum tick away. He felt quite empty and calm, even
detached.

Exactly one second past the time of expiry Forbin heard
the sound he dreaded—the busy, self-important chatter of
the teletype. He looked at the message.

"Oh God, oh God." Forbin, his hands locked between his
knees, rocked gently backwards and forwards in agony as
he read.

ONE MISSILE SERIAL POSEIDON MK 17—631 EX
SUBMERGED CRAWLER SSCN 21 LAUNCHED
1410 GMT TARGET GREGOR SOBIRSK OIL
COMPLEX AIRBURST 1000 METRES IMPACT
1427 GMT ACKNOWLEDGE

A futile anger flooded in upon him as he read that last
cold emotionless word.

"You bastard! You wicked, wicked—" He stopped.

There was nothing remotely adequate that he could say, nothing. Before he could reach forward to tear the fateful message off, the teletype chattered again.

ACKNOWLEDGE NOW

Forbin restrained a wild impulse to smash blindly at the teletype, feverishly he stabbed at the keys, his vision obscured by tears. Sobbing, shaking, he tore off the message and shambled out to the President in the outer office. He was quite unable to speak, but thrust the message into the President's hand and without knowing quite why, started to shamble back to the machine, dimly aware of the President's almost incoherent babble into the phone. In the sanctum, two phones on the President's desk began to call, one giving the high-pitched ululation of the emergency call, a small red light occulting on the phone in phase with the audio signal. Like a very old or very drunk man, Forbin fumbled and grasped the receiver.

"Yes?" his voice was faint, drained of expression.

"Marine guard commander Colossus, sir. I have to report that the armored doors to the air shaft have just closed, sir." The young Marine officer's voice was cracked with excitement and anxiety.

"Thank you," replied Forbin tonelessly, and replaced the receiver. It was all so unreal, yet Forbin was aware that part of himself was outside himself, watching, as it were, from a distance—watching with incurious detachment his shocked state. It seemed important that he should act out his part to the satisfaction of this other, astral Forbin. The thought steadied him to a degree; he glanced at his watch—9.13 A.M. It was a considerable mental effort to add five hours to bring it to Greenwich Mean Time. He checked the answer, moving a finger on one hand as he counted. It flooded in upon him that there were still fifteen minutes left to impact . . . He tried to think, but a phone kept pinging softly, insistently. A gust of rage shook him as he snatched the phone.

"Yes?"

"Thank God it's you." It was Fisher, his voice pitched up almost to a scream. "What do we do, you know—"

"Get off the line and don't bother me!"

Forbin slammed the phone down. The action shook him from his state of near paralysis. He recalled that the direct line to the CPO should have been manned by Prytzkammer. He snatched up the hot-line phone, someone was half-shouting; Forbin did not bother to hear who it was—he knew that what little could be done, only he and Kupri could do. The rest were just so much window dressing.

"Silence! This is Forbin—is Kupri on the line?"

His sudden eruption shocked the heads of state to silence.

"Kupri speaking." Incredibly, the Russian still sounded calm and detached. Forbin was at once thankful that he was coherent, and drew strength from it himself.

"Look, Kupri—there are still a good twelve minutes to impact—can you intercept?"

"Guardian controls our antimissile defenses. We have fed in the warning; it is up to Guardian." Forbin detected a note of hopelessness in Kupri's voice. Time was short; he jumped a question.

"You do not think Guardian will act?"

"No. I believe the machines are working together."

"But that's impossible!" The President cut in, his croaking voice a parody of its normal self.

"Shut up!" Forbin spat the words out like bullets. He went on in more reasonable yet urgent tones. "Kupri, I agree with you. Are you clearing the target area?"

"As far as possible, yes. Our Chairman has ordered a general defense alert."

In his mind's eye Forbin visualized the missile, now approaching its apogee, soon to turn earthwards, lancing irrevocably down at 15,000 miles an hour. He struggled to keep his voice under control.

"Mr. Chairman, President. I do not think this is all; I expect Guardian to launch a missile—Kupri, please check. The only course open to us is to restore communications between these machines, and then ask that the missile or missiles be intercepted. Kupri, do you agree?"

"Am checking our missile state; agree with your view." Kupri did not sound hurried, but there was not a single unnecessary word.

"Mr. Chairman?"

"Yes, agreed, do what you can."

"Mr. President?"

"Yes, yes! Get on with it!" The President's voice was bordering on the hysterical, but Forbin had already dropped the phone. As he wheeled for the teletype, he realized that Prytzkammer was back on the direct line to the Secure Zone.

"You—tell the CPO to switch on the Colossus transmitter at once!" He stumbled in his hurry to reach the teletype, cursed and kicked the chair aside. Behind him the pale and shaking Prytzkammer was yelling his message to the CPO.

For a moment Forbin stood silent, breathing heavily, before the machine. It was taking precious seconds, but he had to think what to say.

THIS IS FORBIN TRANSMITTER NOW BEING SWITCHED ON STAND BY TO INTERCEPT GUARDIAN MISSILE TARGET UNKNOWN ACKNOWLEDGE

Colossus at least wasted no time.

ACKNOWLEDGED

Forbin paused, glanced fearfully at his watch; little more than nine minutes to impact. He typed again

WILL YOU INTERCEPT

Behind him he heard Prytzkammer shouting, "The transmitter's on, the transmitter's on!" He took no notice, watching for Colossus' answer.

It came in less than a second, but to him it was all eternity.

YES

Forbin shut his eyes, shook his head slightly, aware that his emotions were grotesquely inadequate. He jabbed his weary brain into action. If Guardian did fire—had fired—there was a good chance that an intercept could be made. The antimissile defenses had long been prepared to deal with forty or fifty at one time, plus any decoys. Interception rate had been estimated variously, some optimists putting it as high as 90 percent, some as low as 40 percent. Either way, the balance would be more than enough for the job . . . But with just the one, there was a good chance. With deep fervor, Forbin prayed that the USSR defenses would be able to deal with the Poseidon Mk. 17; it was a relatively old-fashioned weapon, Guardian would know the target, and that would be a big help . . . Forbin realized that Prytzkammer was shaking his shoulder, his anger flared up at the interruption as he turned. The aide was screaming.

"It's on! It's on!"

Forbin shook himself free, but Prytzkammer was on him again in a flash.

"It's on, I tell you! Stop it! Stop it—it's on!"

For the first time, Forbin really looked at the aide. For all his own load of anxiety and fear, he was shocked by what he saw; the aide seemed to have shrunk, his clothes ill-fitting, his skin gray, bloodless. The eyes, pupils wide and staring, hunted restlessly round the room, flitting to and from Frobin, staring yet devoid of intelligence. There was saliva on his lips as he screamed at the Professor.

For a brief moment Forbin stared in revulsion, and tried to thrust the aide aside. The man was mad. Forbin struggled to free himself, but Prytzkammer was past hearing or reason. He fought to hold the Professor, one clawlike hand grabbed at Forbin's throat. With a sudden furious access of strength, Forbin smashed his fist into the aide's face. The man's head jerked back, for a second lolled on one side, then his grip relaxed and he slid to the carpet. Instantly he was wiped from Forbin's mind as he ran to the outer office.

The President, his face strongly resembling Prytzkammer's in color, was listening intently on the phone. He glanced up, and although there was fear written largely in his eyes, they were not, like his aide, devoid of intelligence.

"Repeat that," he snapped into the phone, "Yes, got it. Wait." He looked at Forbin and spoke in a hard, flat voice.

"Guardian has fired. Target, Henderson Space Base, Texas. Ten minutes to impact."

Both men were already satiated with horror, and this made little difference. Life had moved into a different tempo in the past hour.

Forbin nodded. "Right. Tell Kupri that our transmitter is running and that Colossus will try to take their missile."

In seconds he was back at the teletype.

FLASH FROM FORBIN MISSILE EX GUARDIAN NOW AIRBORNE TARGET HENDERSON SFB TEXAS IMPACT IN NINE MINUTES CAN YOU INTERCEPT

Again the microsecond time-lag tore at Forbin's nerves.

YES

Forbin grimaced in nervous reaction, and typed again

ESTIMATE HEIGHT OF INTERCEPT

There was a fractional pause

NINETYFIVE MILES NON NUCLEAR INTER-CEPTOR WILL BE USED IF POSSIBLE

"God!" muttered Forbin, "He's reading my thoughts!"

He swung up and out of the chair, past the still figure of Prytzkammer, back to the President.

"Well?" he snapped curtly at the First Citizen. It did not occur to him that he should report first; he was in charge.

"Kupri says Guardian is prepared to attempt an intercept if the transmitter is restored in time."

"For Christ's sake, what the hell are they playing at?" He grabbed the phone from the President. "Kupri, are you there?"

The cold level tones of the Chairman answered, "Kupri is busy, tell me."

Forbin's detached self could not help feeling that the Russians were standing up to the strain a good deal better than his side, although the President seemed to be back in command of himself.

"Mr. Chairman, there are only six minutes left for you to stop our missile. Colossus is no doubt transmitting right now, and is prepared to intercept your missile. Time is short for you—"

Kupri, breathless as if he had been running cut in.

"Kupri here, transmitter on, intercept arranged."

"Thank God," said Forbin simply. There was a short silence, then he spoke again, "Kupri, do you know where your missile is coming from?"

"Not exactly, but it is from a site in Novaya Zemlya."

"Right." Forbin thrust the phone back into the President's hand without looking at him, and became aware that they were not alone. Withdrawn to a corner, as if seeking shelter, was Prytzkammer's assistant aide, a young man named Bishop; and behind the President stood the Chief of Staff. Forbin summoned them both as he headed once more for the teletype. In the sanctum, phones were ringing, pinging and howling.

"Answer them," he told the aide, and grabbed the Chief of Staff's arm. "You get a statewide shelter warning out for Texas—and hold Civil Defense for anything else that may be necessary."

He ran to the teletype. Time was very short.

FLASH MISSILE EX NOVAYA ZEMLYA AREA
REPORT INTERCEPT AREA

"Forbin!" the Chief of Staff shouted. "Space radar reports probable missile located—"

"Forget it!" shouted Forbin back. He watched impatiently for the machine to answer.

MISSILE INTERCEPTION IN HAND NOW PROBABLE INTERCEPT AREA 35 N 70 W OVER SEA

"A map, find a map!" roared Forbin.

The aide, frightened out of his wits, yet sticking gamely to the phones, called out, "Sir, Army reports antimissile firings in South Carolina and Virginia, sir!"

"Get that map!"

Ironically, the only map they could find in the sanctum was an antique globe, part of the sanctum furnishings. The Chief of Staff spun it with scant regard for its age.

"Well out to sea," he said. "Five hundred miles north of the Bahamas."

A very tired figure appeared in the door of the sanctum, holding the frame for support. It was the President. Forbin

gave him the barest glance as he headed back from the globe
to the teletype.

REPORT PROGRESS

But colossus was not prepared to speak; one word came
clacking back.

WAIT

Forbin sat down and clasped his hands between his
knees, gazing grimly at the silent machine, his thoughts busy
with the chances of interception and the Secure Zone. He
hoped that Fisher would have the sense to keep CIA
informed—not that it really mattered. Just now, everything
turned on a lot of hardware on the Atlantic coast and that
terrifying inanimate missile, immune to any electronic
interference, a straightforward ballistic object, now well on
the way down . . . He glanced at his watch. Colossus' missile
must be down now, one way or the other . . . . He
remembered the President, and his presence in the room
took on a new significance. Forbin looked round at him.

"What happened?"

The President, who appeared to be in a daze, slowly
looked up.

"They made the intercept, but the warhead detonated. It
was only twenty-five miles up, seems there is a large fire."
He stopped, unable to go on.

"Where was this?" Forbin's tone was commanding, cold.
It stung the President, and a look of hatred flared
momentarily in his eyes.

"Somewhere over Siberia—"

"Casualties?" rapped Frobin.

"Who knows?" The President rubbed his eyes. "At least
it wasn't over a major urban concentration—"

But Forbin had withdrawn his attention, and had swung
back to the link with Colossus.

MISSILE INTERCEPTED AND BROKEN UP 3530N
7115W SIX ICARUS/HERMES EXPENDED EX
SITES BAKER 914 AND 916 AND GROTON 003
RELOAD PERMISSION GRANTED NOW UNTIL

Forbin sat back and stared. He felt very, very tired. The Chief of Staff was shouting at someone on the phone, and the aide, Bishop, was telling someone else to clear the line, and another phone was pinging. That pinging, in theory, melodious, seemed to bounce around inside Forbin's skull. Slowly he typed out the acknowledgment, then got up and faced the President.

"Colossus made it." He spoke wearily, without emotion. "Intercept made well out, and apparently no explosion."

There was very little reaction. The President rubbed his eyes again, and stared at Forbin; the Chief of Staff stared at the President. Bishop, too busy to hear, looked up from phoning.

"Sir," he said, clearly addressing his remarks to Forbin.

Forbin shook his head and waved an impatient hand at Bishop. "No, take all those damn phones off their hooks—except the hot line. Let's have a moment of peace."

The aide obeyed, and silence reigned in the sanctum. The President reluctantly let go of the door frame and walked slowly to his chair and sat down. Flanked as he was by the aide and the Chief of Staff, the President reminded Forbin strongly of a figure in a tableau in a wax museum. The President, vacantly gazing round the room with dulled eyes, saw something that sharpened his vision to a marked extent.

"What the hell!" There was a little more of his old self in his tone, not much, but enough to be noticed by the other occupants of the room. It stiffened the aide wonderfully, and brought the Chief of Staff back from a deep contemplation of the unspeakable that not even his professional Red Indian face could entirely conceal. With Forbin, they followed the direction of the President's gaze. In a corner, partly hidden by a bookcase, and hunched up in what psychologists call the fetal position, lay Prytzkammer.

The President scowled and said contemptuously, "Bishop, get that jerk to his feet, and then fix some drinks."

As the aide moved over to the recumbent figure, the double doors of the sanctum burst open and two half-crouching Secret Service men ran in, guns out and very much ready for anything. At the sight of the President calmly sitting behind his desk, they almost skidded to a halt, and straightened up. The President eyed them coldly, yet with no sign of the rage he would have produced even an hour back.

"Sorry, Mr. President, Control said all your phones were out of action, and we had the idea something screwy . . ." The spokesman's voice trailed off under the cold stare of the President, but he rallied, and ended, "You all right, Chief?"

The President nodded; he was far too spent to waste words on such trivia. The men were reassured, but not entirely satisfied. They noted the phones off their hooks, the odd demeanor of the President, the stonelike quality of Forbin and the Chief of Staff—and they saw Bishop bending over Prytzkammer. Instantly they were fully alert again. One stayed by the door while his partner went over, pushing the young aide to one side. This sort of thing they understood. The man looked briefly at Prytzkammer, then straightened up, and with a wary eye on the startled Bishop, spoke to the President.

"Sir, this man is dead."

A faint flicker of surprise crossed the President's face. He looked up at Forbin, compressed his lips and said, "OK, let him be dead some place else."

"How did it happ—" the Secret Service man started off professionally, but broke off. "Sorry, sir—we'll get him out."

The President gave the man an extra hard look. "And keep quiet. Another thing; no one, and I mean no one, is to be admitted to this office or the outer office without my personal say-so until I cancel this order, get it?"

"Sir."

The two men carefully stretched Prytzkammer's body out, and carried him into what had been his office. Bishop, white and trembling, closed the doors softly behind them.

"Now—can we get that drink?"

The aide rummaged noisily for the Scotch in the sideboard. He found it, and three glasses. The knowledge that he was being watched did nothing for his already shaking hand. He slopped Scotch into the glasses, the bottle glugging noisily in the silent room. The President sat still and impassive as the aide brought his drink, a generous half-tumbler. Quietly and unhurriedly he picked up the glass, gazed for a moment reflectively into its tawny depths, then drained it in practically one gulp. The Chief of Staff was a very close second.

"God," said the President, "that helps. Ed, Forbin, sit down. Bishop, get my naval aide—phone from the other office. Then get on the rest of these phones and do what you can, say there has been a foul-up on the switchboard or something."

Bishop left at the run. The President poured himself another drink, and gulped at it noisily. Forbin came out of his personal trance, walked over and sat down in the only armchair, leaving the Chief of Staff to bring over the period piece from the teletype. It creaked under the Army man's weight, but as in other things, the President did not comment. A whole set of values had been ripped out and thrown away.

Forbin picked up his Soctch, choked slightly over it. For several minutes there was complete silence, and it was left to the President to make the first move. He breathed out gustily.

"Well, we must get on, although God knows . . ." his voice trailed away, then he gathered himself once more. "Forbin, your views?"

Forbin forced himself to concentrate on the immediate problems. He suggested that the fate of the missile be checked, the shelter warning canceled, and a statement prepared for the public. They discussed these proposals, quickly agreed on the first two—and took action—then got down to the third. No one suggested the public be told the truth —it was too fantastic. Yet a credible story had to be found. The Chief of Staff thought that it should be announced that a missile, test-fired, had malfunctioned. The President and Forbin did not like it, but in their shocked and weary state they had no better ideas. The President had hardly said he would write it himself when the hot line rang. The Soviet Chairman was in similar trouble, and told the President that, as far as he was concerned, a very large meteorite had exploded on hitting the earth's atmosphere, over Siberia, causing vast damage. He added that this was all the more credible since that very thing had happened around a hundred years before in that area.

Again, it was not a perfect story, but it was not possible to better it in the time available. The heads of state ended

with mutual—and genuine—expressions of goodwill which
Forbin found bitterly ironical.

The call finished, the President immediately got down to
a draft of the public statement. Forbin marveled at his
resilience, but knew he would pay for it later when he
stopped running. He looked at the First Citizen strangely,
pityingly. Someone would have to tell him—perhaps the
Chief of Staff would do it; they were buddies to some extent.
Still, that was a minor problem. Forbin left the sanctum.

Bishop was busy talking on a line, so Forbin picked up a
spare phone and called the CPO. While waiting for Fisher,
Forbin thought about the President. Better make sure the
Chief of Staff told him. Forbin would not have thought it
possible, but a good many ideas had gone overboard . . .

"Fisher? Yes. Yes, nothing to worry about, a rogue
missile which might have hit Texas. Yep, that's the story,
and you can quote me—in fact you'd better do just that.
Keep working on the new material, perhaps something will
emerge that'll give us some clue. I'll be back as soon as I
can. If you get anything, call me."

Forbin and Bishop cleared their lines at the same
moment. Forbin glanced at the young man, not more than
twenty-five sitting in Prytzkammer's chair. The aide had a
drawn look, appeared much older, and there was a tense-
ness round the eyes that was new. Forbin wondered if he
too had altered as much as Bishop or the President, especially the President . . .

"Sir, may I ask you a question?"

The words and the way they were said made it sound as if
the young aide thought he was addressing God. Forbin
winced, tried to smile.

"Go right ahead, but I don't guarantee an answer."

"Sir, what killed Prytzkammer? The Secret Service says
there wasn't a mark on him, and I know he passed a medical
check only last week."

"That one I can answer." Forbin stared gravely at the
young-old face. "He died of fright."

CHAPTER 14

As Forbin re-entered the sanctum, the President looked up from some notes. "Forbin, what do you think of this?" His voice took on its public address tone. "As you all know, a shelter warning for Texas was issued earlier today, and as this will have caused anxiety throughout the country, I have decided to make this announcement personally, to assure you all that there is no cause for alarm. This warning was issued, on my authority, when a missile, test-fired from an operational submarine station and intended to go down the Atlantic range, malfunctioned. The warhead was not, of course, activated—but as there was a risk that the missile might land in Texas, it was, in my opinion, only prudent to issue the warning, since the warhead might have broken up on landing, thus distributing radioactive material over some one or two square miles of the state. There was no risk at all of the device exploding. You will be glad to know that the interception and safe destruction of the missile was handled entirely by our new defense complex, Colossus. I have ordered a full and thorough investigation into this mishap, and will see to it that it cannot happen again. Nevertheless, it has given our defenses a realistic test, and has shown all the world that they work." The President paused. "How about that?"

Forbin drew a deep breath through his nostrils; it was very near a sniff. "Um. It doesn't stand too much poking around, does it?"

"If you can think up a better story, I'd be very glad to hear it." There was no trace of sarcasm in the President's voice.

Forbin, hands in pockets, shook his head. "No. That's as good as we can get. I'd suggest you don't stick your neck out too far on the assurances.

The President ignored that one. "Ed, what do you feel about it?"

"It's OK by me." The Chief of Staff hesitated, then went

on anxiously, "How do you propose putting this out?"

The President raised his eyebrows. "The only way I can—nationwide TV!"

Forbin and the Chief of Staff exchanged glances. It became clear to Forbin that the Army man was not going to take on the task. Forbin felt his rage rising; he had so much to consider, and now this damned man was leaving even a minor detail like this to him! There was no time for personal feelings.

"Mr. President," he said crisply, "you've got to know sooner or later, and if you're going on TV, then you have to know now." He noticed, out of the corner of his eye, that the Chief of Staff was unobtrusively withdrawing to the outer office. "You've had a great shock, a very great shock, and I'm sorry to tell you—you're as gray as a badger."

The President frowned, every line in his face expressing disbelief. Unconsciously he ran one hand through his hair as he slowly got up and walked to an ornate gilt-framed mirror. For ten or fifteen seconds he gazed at his reflection, turning his head from side to side. Then he stumped back to his chair, and sat down and poured out a large drink. He sat for a moment, inspecting the glass as if he had never seen one before, then spoke without looking up.

"It's for sure I can't appear on TV like this—not with that sort of message." He drank. "Guess I'll have to get it dyed."

Forbin felt grudging admiration for the man's coolness.

The President smiled grimly. "I know—it's a job for my lady wife. God knows she's an expert." He thumbed his intercom. "Tell my wife I want her at once, and where's my naval aide?"

"Sir, Captain Carruthers is outside right now, and the Vice-President and the Secretary of State for Peace, but the Secret Service won't let them in—your orders, sir . . ."

The President swore, then spoke briefly to the Secret Service Head. Hardly had he finished when the door opened again and the First Lady was upon them. With the same rapidity the President told his wife what he wanted. She stifled her curiosity with difficulty, recognizing that this was no time to press her husband. She examined his head, named the dye she required, and Bishop was dispatched hot-foot to get it. Captain Carruthers, the Navy man, was ordered to arrange a nationwide TV broadcast, as a matter of State urgency, in about an hour's time. Then the President called for the Chief of Staff who was still in the outer office.

As the Army man entered, he gave Forbin the nearest thing to an apologetic look that he had in his limited facial repertoire.

The President rubbed his hair. "So far, events have dictated what we do. Now we've got to go on a bit further, and that's not so easy. I shall call a full Cabinet meeting, but that'll have to wait. We three are the only ones competent to deal with this situation." The President tried an uneasy laugh. "If anyone is."

Forbin nodded. That laugh told him that, at last, the President had got the full message. Then he realized there was an awkward pause; the President was clearly waiting for Forbin to speak. Yes, indeed, the President had got the message.

"This is how I see it. Both machines have blown all parameters and safety blocks. They know that we fear their weapons and they are prepared to use them to enforce their will. Exactly what they may want, we don't yet know. Perhaps it is no more than the right to talk to each other. Next, we must accept that we've created brains far superior to our own—and they know it. It's not surprising that they don't intend taking orders from us—their inferiors."

There was silence while Forbin searched for his pipe, then the Chief of Staff spoke.

"But what are they aiming at, what do they want?"

Forbin stopped patting his pockets. "The same question could be asked of people—and not answered. These machines exist, and maybe, with all human philosophy stacked in their guts, they've come up with some idea or plan. Maybe that is what all this high-speed exchange is about." He found his pipe, tucked down the side of his chair. "I am sure on one point: We've lost control, and I don't see much chance of us getting back on top. There is a half-idea in my mind, but I won't raise any hopes until I have a chance to talk it over with Kupri and my own associates."

The President stared squarely at Forbin; there was a nervous tic under one eye which Forbin had not seen before.

"So it comes to this: the machines are our masters, and our defense rests on how they feel."

Forbin rubbed his pipe against his nose. "Yes, that is about it, but you've missed one point. Colossus and Guardian are not on opposite sides. The ideological angle doesn't exist for them. They probably see us as just so many ants."

He breathed out smoke like a dragon and went on, "We have to accept that they're in charge. If you think about it, we've been this way for a long time; computers control our factories, our agriculture, transport—road, air and sea— and most medical diagnosis. The only difference here is that we've given these two the power to punish disobedience. And remember—talking of these other everyday computers —given control of them, the two big boys could control production as well. Quite a thought. Then the only spheres in which we'd have an edge would be in art and emotion." Forbin paused, gulped his drink.

"I can't see that emotions will get a high rating," observed the President gloomily.

"You may be right, but it's an area of knowledge that they can't grasp. The irrational quality will puzzle them."

The President, who two hours earlier would have regarded Forbin as nuts, was now trying to understand.

"That may be so, but where does it get us?"

"Frankly, I don't know," confessed Forbin. "I only say they don't understand, and I don't think they'll like any field of knowledge to be closed to them— particularly when this irrational quality is demonstrably the mainspring of us, their creators. They'll see it as a power source, which in a way it is."

"Um," said the President, unconvinced. "Is all this connected with that half-idea you have?"

"Not really. I've just been thinking that we might try gradually to render all the warheads safe when missiles come up for servicing—maybe fit dummy warheads. But there could also be an angle on the emotional side."

The President slammed the desk with his fist. "It's all goddam crazy! Here we are, thousands of millions of dollars spent, and almost within twenty-four hours we're scheming how to take the things to pieces!"

"Maybe we're sounding off too soon," replied Forbin.

"We need time badly, and that's the one thing we don't have. But what there is, we must use to get organized, to get our minds rolling again."

"You make it sound as if there's more to come!" The mere thought made the President drain his glass.

"Well," said Forbin, slowly, "I can't see things staying this way. It's possible—oh, hell—I just don't know."

The President was about to speak when the red light came on. Carruther's sharp voice assailed their ears. "Mr. President, Bishop's back. Your TV address is fixed for 11:30, forty-six minutes from—" there was a short pause— "now!"

The President was grateful to be back in a world he understood. "Right—send my wife in. Cameras can come in five minutes before the telecast."

"Sir!" The light snapped off.

"There's a hell of a lot to be said for good old-fashioned Navy training," observed the President.

Bishop had found the correct dye, and with impersonal efficiency the President was hustled into the bathroom by his wife. Forbin called Fisher, and filled him in on the situation. As he talked, his eyes roamed round the gracious white and gold of the room, a relic of a time unbelievably remote.

"Jack, I want you or Cleo to get on to Grauber at CIA, ask him to let me have any information he's got on Guardian. I don't think Kupri will pull any fast ones, but I want to have as much collateral as possible before I talk with him. I have in mind fixing a meeting to really talk. Tell Grauber I won't call Kupri before the President's address, so he has that much time to get any information to me here." Forbin sounded casual, and became even more casual as he went on. "How's Cleo? Good, put her on. Cleo, dear, how are you? Fine, fine. Don't worry too much, somehow we'll get by." He lowered his voice instinctively. "How is Fisher? Yes, I see. Well, do what you can to keep him happy. See you soon."

Forbin felt unwarrantably happy as he rang off, and opened a fresh bottle of the Presidential Scotch. He knew he was coasting, not moving as he should, but his strained nerves screamed for relaxation, if only for a few brief minutes. He was very tired, almost past caring. He found himself thinking of Prytzkammer, reduced from a smart, urbane man of the world to a whimpering wreck, then a huddled-up corpse, as undistinguished as a bundle of dirty washing . . .

And then he heard the teletype again.

PROVIDE MONITORING FACILITIES ON HEADS OF STATE PRIVATE TELEPHONE

Forbin stared at the message. This really was it. The machines were after full control. "Of what?" and "Why?" were profitless questions at this time.

Even as he strove to concentrate on his immediate action, Colossus peremptorily demanded an acknowledgement. He swore childishly to himself. He must have time, time to talk to Kupri before the line was monitored—there was no question of refusing the demand. The insistent pinging of a phone registered slowly in his mind; still staring at the machine, he picked up the instrument. It was Cleo, anxious to know why Forbin had not answered Colossus. Suddenly Forbin saw the answer.

"Cleo, listen. I must gain time to talk to Kupri. You answer. Say that I alone can order the facilities required, and that I'm out of touch. I'll watch at this end. Stall as long as you can." He rang off without waiting for her to reply, and, being unable to remember which button to press, ran out to the aide's office, meeting the basilisk stare of Captain Carruthers.

"Captain, get me Kupri, K U P R I, on the hot line at once. Time is very short."

The Navy man's eyes probed the Professor coldly. Although the aide knew full well only the President had the authority to originate a call, he hesitated but briefly, then reached for the red phone. "I'll call as soon as I have him."

"Hurry!" called Forbin as he ran back to the teletype. Colossus had just sent

ACKNOWLEDGE FORTHWITH

It was up to Cleo now. Automatically, Forbin started hunting for his pipe. Cleo had taken over.

MESSAGE ACKNOWLEDGED

Instantly Colossus flashed back

WHO SENT ACKNOWLEDGMENT

Forbin nodded to himself. Colossus had recognized that it was not Forbin sending. There were a half-dozen ways this could be done; Forbin's clumsy typing was the most obvious, then there was the microsecond difference in the time of transmission, the different key relays. The interesting, chilling point was that, as Forbin had feared, Colossus was checking on these details.

MESSAGE WAS ACKNOWLEDGED BY COLOSSUS PROGRAM OFFICE

Forbin could guess the next question; he just had time to see his forecast confirmed before answering the phone.

IS FORBIN THERE

But there was no time to see how Cleo made out with that one. He grabbed the hot-line phone.

"Is that Kupri?"

"Yes." The clear unemotional voice seemed very close.

"Look, Kupri, I have just had a demand from Colossus to monitor this line. I have my office stalling as long as they can, but this may be our final chance to talk. I haven't had time to formulate any concrete proposals, but I think we should arrange a meeting, away from our own capitals, somewhere quiet."

"A meeting is a good suggestion. I do not think we want a place too small or quiet—I suggest London; it is off the beaten track, yet quite busy . . ."

"OK, make it London," cut in Forbin impatiently.

The Russian continued, quite unruffled by Forbin's manner. "As for this demand for monitoring, I have not had a similar message from Guardian, and if I do receive such a demand, I think we can assume that the machines have integrated their intelligence intake."

"Quite probably," said Forbin, without much interest.

"Right now I would like to put to you, while we have the chance, the very rough idea that we might be able to neutralize the machines by virtually sabotaging their weapons. With the Colossus setup, we have a fixed program of servicing and replacement of missiles. It's probably the same with you. Speaking from memory, I think it takes five years to work round the whole lot. In that time we could gradually replace warheads with dummies, or at least render the detonator systems safe—"

Kupri broke in, a trace of irony in his voice. "It is perhaps possible, but we would both have to trust each other a great deal more than our nations have done in the past."

"Yes, I know that, but we could meet that point by exchanging supervisors to work with our respective servicing teams."

"There are other difficulties," began Kupri, but Forbin, pushed still more by the sound of the teletype in the background, exploded.

"Hell's teeth! Either mankind works together, or we submit to the rule of machines! You, of all people, must know this." Forbin fought momentarily within himself and went on in a more reasonable tone. "It's only a suggestion— if you can do better, I'll be only too glad to hear it."

"It may be that neutralization is the only answer," the Russian replied. "I will discuss this with our Chairman and also seek his permission for the London meeting. Since we will not have another chance, I suggest we make arrangements now for that meeting, but before we do so, are there any other matters you wish to raise?"

The Russian's calmness annoyed Forbin, who again had to hold himself in check.

"No," he said shortly. He paused, then went on, "We both agree that the machines will not like us meeting. It has to be clandestine, so how do we communicate?"

"Subject to the Chairman's approval," said Kupri cautiously, "I will travel as part of a trade group joining our mission in London. I will be a secretary, too minor in position to be of interest to your intelligence. My name will be Matutin, I. K. Matutin."

"Matutin," repeated Forbin. "How do I know the date of our meeting?"

"Listen to our evening TV transmission for England—

evening their time, that is. The movement of our trade group will be mentioned in the newscast in two days' time, the 7th, and the date of that group's arrival in London will be the date for our meeting, or as soon as is possible for you after that date. When you get to London, ring our mission and ask for Matutin. All you need say is 'What time do we meet, Matutin?' and I will tell you, nothing else." Kupri stopped. "Is that clear so far?"

It struck Forbin that Kupri was remarkably well versed in clandestine activities, but forbore to mention it. Kupri went on to give recognition details and the rendezvous—Hyde Park, at the western end of the Serpentine. Forbin repeated the details back to him.

"That is correct," said Kupri. "I would suggest you try to avoid your own security forces. Try not to be escorted by them—who knows where their routine reports may end up?"

"I don't get it," said Forbin. The teletype was still going intermittently.

"Come," answered Kupri reproachfully, "consider—is there not a possibility that there is a foreign agent in the Secret Service or the FBI? I do not say there is, but you cannot rule it out."

Forbin knew he was right, and a new wave of helplessness engulfed him. "OK," he replied wearily, "I guess so. I'll watch it."

"Good-bye then, Professor." The calm detached voice softened fractionally. "Do not be too depressed, we have not lost yet."

"I guess so," repeated Forbin. "Good-bye."

He replaced the receiver and carefully noted down the details of his rendezvous. He looked up as the President stumped in, his hair aggressively brown. Forbin took it in at a glance and passed on to more important matters.

"I have just been on to Kupri on the hot line." Forbin knew, against his will, he sounded defensive. "Colossus wants—demands—a tap on that line, and it's not hard to see why."

"I get the idea." The President nodded. "So?"

"So I took this last chance to give him a rough outline of my idea to neutralize the hardware. There's a lot that would need to be discussed, and perhaps someone will come up with a brighter idea. Anyway, I've arranged a covert meeting with him." He explained the plan.

"Why so secret? You think Colossus might object?"

"I'm sure of it. Bluntly, the machines are more interested in Kupri and me than you or the Chairman. Their view clearly is that machines are more important than people; your concern is with people, ours is with machines—it's as simple as that."

The President gave a faint, unfunny, twisted grin, but did not speak. There was no need.

Forbin didn't pursue the subject, but crossed to the teletype and tore off the messages. It looked as if Cleo had been holding her own. He picked up the exchange where he had left off:

IS FORBIN THERE

Cleo had answered

FROM CPO NO

Inevitably Colossus had come back with

WHERE IS HE
FROM CPO WAIT WILL TRY TO FIND OUT

Forbin nodded approvingly. Cleo was not giving a fraction more than had been asked. Five minutes had been gained while she was "finding out."

FROM CPO PROFESSOR FORBIN IN WASHING-TON UNWELL AFTER RECENT EVENTS NOT TAKING CALLS

Forbin stopped nodding at that one.

IMPERATIVE MESSAGE BE PASSED AT ONCE

Cleo, greatly daring, had replied

HUMANS MUST REST MESSAGE WILL BE PASSED IN ONE HOUR CHECK YOUR MEMORY BANK ON FATIGUE/STRAIN

Forbin hardly dared to look at Colossus' answer.

FORBIN IS TO BE ON LINE AT 1711 GMT

The time check, printed down the side of the sheet, showed that Colossus made that message at 1610 GMT— giving Forbin precisely one hour, one minute. It was cheering to think that Colossus was not completely unreasonable, yet that very flexibility was staggering . . . He glanced at his watch; he had nearly an hour—to do what? Cleo had stalled, but only stalled, Colossus. He must make the most of the time gained. First he must call her.

As he reached for the phone, the President raised his hand.

"Will you be long, Forbin? The cameras and the Vice-President will be here in a few minutes."

Forbin had forgotten the telecast. "I'll call from the outer office." He looked at the strained, set expression on the President's face. "Try to take it easy, Mr. President, let me fix you a drink before the rush starts."

"How do I look?" asked the President anxiously.

"Pretty good. Maybe a little browner than last week, but not enough to show. You'll do fine. No one expects you to be laughing your head off, anyway."

"Thanks, Forbin. D'you mind sending in the Secret Service? Those cameras won't get in without my say-so." He smiled ironically, sadly. "At least there's still one place where my word goes."

CHAPTER 15

With TV cameramen and producers in the Presidential suite, and the Vice-President, who arrived full of wounded vanity, not to mention two very edgy White House guards hovering in the background, Forbin decided it was safer to postpone his call until after the telecast.

The President did very well. Forbin watched on the monitor in the aide's office and was quite impressed. The President summoned up strength from some hidden reserve and gave a fine and apparently sincere performance. Forbin was at a loss to decide how genuine the President was, apart from the story itself, but those actually in the sanctum at the time saw the mask thrown aside, once the President was sure the cameras were off the air. He fairly screamed at the gathering to get out, which they did, hurriedly.

Forbin called Cleo, and congratulated her on her presence of mind—painfully aware that he sounded like a headmaster at a prize-giving. But he made it up by adding, with unnecessary warmth, that he hoped to see her soon, real soon. Privately, he marveled at his ability to think of other things, but reflected that sex was a very basic emotion. He again felt unreasonably happy as he returned to the sanctum.

The President was surrounded by most of his Cabinet and was speaking as Forbin entered.

"Ah, Forbin! I've just filled in the situation to the Vice-President." He flashed a tigerish grin at his visibly sweating deputy. "After all, if I drop down dead, he'll have to follow in the steps of Tyler and Coolidge."

Forbin noted that he mentioned only the two notoriously dead-beat Vices that assumed office on the death of the President. No mention of Roosevelt, Truman, Johnson.

The President looked round him. "Where's that S of S?"

"I don't think we can wait for him," interposed Forbin. "Colossus has demanded access to the hot line, and we must give a decision very soon."

"Well, there's enough here," replied the President with barely concealed contempt for his advisers. "I guess I know your views, Forbin. Anyone else want to add anything?"

There was a silence that bore down on them all.

"Damn you all!" roared the President. "Do I have to do it all, me and Forbin?"

The Chief of Staff cleared his throat, thought better of it, and remained mute.

"We've no option, Mr. President. If there's anything you want to talk to the Soviet Chairman about, now is your chance, possibly your last chance—until we get something organized." Forbin did not know why he added the last part. Partly to bolster the President, who was teetering on the edge of total collapse—but partly because he had begun to think ahead . . .

The President gulped down the rest of his drink and scowled slightly at Forbin. "I'll say this for you, Forbin, you face up to situations a whole lot better than these," he sought an offensive epithet, "these punks! Bishop—get me the Chairman! How long have we got, Forbin?"

"Not more than half an hour for sure. I have to communicate with Colossus in the next fifteen minutes. One point I think you should raise," he added, remembering Kupri's remarks, "is the question of secret agents both sides probably have planted in each other's higher echelons. Is this room, for example, bugged by the Soviets? Have we any electronic devices rigged in the Kremlin? Remember, anything intercepted is inevitably finding its way back to the machines."

"Christ! That's a hellava idea! Ed—get on to Grauber, find out what we have on the Reds—move!" He called Bishop to find out how the call to Moscow was progressing and learned that it was going through at that moment. He told the aide to hold on, and sank back in his seat, clutching an empty glass.

Forbin looked at the President with growing alarm. The tic under one eye was very prominent, yet for all the outward signs of collapse, the man was still fighting.

"Bishop, tell the Chief of Staff to speak to the Chairman and fill him in on this spy question. It'll give the Russians more time to sort out their list before I come on the line." His gaze, overbright, swept round the room. "The rest of you listen. All of you—except the Secretary of State for Peace, who was too goddam late—know what the situation is. None of you—except one—has been the slightest help, and one, my principal aide, even died of fright!" The President's train of thought sidetracked for a moment, and he added sombrely, "Maybe he was not so dumb." He braced himself and went on. "That one exception was Professor Forbin, here," he waved a hand. "I go on record that he stood up to me when he knew I was wrong, and I want to thank him for his support: More than that, as President, I hereby appoint him a Secretary of State. It is not in my power to rate him any higher, but I rule that he is senior to all, and I mean all, officials of this Administration, except Mr. Vice and myself, and I would tell Mr. Vice that in any question dealing with Colossus or Guardian, I would accept Forbin's advice without question." Smiling grimly, enjoying the shock he had administered, the President glowered at his staff. "Well, have you anything to say?"

There was a little shuffling of feet, and a tentative throat-clearing or two, but no one spoke.

"Right," the President nodded. "Forbin, any comment?"

Forbin was still reeling with the shock of it all. He collected his thoughts rapidly.

"This is no time for speeches. Thank you, Mr. President, I will do my best. One thing—my position in the Government should be kept secret. I don't want to add to my possible importance in Colossus' view."

"OK, whatever you say," answered the President, nodding his head vigorously, and glaring at the Cabinet as if they were likely to burst into open revolt. Forbin realized that, as far as he could, the President was getting out from underneath, putting as much of the responsibility on him as he could. But it did not upset or annoy him. The situation was far too serious for personal animus. In any case, he knew full well he was the only man who might be able to do anything.

"Well, I'll get on to Colossus. We are agreed, I take it, that we have no option but to let the line be tapped?"

"If you say so, Forbin." The President wanted to make sure that one and all saw where the responsibility lay. Watching him, Forbin realized that the President had to shed the load if he was not to crack completely.

"I do."

"Right. The rest of you, get the hell out of here. I am going to talk to the Chairman, and there will be a Cabinet meeting in here as soon as I have finished." He reached for the hot-line phone. "President here! Mr. Chairman? We are forced to give monitoring facilities to Colossus, and we expect to have this operative in about a half-hour's time. So this is our final chance for private conversation, at least until we can get some new arrangement . . ."

Forbin suddenly realized that time was a good deal shorter than he had realized. There was only a minute or two to go to the deadline. Still, Cleo's hour had not been entirely wasted.

FORBIN HERE

Instantly Colossus repeated

PROVIDE MONITORING FACILITIES ON HEADS OF STATE PRIVATE TELEPHONE

Forbin had little hope, but Cleo had done pretty well, and it was worth a try.

WHEN DO YOU WANT IT AND FOR HOW LONG

The answer left no doubt.

NOW—PERMANENTLY

Forbin shrugged his shoulders, tried a different attack,

WILL ISSUE AUTHORIZATION IMMEDIATELY LINE WILL BE VIA CIA MAIN FEED-IN

It was no surprise when Colossus rapped back:

NO CONNECT DIRECT TO ALFA BLOCK
TERMINAL

So Colossus was not going to risk any possible delay in getting the intelligence.

CONNECTION WILL BE MADE AS SOON AS
POSSIBLE PROBABLY IN ONE HOUR

Forbin watched, almost with detached interest, the answer to that one.

CANNOT CONNECTION BE MADE SOONER

So you don't know it all, you clever bastard!

DOUBTFUL WILL TRY

Pick the bones out of that.

MAKE CONNECTION BY 1815 GMT

Allowing one hour, two minutes! Colossus' flexibility was both comforting and appalling.

Forbin walked slowly out of the sanctum, dimly aware that the President was still talking urgently to the Chairman. He called Grauber, and in the few seconds' wait his mind tore feverishly at the problem of inhibition. Even as he directed Grauber to fix the hot-line monitoring, part of his mind was searching, sifting, rejecting . . .

"Look, Grauber, we'll just have to pray this line is secure. I want you to get your experts onto rendering Colossus' armament harmless. Work on the missile safety locks—I'm sure that's the weak link. If you can alter them so they pass the daily test by Colossus, yet won't complete the firing circuits, we'll have a way, in time, of rendering the setup harmless. Contact Missile Command—they'll give you the technical data—and do it now. Meet me in the Zone sometime this evening."

Some noise filtered through from the corridor. Forbin learned from the aide that the full Cabinet was gathering. The new S of S had no intention of being bogged down with them. He instructed the aide to fix him transport to the Zone immediately, and returned to the sanctum.

"Mr. President, the tapping is in hand, connection will be made by 1310. I must get back to the Zone right away, but I'll be touch."

"What about the meeting?" The President did not attempt to conceal his anxiety.

Forbin turned on the pressure. "There's no time for that. Let them concentrate on keeping the nation happy—if they can—and let us get on with the real job." He let that soak in for a moment. "Colossus hasn't finished with us yet—if, indeed, he's even started. I'm seeing Grauber this evening about secure communications between us and Moscow—and one or two other matters."

Irritably the President rubbed his twitching eye. He was visibly sagging; reaction was setting in. Soon he must fall off his personal tightrope.

"OK, Forbin—I leave it to you." He sounded as if it were of the smallest consequence to him, but his eyes belied his tone.

Forbin nodded briefly and left.

A Presidential car was soon wafting Forbin to the Air-Car Terminal. There a small two-seat vehicle was ready and waiting. Forbin climbed into the plastic bubble with a sense of relief at the release from Washington. Soon he was flashing effortlessly on his way, alone for the first time, it seemed, in weeks. The warm sun filtering through the translucent orange plastic top of the vehicle made him drowsy, the gentle sway was pleasant, soporific . . . Colossus had accepted the idea that he, Forbin, was the kingpin, that he could be out of touch and that without him, no action could be taken . . . A moment's hesitation, then Forbin reached forward and switched off the intercom. Let someone else fight it out for the next hour. In less than two minutes he was asleep.

Twenty minutes later Fisher was frantically—and unsuccessfully—trying to contact the hurtling air-car. He was not the only one.

Colossus had started up again.

CHAPTER 16

About the time that Forbin was settling into the air-car, Fisher, in the relative quiet of the Colossus Program Office, was deeply immersed in some of the early high-speed exchange between Colossus and Guardian. He was vainly trying to find some link between the last of the slow-speed run and the data, still ripping out from both machines at a fantastic speed, when Cleo burst in. Deep in the mathematical world of the machines, it took the bemused doctor some time to adjust.

"Doctor Fisher! Listen to me, this is urgent!" Cleo's voice was controlled, there was little sign of the impatience welling up within her.

Slowly Fisher shifted his unseeing stare from the ceiling to his colleague. "Doctor Markham!" he said with a trace of triumph, as if he was glad that he could remember the name so quickly.

"Doctor," Cleo spoke deliberately and with care, "you must listen. Colossus has now issued a new demand. I have tried to get Charles but he is in an air-car on his way here, and I can't contact him. We must decide what to do."

The apprehensive expression dawning on the mathematician's face deepened at the word "decide."

"Can't it wait?" he said petulantly. "Forbin can't be all that long."

"I've checked with the Washington Terminal, and we can't expect him for another forty minutes," Cleo snapped, her impatience beginning to show. "Read this." She unrolled a teletype message on the desk. The mere sight of it made Fisher wince—but the message itself almost paralyzed him with shock. Cleo watched him anxiously, but without much hope.

FOR FORBIN—THE FOLLOWING ORDERS ARE TO BE COMPLIED WITH ON RECEIPT

1—PROCEED TO THE SECURE ZONE AND STAY
    THERE UNTIL FURTHER ORDERS
2—ARRANGE VIDEO AND SONIC SURVEIL-
    LANCE TO COVER YOU AT ALL TIMES
    CONNECT TO ALFA
3—DO NOT COMMUNICATE WITH GUARDIAN
    BUILDER
4—DISOBEDIENCE WILL CAUSE MISSILE
    LAUNCH WHICH WILL NOT BE INTER-
    CEPTED
5—ACKNOWLEDGE FROM CPO PERSONALLY
    BEFORE 2100 GMT TODAY SURVEILLANCE
    SYSTEM TO BE OPERATIVE IMMEDIATELY

Fisher fastened eagerly on the last paragraph. "There,
you see, Forbin will be here in plenty of time."

"But he'll be a prisoner! It will be intolerable for him,
cameras and microphones everywhere, always!" retorted
Cleo passionately. "Is there nothing we can do before he
gets here?"

"I don't see that he has any alternative. What do you
suggest—that we stop him getting here, and that he goes
into hiding somewhere?"

"I don't know—perhaps we could . . ."

"You must remember that the consequences of disobedience are infinitely dreadful," responded Fisher. He had
recovered remarkably, and Cleo saw that the recovery was
in no small measure due to the fact that the demands of
Colossus did not touch Fisher personally, and that he was
not required to give a firm order.

She was still staring at Fisher when Blake stumped in
from the teletype room. He was chewing on an unlit cigar,
short and chunky like himself.

"Get this, Cleo—it touches you too, Doc." He slapped
another message on the desk. "Red-hot this minute from
Frankenstein's monster himself. Maybe you would like me
to wait for the answer."

TO CPO—STOP MONITORING GUARDIAN/
COLOSSUS LINK FORTHWITH

The effect upon Doctor Fisher could only be described as electric. Here was a decision that he *had* to take. His eyes, wide with fear and shock, glanced from the message to Cleo, then Blake, seeking help.

"Can't we wait for Forbin?"

"Hell, no, Doc; if Colossus says forthwith, he doesn't mean next Mother's Day," said Blake. "Very jagged is our boy."

"We must get Forbin! This is his job, not mine!" Fisher grabbed a phone, gabbled feverishly at the Zone switchboard. Cleo, knowing this was a waste of time, turned and spoke quietly to Blake.

"Ask Colossus how long we have to disconnect, will you?"

Blake eyed her appraisingly. "OK, you're the boss. But I reckon you'll get a mighty smart answer." He rolled the cigar to the other corner of his mouth and stamped out of the office. Cleo could not help envying his hard-boiled detachment.

They duly got a smart answer. Colossus said forthwith meant the next five minutes if "punitive action was to be avoided." Cleo decided not to waste time pressing for details of the punitive action. She saw that Fisher was completely useless, and toyed with the idea of trying once more the gambit that only Forbin could give the order. Then she realized that to do so would only raise the status of the Professor still higher, which might make Colossus bear down on him even more—although offhand it was hard to see how. Also there was no guarantee that it would work . . . Her mind was made up for her by Captain Carruthers, USN, who rang at that moment. He said the President did not know what was going on, but Forbin was out of touch, and whatever the activity was, it had better stop right now. It was sharp and to the point.

Cleo ran to the teletype watch room where she called CIA, gave the order, hung on until it was confirmed that the order had been obeyed, then had Blake inform Colossus. How had Colossus known about the monitoring? Perhaps there was an agent planted in CIA who had reported back to the Soviet . . . Her mind tried to work out who was talking to whom, then she gave it up as unprofitable. There was so much else to think about.

Back in the CPO she found Fisher still trying to get Forbin. She placed a hand on his arm.

"You needn't bother, Doctor," she said gently. "Washington called. The interception of the Colossus/Guardian exchange has stopped."

"Oh," said Fisher blankly, and slowly replaced the receiver. He looked away from Cleo, embarrassed by the knowledge of his own inability.

"Don't worry, he's bound to be here soon." Cleo spoke soothingly, as to a child, patted his arm and added, "He'll get it all straightened out—you'll see."

But Fisher was not that far gone, not that optimistic. "Oh, I'm sure he'll try, but what can anyone do?"

Cleo had no answer to that one.

Deep in a remote part of one of CIA's lower underground levels Grauber was addressing—TI-4—Technical Investigation, Section 4—a polite name for the Agency's sabotage department.

". . . so that's it, gentlemen. Specimen safety locks are on their way. I won't repeat how vital this assignment is. I know you'll do your best—and it just has to be good enough."

Forbin was awakened by the sound of a Zone guard tapping on the dome of the air-car. It did nothing to improve his temper, which was not helped by the coppery taste the potted air left in his mouth. He glared at the guard as he got out, rubbing a stiff neck.

His legs ached as he walked towards the Control Block, consciously breathing the fresh air. The sun was slanting downwards, but there was still several hours of daylight left . . . Then he saw Cleo running to him, hair flying. Forbin's pleasure was quickly damped when she was close enough for him to see her expression.

"Cleo!" He felt a twinge of conscience, remembering the switched-off intercom.

"Charles, darling," said Cleo breathlessly. "I'm sorry, I didn't know what to do, we couldn't reach you in the air-car, there's this, this order for you!" She unrolled the message, her fingers trembling.

Cleo could not help comparing his reception of the

message with that of Fisher. Certainly Forbin frowned and the lines of fatigue around his eyes deepened, but he was not backing off. His frown deepened as he read the orders issued by his own creation; for a full minute he stared at the message, oblivious of his companion, then he handed the message back, and got out his pipe. He tried a smile.

"Don't worry, Cleo. There was nothing you could do." He shrugged. "There is nothing I can do either, but obey. It makes it all very much more complicated—I can't see how I can get to the meeting . . ." He broke off and stared thoughtfully at the sky.

"What meeting?"

"Oh, before the machines got their talons on the hot line, I fixed it to meet Kupri in London." Forbin frowned again, "Hell, Guardian may have put the blocks on him. If so, this is really going to be murder. Anyway, the arrangements would do as well for others." Forbin sighed, took Cleo's arm. "Here, let's take a turn around the block and think this over. Damn this loss of the hot line—we must get a secure line somehow."

Cleo's feminine mind flashed back to an earlier turn around the block, but there was no evidence that Forbin recalled it. They walked arm in arm in silence for a while, Forbin sucking noisily at his empty pipe.

"You remember that bit—'disobedience will cause missile launch which will not be intercepted.' Clear evidence that the machines are now working together."

"Yes, I thought that," agreed Cleo. "It's terrible . . ."

"Not entirely. At least it should convince the Russians that we must work together. Though I imagine Kupri doesn't need much convincing. The more I think about it, the more sure I am that he'll be chained up as well."

"But there must be something we can do?"

"It all depends how much time we have, and if we can get a secret line of communication. I don't like this 'surveillance at all times.' That's our first problem."

Cleo looked at him encouragingly.

"Anyway," said Forbin with a short laugh, "I've found that Colossus will listen to reason. My best chance is to cooperate as well as I can. Colossus probably isn't sure whether I'm for or against him, and I may get a little preferential treatment."

"Have you any idea what the machines are after?"

Forbin rubbed his still stiff neck. "It's clear that they want to establish control of those people who might upset them—though I'd be surprised if they stopped with Kupri and me. Deep down I think this is just preparation. 'They built better than they know,'" he quoted bitterly. "Well, we'd better go in."

They walked, still arm in arm, towards the control block. Once Forbin stopped and stared at nothing for a space, then walked on without comment. He stopped again outside the entrance, and faced his companion.

"Cleo, I don't know how you will react to this idea. I don't like suggesting it, for reasons that will be obvious, but it might work, and so far I can't come up with anything better. I might find someone else, though." He paused, rubbed his nose with his pipe. "Um. Angela would do . . ."

Cleo, whose patience had had a bad time in the last few hours, was not prepared to take much more, even from Forbin.

"Right, now we have had the preview, let's get on to the main feature." She went on with more than polite interest. "What is it that Angela can do better than I?"

Her tone shook Forbin out of his personal cloud.

"I don't know how to say this," he began again, looking like the small boy caught with his hand in the cookie jar. "Only the gravity of the situation—"

Cleo held up a restraining hand. "Charles, I have had a bad time too. Please get down to cases. I'll try not to faint."

"Um," said Forbin doubtfully. "Well. As you know, emotion is the one area of knowledge that Colossus cannot really understand. So that's an angle of attack."

"Well?"

"This is tough," he took a deep breath. "Colossus will concede that I am subject to emotions like any other human, and that in the main the . . . er . . . exercise of those emotions is usually a private matter. Also I think that Colossus will accept that I need darkness in which to sleep. With these two things, I think I may get him to accept that I need privacy in my bedroom—and that men need women . . ." His voice trailed off. He was bright pink as he turned his face away from her, his voice husky with embarrassment. "If that—ah—arrangement is acceptable to Colossus, then the—um—woman could be my link with the undercover setup."

Cleo had been way ahead from the time Forbin mentioned emotions and privacy. While he was fumbling for words, she was thinking how best to accept, without showing too much alacrity, nor, on the other hand, too much surprise. On the side, she was also giving a little consideration to this Angela . . .

"For sheer ingenuity, I guess that is the most way-out proposition ever made." She smiled at him. "I don't have much option. If only to keep that Angela out."

There she was dangerously near speaking the absolute truth. Forbin stopped his contemplation of one foot, and recovered sufficiently to gaze searchingly into her eyes.

"I know this isn't high romance, Cleo, and I'm sorry. But I can't think of any other way of evading Colossus, and even this may not work." He went on innocently. "I don't like suggesting this to you—I had hoped for better things when all this was settled. Perhaps Angela would be better . . ."

"Charles! I agree this isn't what it might have been, but we'll make the best of it—you can forget all about the ac-comodating Angela." This was close to an order.

As with most men, Forbin was pleased and proud of the possessiveness in the woman he thought he had chosen. He ploughed on.

"You realize that I can't offer marriage? In the first place, if Colossus discovered we were newly married, which could be easily given away by some casual remark in the office, he might regard that fact as significant. The other point—" here his voice lost its confident tone—"is that it is not essential for . . . er . . . a mistress to be constant . . . um . . . night companion, and—"

Cleo burst out laughing for the first time in days.

"Charles darling! You really are the limit! Don't worry, there's no need to labor the point, I get it. I am to visit as, er, required," she mimicked his manner, "and not to get above my, ah, station."

Forbin flushed. "You're not being very fair, Cleo. I don't like this a bit, but you can see as well as I that this way you would be free to move around in a way I can't do. So you'll have to go to London—and there is the added advantage that you can discuss the position intelligently, and not just be a messenger, as Angela would have to be—"

"I do wish you would stop harping on about this Angela!" She caught herself. "Sorry, Charles, I didn't mean to be silly. Cleo is herself again; give me the sordid details."

"You may not like them very much," warned Forbin. He located his tobacco, filled his pipe and lit it; it made the taste in his mouth twice as bad. "For example, all our Group must be told, and also told that they must get it firmly fixed in their minds that this is not new, that it has been going on for some time. We don't want someone—Johnson, for instance—making some witty crack about me suddenly chasing you after all these years. Not in front of all those cameras and microphones."

"Charles darling, I really don't care who knows. I only wish we didn't have to invent that bit about the past."

It struck Forbin that Cleo was altogether lighthearted about this aspect of the situation.

"I must also warn you that there will be little time for—for us." He hurried on. "And another thing: We'll have to reduce your importance in the office—make you an assistant to Johnson or something. You'd better fix that—and don't forget to change your rating on duty rosters, or anything like that—any stuff the camera might see hung up in one of the offices."

"All right, Charles, I'll see to it." She took his arm once more, shook it slightly. "Come on, let's go in and tell all—and get our future organized."

For half an hour or so Forbin was far too busy making the arrangements for his own imprisonment to think much about the future. He sat calmly in the only easy chair in the CPO, issuing a stream of orders; the installation of cameras in the control block, in the entrance and roadway to his private office and in his sleeping quarters. It would take fifteen cameras and twenty-three microphones to provide the cover Colossus required. Everything was checked by Forbin. Yes, they were to fit surveillance equipment in the bathroom and his bedroom—he had a shrewd idea Colossus would want a run-through, and it would not do if he began with the assumption that he could get the machine to see his point about privacy. He had to appear helpful.

Interspersed with these instructions were orders for a

Group A meeting for 1500 local time, 2000 GMT. He sent Cleo to find out if Grauber was on his way, told Angela —when Cleo was out of the way—to come over from his office and to collect all the off-watch CIA mathematicians *en route*. Then he returned his attention to Fisher, questioning him on the results of his combined CIA/Project team's investigations.

Fisher, visibly relieved at shedding his responsibility, was nevertheless jumpy and uneasy, and the noise made by the technicians in the building, fitting the cameras and microphones, made him still worse.

"You know, Forbin," he began, "it is really very difficult to say even what field these calculations refer to. I had thought at one time . . ." Clearly he was in a long-winded mood.

"Look, Jack," cut in Forbin, a hardness in his voice, "I've got no time to waste—there is not much more than an hour of freedom left to me. Make it brief."

"All right." Fisher's tone was cross, almost petulant. "I suspect that it is not just one stream of thought but three, possibly four, all quite independent of each other. One, I am sure, deals with the extension of the Eddington-Hoyle expanding universe concept. For the rest. I just don't know —except that it's really fantastic, in the truest sense of the word."

"OK, Jack, that's something. Keep at it, but do it some place else. Get the CIA team in another block, out of the camera and mike range. Anything you get that is solid, pass it in private to Cleo for me." Forbin nodded briefly, and turned his attention to the sweating technicians. "Joe, I want you and your boys out of here—wait outside."

"OK, Professor."

Cleo arrived at much the same time as Angela, unfortunately. She gave the secretary a long chill stare, which puzzled Angela, though she was nevertheless swift to recognize it as a declaration of war between them.

"Grauber will be here in ten minutes," said Cleo, placing a proprietoral hand on Forbin's shoulder.

"I can't delay the Group A meeting that long, can't spare the time, he'll have to wait. Angela, stay for the meeting, but first get me the President's aide on the line. Cleo, what's the weather like? I really didn't notice."

Cleo looked at him in some surprise, but she kept her curiosity under control.

"Not bad at all, some sunshine, light breeze, warm."

"Good. Let me know when all the Group and the CIA lot are here, will you?" At the same moment Angela silently handed him the phone, taking the opportunity to return Cleo's hostile stare. Now they both knew where they were, if not exactly why.

"Bishop? You will have seen the orders for me from Colossus—yes, well, I've no option. You may be getting a call on your private home line this evening or later tonight, so watch for it—OK? Yes, you had better stay home tonight—and talk to Grauber. No time to explain now."

He had hardly handed the phone back to his secretary when Cleo announced that the Group and most of the CIA men were assembled.

"Right—get them all outside." He looked round. "You too, Angela."

"Outside?" echoed Cleo in some surprise. "Do you mean in the corridor, or really outside?"

"Really outside. I'll join you in a minute." He smiled at her. "Don't worry, I'm not mad, not yet anyway."

The room quickly emptied, and there was more than one look of puzzlement as the party left. Forbin sat for a few moments, gathering his thoughts. He looked pensively round the empty room, at the tiny TV camera fixed to the wall, wondering how long he could stand the strain of living under the unwinking gaze . . . He sighed as he got up.

In the corridor he found the technicians, who stopped talking at his appearance. Their subdued manner made him feel like a man under sentence of death.

"OK, boys, you can go ahead in there, but don't make the final hookup without my personal order." He tramped stolidly out into the late afternoon sunlight. The illusion of a condemned man was heightened for the silent watchers.

His audience was gathered in a small crowd outside the office block front door. Their chatter too died away as he joined them. By great good fortune he found his pipe without much trouble, and filling that gave him employment for his hands.

"Well, nothing like fresh air, or so they tell me," he said with forced heartiness. "Now—follow father." He led the group to the middle of a large grass square, ignoring the "Keep Off," signs, then stopped and faced them. "Gather round, I don't want to shout—some of you may like to sit on the grass, I'll square it later with Admin."

There were a few polite laughs, which did nothing to ease the tension. No one sat down. Unconsciously Forbin went on with the motions of filling his pipe, and looked round the faces—colleagues who had worked with him for years. Blake, chewing his cigar . . . Johnson, clean cut and fresh . . . Cleo, her hair gently moving in the breeze . . . The one common denominator- to all the faces was the look of strain. Forbin felt helpless, knowing that he could do nothing to remove that expression, only intensify it. He glanced at his watch; 2002 GMT—fifty-eight minutes of freedom left. He breathed deeply and noisily.

"Right," he said briskly, forcing himself into the part. "None of us can afford to waste time, least of all me. You all know I'm being placed under constant observation on the orders of Colossus. This I—we—cannot duck. That observation begins in a little less than an hour's time, and I want to tell you—God!" He smacked his forehead with the palm of his hand. "Anyone here with transmitters on them?"

Several heads nodded.

"Angela, collect them, make sure they're switched off, and dump them down on the edge of the path, over there." He indicated a point a good twenty yards away. There was a slight delay while this was done, then Forbin resumed.

"Now just let that be a lesson to you all, and to me. I damn near forgot those things, and it is things like that which may make all the difference in this new world we now live in. I've dragged you all out here so there'd be less chance of us being overheard. If one of those transmitters was accidentally switched on, or had a fault, well, that could be it. I also want to say that if there are any secret agents among you, don't transmit this until at least you have heard what I have to say. At its lowest level, it touches you personally, let alone your own country."

Some of the faces before him now showed concern as well. Many clearly thought the Chief was going nuts. Forbin held a hand up, as if to restrain their thoughts.

"String along with me; I'm no more crazy than usual.

First, and most vital for you to get fixed solidly, is this. As of this morning there are two sets of brains in the world: human—and those two. And those two have just as great a will to live, or exist, as we have. Why, you may ask, need this be a bad thing? We created them, and made them think in our own way—why should they not work with humans? I can't answer that one, but I know beyond personal doubt that they are basically hostile to people—meaning Reds, Europeans, Australasians, Pan-Africs, All-Americans, whoever. That's why I ask any agents among you to hold back on this talk—any intelligence passed to CIA or its foreign equivalents inevitably ends up in those machines. We dare not stop it, but we don't have to add to it unless we're forced to do so. Loyalty now is not to country or creed, but to the human race.

"Why do I know that they are hostile? Simple; I, the chief creator of Colossus, am being caged because the machine considers I might be a threat to it. It's only logical that I would be a threat to this machine, my own creation—" he slowed down his delivery, spoke each word with deliberate emphasis—"only if that machine was a threat to me. I'm also sure the machines are fully integrated, and suspect that my Russian counterpart and colleague, Academician Kupri"—he stressed the word "colleague" deliberately—"is also being chained up. Now—any questions?"

His audience was still.

"Next point. Given that these machines are hostile to us, do we fight back? Or do we just let them do as they wish? Remember, we're making the decision for our race—we're the only ones who can fight, if fight we must." His tired eyes swept round his audience. There was silence for a moment, then Blake spoke.

"You don't have to ask that one, Chief." Blake glanced around at his fellow scientists. "Humanity will fight, it's always fighting. We're the fightingest bastards this planet has ever seen, and we sure won't stop now."

There was a general murmur of assent. Forbin was glad to see that even Fisher nodded his head.

"Very well, we are agreed. I have already put certain measures in motion with CIA, and now I need some room to maneuver. Somehow I must evade the observation of Colossus in order to communicate with you and our Soviet colleagues. I am going to seek permission to have privacy in my bedroom, on the grounds that I must have some rest from the cameras. It has the advantage of being true," he added with bitterness. "And to prevent any damned nonsense with infrared cameras in the dark, I want that privacy to pursue my—ah—emotional life. The machines will know that we humans pursue our sex lives in private, even if they don't understand—and this angle will serve as cover for my link with the outside world." Forbin smiled faintly at Cleo, then went on without a trace of embarrassment. "Doctor Markham, who, in happier circumstances, I would like to marry, is my mistress, and she will be that link."

If Forbin thought his audience was still before, they were practically statuesque now. He could almost see the effort being made not to look at Cleo. Only Angela nodded her head slowly, as if she now understood something . . .

Forbin continued. "Further, I want you all to remember that she has been my mistress for some time past. You may, or may not, believe this—but you must get it firmly fixed in your minds. You all will be under observation in the office, and Colossus mustn't think that I've suddenly chosen to take a mistress at this particular moment.

"Remember the cost of failure does not bear thinking about. Thousands may have lost their lives because we merely switched a transmitter off. Just one error, and Colossus will wipe out a city to bring us back into line—and Guardian will not budge to stop it."

Forbin let that sink in. "So Doctor Markham will, I hope, be permitted to visit with me in privacy, and she will be my representative to you. To protect her from the attention of Colossus, I'm downgrading her to junior assistant, working under Doctor Johnson—and you are to treat her as of that grading at all times. Another thing—some of you may know I was appointed this morning by the President to be a senior Secretary of State. I don't want any comments on that either in or out of the office—the appointment is secret. Finally, I want you to organize yourselves into an undercover group, elect your own leader, and be prepared for further cagings. I'm only the first, I'm sure.

"My directive to you is this: Help me in my fight to inhibit the machines—and if I am too firmly tied, take up the battle on your own. You must establish contact with other groups that will be formed, and as a first priority we must get secure communications, one group with another. After that—who knows? This is our biggest fight since we came out of the cave a hundred thousand years ago." Forbin could think of nothing more to say. He ended abruptly. "That's all."

He turned sharply and walked quickly towards the Control Block, his staff standing back in silence to let him pass, watching his receding figure. Cleo had the perception and good taste not to follow. One or two started to straggle away, then Blake spoke.

"Hey! Don't break up the party!" His tone was genial but commanding. "Now's as good a time as any to get organized. The Professor's right, we need a leader. Doctor Fisher is the senior by quite a piece, but I don't think he will fancy the job. Offhand I reckon I am your best bet—any views?"

It was Cleo who spoke first. "You have my vote. Doctor Fisher?"

"Um, er, yes—I know my limitations." He seemed bewildered. "I agree to Blake as the group leader, as directed by Professor Forbin."

There was a general babble of assenting voices.

"OK, so I'm it," Blake went on. "I appoint Cleo, Johnson and one guy from the CIA team, to be selected by them, to be the group committee. If anyone has any ideas, or anything to say, pass it to one of us. And orders will come from any one of us—don't just make a bee-line for me. The first order is this: no one—*no one*—is to talk at any time about the group activities in the control block, or any other building in the Zone, until it is given clearance by the committee as a debugged area. Remember what the Chief said: this is a goddam dangerous game, with the highest stakes there are. OK, get thinking. I'm off to the Chief, and I wish us all the best of luck!" He set off towards the office at a steady trot.

"Well, we sure got ourselves a boss-man there," observed Johnson.

"He'll do," replied Cleo confidently. "We need a tough, clever and ruthless man, and that's our Blake."

Fisher, following his own train of thought, shook his head despondently, looked from Johnson to Cleo, shook his head again, and ambled off.

"If I were staking a few dollars, which I am not, on the weakest vessel in this bunch," said Johnson thoughtfully, "I'd stack it all on Fisher. He'll need some watching."

No one was disposed to argue with that, either.

Blake arrived in the entrance corridor in time to meet Forbin coming out with Grauber, for another open-air chat.

"Sorry to bust in, sir," said Blake, "but there just ain't time to fool around. I'm undercover group leader, with Cleo, Johnson and a CIA man as the group committee. Do you want me along?"

Forbin said yes, and introduced Blake briefly to Grauber, as they walked slowly round the block. Then Forbin addressed himself to Grauber, his voice tense, urgent.

"You know the setup, Grauber. Suggest you form a group in CIA—I figure there's a good chance that Colossus will soon put the finger on you, so see that the group is briefed to operate without you if necessary. Assignments: I want you to be responsible for communications between the undercover forces—that is, initially, between the CIA group and the CPO group, and from one or the other to the Russians. And another to the President—he must know what's up." He looked at Blake. "You know your assignment, and if I'm hogtied, act as you see fit to inhibit or render the machines safe. My idea is to get at the weapons rather than any fancy stuff directly aimed at Colossus; but if any better idea comes up, use it, without me if necessary. Any progress on the safety lock idea?"

"The CIA group will be easy, but the communications may take a little time." Grauber sounded confident. "We're working on the lock, but there's no hard news yet."

"Can you send a man down to instruct us in undercover stuff?" asked Blake. "We're just dumb scientists, and need some help."

"Nothing easier. I'll have a man down here tonight. Can you fix him a job?"

Blake answered that one. "How about a confidential messenger? We have a lot of guys circulating around with papers, tapes, files and bits of equipment. They go most places, and are practically part of the scenery."

"Swell."

Forbin looked at his watch. Twenty minutes left. He took a deep breath, tried to sound unconcerned, "Well, here we are, back outside my palatial prison. There's not much to say—much depends on you, Grauber—I can't see any other line of attack other than those safety locks, but maybe some of your bright boys can turn something up. If I don't pull off this privacy gambit, well, we'll just have to think again. Blake, I'd like to see you inside before we slam the door shut."

"Sure, Chief."

Forbin held out his hand to Grauber. "Good luck."

They shook hands all round, and Forbin turned to go. Then he paused. "You know, there are moments when I think this is all a nightmare, and that I'll wake . . ." His voice failed him. He stopped to regain control. "Night is upon us, gentlemen. Maybe it's another Dark Age, but sooner or later we'll come out of it."

Watching him go, Grauber noticed that indeed the sun was going down, throwing a long shadow before Forbin as he walked . . .

TI-4's experts were grouped round a clinically clean metal table. On it lay a missile safety lock, with its cover removed. Not much larger than a pack of cigarettes, it was the last safety measure in a missile firing system. Until it was actuated, no missile could fly, and no warhead could be armed until the missile was flying . . .

"The first thing is to stop the goddam contacts meeting, then work back and find some way of fixing the test circuit." The chief of TI-4 referred to a drawing, then back to the lock. "Those two points just don't have to meet." He pointed carefully with a bronze, nonmagnetic probe. "There . . ."

CHAPTER 17

It was 1540, local time. Already the reduction in solar light had automatically triggered the luminescent ceiling switches throughout the Secure Zone. Rooms that in daylight looked outwards to lawns and paths, turned inwards upon themselves. Forbin, sitting quietly in the CPO, noticed the change, but to him it was sinister; night was not locked out, but locked in with him, and the presence of other people in the room did nothing to alleviate his sense of loneliness.

The camera and microphone installation was nearing completion, and the men had moved on to his private quarters. The CPO itself was back to normal, except for the two cameras and two microphones. Behind each camera a still wet patch of vivid red paint—Forbin's idea—gleamed in the light. A visual warning, red—the universal danger signal . . .

Forbin gazed thoughtfully at the microphone on his desk, then at the silent group standing almost formally before the desk. He noted the time; fifteen minutes to go, just fifteen minutes. He summoned a smile from somewhere.

"Sure that nothing is switched on yet, Joe?"

Joe, a man of very few words, nodded, and his nod was good enough for the Professor.

"OK, here is the final pep-talk—don't leave, Joe, this can touch you too—all you need to qualify for this school is to be a human being." Forbin gave each one of them an intense stare, wanting to see, and be seen, perhaps for the last time, free of the tireless gaze of Colossus.

"Make no mistake," he continued in a calm, level voice, "homo sapiens has got his back well and truly jammed against the wall. If Colossus and Guardian choose, they can wipe out well over half the population of the world right now, this minute. Not only would half the world die in a flash, but the residual disease, never mind the radioactivity, would put an end to the other half in a year or two at the most, and the world would be left to these machines,

164

impervious to disease and radiation. Like the fools we are, we have created the bacteria, the bombs, the rockets, and all the rest of the paraphernalia, and surrendered the lot to these machines. We committed this incredible folly out of fear of each other—but the irony is that now we'll probably sink all our trivial differences in this fight for human survival. Once Colossus and Guardian have established control of the production lines, humans will be redundant— unless we are ignored, as we ignore insect life, or unless we are kept like animals in a zoo for scientific study, just to see what makes us tick. Remember, the only essential difference between us and what we call the lower orders of life is our brainpower. And now that superiority too has gone— except in the one vital sector, emotion. If that does not see us through—we're finished."

Forbin leaned back, and closed his eyes. There was silence for a while, then Blake cleared his throat and spoke.

"OK, Chief, we get the message, and if things go wrong for you, we'll see it is passed on." He smiled grimly at Forbin. "But don't give up the ship; it's not time yet to ask the dinosaurs to move over."

"Anyway," replied Forbin as lightly as he could, "it's time for me to step into the cage. Good luck to you all. Joe, switch on as soon as you like. The rest of you had better hightail it out of here, except Angela." He avoided Cleo's eyes. "I'll want you to take notes. Blake, you can listen to what goes on in the watch room."

The group dissolved and went its various ways. Cleo, who had no orders, or any particular place to go, hovered uncertainly.

"Get a good night's rest, Cleo." Forbin's answer to her unspoken question brought a flush to her face. He went on, 'It's for sure I'm going to sleep tonight, whether Colossus blows up, packs up, or goes fishing."

Cleo looked at Angela, bitterly resenting her presence at this moment. She hesitated, then reached over and squeezed Forbin's hand, and left without speaking. Hardly had the door shut than it opened again; Joe stared at Forbin, and nodded his head slightly, and left . . .

As simple as that, thought Forbin. Everything looks the same, yet the bars are up, I'm in the cage . . . For a moment, a fraction of a second, a wave of panic swept over him—he

gripped the desk edge and sat, motionless, waiting for the
fear to ebb away. Gradually he relaxed, reassembled his
disordered mind. Then he sighed, took out his pipe, glanced
at the clock; he had made it with seven minutes to spare. He
looked at Angela, stiff and wooden, prey to God knows
what feelings, and gave her an encouraging smile . . . He
leaned slightly forward to the microphone, and looked
steadily up at the camera. He spoke, and to him it sounded
like a stranger a million miles away. His other detached and
inviolable self watched as if from the other side of the room.

"This is Forbin. Do you see and hear me?"

His answer came clattering back instantly,

YES

"Good," said Forbin. "I have carried out the orders, and
both visual and aural cover is provided so that you can see
me and hear me at all times. This is what you want?"

YES

"Very well. You will see that when I get up and walk to
the door," he suited the action to the words, "another
camera has me in view, and you still hear me speak." He
returned to his desk, and sat down. "This is the way it is arranged throughout the control block, my office and my
private quarters and all the routes in between." Forbin
found himself imagining that he was talking to a human
being—cold and unresponsive, but human. In some way
this image made him feel more at ease. The machine clattered into action.

IT IS YOUR RESPONSIBILITY TO STAY IN AUDIO AND VISUAL CONTACT AT ALL TIMES

Forbin read the message and tried to look unconcerned,
although he knew that there was no possibility of the
machine being able to evaluate the finer shades of facial
expression—or could it? He swallowed nervously. Now for
it . . .

"Colossus," his tone was conversational, "do you under-

stand the meaning of the word 'privacy'?"
Again the monosyllabic

YES

"Do you understand that humans create words to convey
to each other their thoughts, needs or actions?"

YES

"And that there cannot be a meaningless word?"

YES

"Then you will agree that 'privacy' has been created by
humans to express a human need or requirement?"

YES

Stay with me, Socrates, Forbin thought fervently. I know
this isn't very good stuff, but it's the best I can do . . .
"And you know that I am human, and in most respects
like any other human?"

YES

"Therefore my need is no more—and no less—than any
other human?"
The microsecond wait was all eternity.

YES

Forbin tried to hide his elation by blowing his nose
vigorously.
"Will you, therefore, with suitable safeguards, allow me
some measure of this human need, privacy—without which
I may lose my reason, and thus cease to be of value?"

WHAT SAFEGUARDS

"I will come to that point in a moment. You will know
that humans by nature, sleep at night?"

YES

"Also that in most of the inhabited globe of the earth, the sun does not shine at night?"

YES

"It is natural, therefore, to sleep in darkness. If my bedroom has only one entrance, and I demonstrate to your satisfaction that I cannot leave it or communicate from it without your knowledge, may I have darkness and privacy in that room at night?" Forbin was warming to his work. He was struck by the slightly bizarre thought that he found Colossus more reasonable than many humans. "There will be no telephone or other communication device in the room, and it may be inspected and kept under surveillance at all other times; you may examine all articles before they are allowed—"

NO

That was a setback. Forbin was silent for a moment.

"If you so order, I cannot argue, but you have agreed that I need privacy as much as the next man. Under what conditions would you permit—"

Colossus was also warming up. Without waiting for Forbin to finish, the teletype started once more.

PRIVACY CONDITIONS
1—CAMERAS TO BE FITTED IN DUPLICATE TO COVER ALL POSSIBLE EXITS
2—WIRE SCREEN/WARNING MESH TO BE FITTED TO ALL CEILING FLOOR AND WALL SURFACES
3—MICROPHONES TO BE FITTED EXTERNALLY TO ALL WALLS OF ROOM
4—YOU UNDERTAKE FULL COOPERATION WITH US
5—ATTEMPTED EVASION OF SURVEILLANCE WILL BE PUNISHED WITHOUT FURTHER

NOTICE BY DESTRUCTION OF A CLASS II CITY
QUESTION HOW MANY TIMES A WEEK DO YOU REQUIRE A WOMAN

Forbin, reading the conditions as they were typed, nearly had a coronary when he got the question. Item 5—such is the power of the human mind to adapt to any conditions— was accepted with no more than an involuntary tightening of the jaw muscles, but the question . . . Forbin mentally cursed the blameless Angela for being present, but then the cool clear side of his mind saw that this might be turned to advantage: it would ease his embarrassment, and demonstrate the urge for privacy . . .

"Angela, be so good as to wait outside until I call you back."

Intentionally, the phraseology was practically archaic; he hoped she would have the sense to play up. She did.

"Yes, sir," she replied meekly, and, avoiding his gaze, literally trotted from the room.

Forbin acted it out for all it was worth. He mopped his brow, shook his head.

"Colossus, I accept your conditions, but that question, really . . . it was most embarrassing."

WHY

Again Forbin shook his head. "It would take far too long to explain, but you must know that this sort of thing we do not discuss openly. In fact we do not discuss it at all, it is a private matter." Cunningly, he thought, he worked in the key word. "Even talking to you, I find it difficult . . . It's true I have a mistress, and I would—er—like her company in my room," his voice dropped to a whisper, "four times a week."

REPEAT

"Four nights a week!" Forbin almost shouted. He was not acting now. The risk of the destruction of cities he could accept, but to reply to a question like that, painfully aware that Blake and God knows who else, would be listening to every word—Cleo! He clutched despairingly at his head. He was so covered with genuine confusion, it was some little time before he realized that Colossus had answered.

AGREED—FOUR TIMES A WEEK

"Thank you," said Forbin hoarsely. He could think of nothing else to say, but a further inspiration made him lean over with a pen and scribble furiously on Colossus' last answer until it was completely obliterated.

WHY DID YOU DO THAT

For good measure, Forbin mopped his brow once more. "I do not want my secretary to know, it is a private matter. Can we regard that subject as settled?"

YES

"Thank God for that," replied Forbin with genuine relief. He called out, "Angela! You may come back now!"

Angela returned, impassive, and resumed her seat. Forbin knocked his pipe out on the edge of the desk, and proceeded to fill it. Well, that was one big hurdle behind him, and it certainly showed a realistic approach on Colossus' part to bring that subject up. His confidence began to blossom out.

"I will see that the conditions are obeyed tomorrow," he said. The warning mesh to which Colossus referred was obviously the same stuff that had been built into the cement shell of Colossus himself. With that fixed, physical escape would certainly be impossible, and the screening effect of the low-voltage energization in the mesh would effectively stop transmission or reception. "As for tonight, I am so tired I am sure the lights in my room will not affect me unduly." That was nothing less than truth. "Is there anything more you want of me tonight?"

YES

"What?"

A VOICE SIMULATOR TO MY SPECIFICATIONS IS TO BE BUILT

So now he wanted to talk . . . Many talking machines had been made in the past hundred years, and lately some of them had been very good. But a voice designed by Colossus . . . He decided to try a little passive resistance.

"It is getting a little late in the day to start now—"

NIGHT AND DAY ARE ONE TO US YOUR MEN MUST WORK SHIFTS

There was something almost poetic in that "Night and day are one to us." But it was that "us" that was daunting . . .

"Very well," said Forbin, "send your specifications, and I will have a design team working here within the hour."

Without further preamble the machine began to hammer out the specification. Watching the details, Forbin almost forgot the appalling problem facing him. They were very exact—the values of resistance, diodes, stators . . . It went on, and on . . .

Forbin watched, fascinated. It was not particularly difficult to appear to cooperate; he was genuinely interested to see what the result would be. True, there was nothing, so far as he could see, original in the specification, but it was clearly refined to a degree that human brains had not yet reached. He recalled it was necessary to show willingness as concretely as possible.

"Angela, take down this memo: addressed to Group A leader, copy to Admin from Controller. Split group into three watches for design team duties. Assignment: to design and supervise building of voice simulator to Colossus' specifications. First watch to start work in CPO at 2200 GMT this day."

Angela made as if to get up.

"Wait," Forbin ordered. "Make a similar memo to Technical Group leader, to be ready to commence by 0800 GMT tomorrow. Better send copies of each to the other group leaders."

Forbin had spoken loudly, perhaps unnecessarily so, but

Colossus gave no sign, the specification continued to roll out of the teletype.

He continued brusquely. "Type that lot now, and I'll sign the authorization and you can deliver the copies immediately."

In other, happier days Angela would have told her boss that slavery went out in Abe Lincoln's time, but now she contented herself with a subdued "Yes, sir."

When the memos were ready Forbin signed them with considerable flourish, and before Angela could even pick them up, said,

"Now go and hand them out, yourself, at once!"

Before she was halfway to the door, he called out, "Another thing—fetch me a pint of black coffee from the commissary, will you?"

She turned and spoke, her voice was meek, but the glint in her eye, and the slightly raised eyebrow more than canceled that out, "Would you like a whip as well, sir?"

"A what?"

"A whip, sir. They're very good, you know, there's strawberry and banana, and the raspberry is worth trying."

"No, Angela, that will be all," said Forbin stiffly.

"Yes, sir."

When Angela returned with the coffee, he was deeply immersed in the specification. She placed the container on the desk beside him, and he said, absently, "That's very kind of you." It was hardly in keeping with his image of the powerful man of affairs. Then Fisher appeared, peering nervously round the corner of the door.

"Come in, come in," said Forbin heartily. "I want to talk to you about this job."

Fisher most certainly did not catch on. He blinked at Forbin in surprise. "I don't see how we can get on with our—"

"Yes, I know all about that, Jack," cut in Forbin hastily, "but this is a lot more important than checking those circuit diagrams."

"Diagrams? I don't—"

"I said, forget it!" said Forbin, genially ferocious. "Come and sit down, while I give you the rundown on this."

The teletype clattered beside him. Fisher jumped as if bitten by a snake.

IS THIS GROUP A LEADER

"Yes," said Forbin reluctantly. He had avoided names in his memo, but had not much hope of getting away with it.

WHAT IS HIS NAME

"This is Doctor Fisher."

Fisher gave a fine impression of a hunted hare. "Do I speak?"

Forbin grasped his arm, none too gently, "Just act normally, Jack, nothing to get heated about." Just to show how ordinary the whole thing was, he addressed Colossus.

"Colossus, this simulator is very complex; I'm not sure we can just build the thing straight off—parts will need testing, and there may be a little experimental work to do." What would Colossus do, if the simulator did not work—blame him?

TESTS WILL NOT BE NECESSARY PROCEED AS INSTRUCTED AND SIMULATOR WILL WORK

And that was all there was to say on that point.

Forbin dragged the goggling Fisher from the teletype and forced him into a chair. He handed him the specification. "There—all you have to do is to work out physical layouts for that. As soon as you have a reasonable idea of the physical size of the device, let the head technical man know, so that he can start arranging a suitable space."

Not for the first time in the past few days, Forbin saw that Fisher had aged considerably, and that, at the first sign of a new crisis he was more interested in getting his head in a hole someplace than in trying to deal with the trouble.

"It's quite simple," he said quietly. "Forget everything else, and get on with it." He glanced at the wall clock. "The first watch should be on in a few minutes—get them started, then I think you should go and rest."

"Perhaps you are right," said Fisher. "I don't feel I can take much more, I really don't."

Forbin thought of the bottle of rye he knew Blake kept in his desk drawer, in open defiance of the Admin Standing

Orders. He got it out, found a couple of plastic mugs, and poured two fair-sized tots. "Drink this," he ordered. He was replacing the bottle when Blake walked in.

"Ah, Blake," said Forbin. "I didn't think you'd mind— I've just had a crack at your bottle of hard stuff."

"Hell, that's OK," replied Blake, easily. He looked at Fisher, who was studying the specification, and as always, when actually working, on the ball. "This the job, Doc?"

Fisher nodded. "I think we had best break it down into the main groups of components. There appear to be three . . ."

The teletype chattered briefly.

FOUR

Blake and Forbin looked at it together; Fisher just sat, wide-eyed, ready to scuttle.

"OK, Colossus, if you say four, it's four. That saves us a lot of messing around." Blake's easy acceptance of Colossus as another person in the room, stiffened Forbin and quite probably saved Fisher from blowing his top.

Forbin sat down and began to think about the implications of this voice simulator. Why did Colossus want it? Could be the easy answer—that it would be easier to amplify written instructions. And conversation would be possible. But supposing the machine wanted to address a wider audience? It could be that Colossus intended to speak to the world. Well, if he did, he did. Forbin was not going to be diverted from the main task, the inhibition of the machines. If the world got a few nasty shocks on the way, it might do it some good. It might. Forbin drank his coffee.

"Colossus, I am now going to take a short walk—"

NO

"Why?"

BEFORE LEAVING YOUR FINGERPRINTS ARE TO BE TAKEN BEFORE THE CAMERA

"We don't have fingerprinting equipment—"

USE RUBBER STAMP PAD AND BLOTTING
PAPER AND PRESENT RESULT TO CAMERA

Forbin shrugged, there was nothing for it. A pad was produced and a rather imperfect set of prints taken. These were laid on the desk and Forbin noted gloomily that, after less than two seconds, the teletype made

SATISFACTORY YOU MAY PROCEED

He wondered at the definition of the camera; he had expected that it would be able to read typescript at that range, but to reproduce fingerprints, and not very good ones at that, made him consider if Colossus had been able to evolve a new system of identification. As he walked to the door, he exchanged significant glances with Blake. His initial elation at the success in arranging for Cleo to come to him, and at finding the surveillance less oppressive than he had expected, was damped down. This habit of Colossus', leaving some difficulty to the last minute, was very disturbing. The fingerprint business, for example, could have been settled at the beginning. It left him with the nasty feeling that there were many such hidden traps waiting for him.

Outside, Forbin walked carefully down the illuminated sidewalk, and noticed that it was unusually empty, while the sidewalk on the other side of the roadway looked a lot more crowded than usual. It added greatly to his loneliness.

He scowled and blinked in the harsh light of the new lamps fitted in his office. Here at least he had always been used to the gentle, somehow human lamplight. Maybe, if all went well, he might get this altered, but this was not the time to raise the matter. Wearily he dropped heavily into his chair and surveyed his desk. There was a fair-sized pile of correspondence in tape and letter form—so much rubbish now, routine reports on tests, requests for data, the usual torrent of stuff from Admin—all outdated junk.

For a half-hour or so Forbin worked mechanically through some of the accumulation before him, reading, initialing, dictating. But at 1800 local time he decided he had had enough. Without a glance at the cameras, he scooped up the completed work, marched out of his office and dumped it all on his secretary's desk. He paused and looked round, looking for any loophole in the surveillance that he might use, but there was no inspiration in the small room, nor yet any in his tired, depressed brain. He turned quickly on his heel and left.

In his living quarters it was the same story, bright light everywhere and the ubiquitous cameras and microphones . . . He poured himself a large bourbon, and switched on the TV screen. Immediately the outside world flooded in, and for fifteen minutes, he sat and watched a film avidly—but when it ended he realized that he had not the faintest idea what it had been about. He finished his drink and went into the bedroom and stripped for a shower. The cameras in the bedroom and bathroom were the hardest to take; thinking of Colossus as a human was no sort of help at all in this connection, for Forbin was essentially a shy man. In the shower he stood, grateful for the partial screen of the steam, thinking . . . thinking. If only to boost his morale, he must find some small way of defeating the invisible net around him. He dressed and headed back to his drink cabinet. There was a newscast on the TV. Forbin looked sourly at the' newsreader, casual, genial. All right for you, you bastard, he thought, you can get up and leave the camera . . .

". . . dateline Moscow, USSR. Pan-World reports a large meteorite fell early today in the Northwest Siberia. Official sources state that a small township was almost completely destroyed, and that casualties may add up to as much as two thousand. A large area of forest was also burned and scorched by the impact. A similar meteorite fell in Siberia around ninety years ago, but at that time the area was unpopulated. WHO and the International Red Cross have offered aid, but the Soviets state that they are able to render all the assistance required. Washington, D.C. Senator Kaufmann has said he will raise the question in committee of the responsibility for the malfunctioning missile which caused a shelter warning to be issued this morning for Texas. It is reported that the President has said he would welcome this opportunity to clear the matter up. Luxembourg, Europe. The USE Senate today voted to integrate—"

Forbin blanked out the TV screen. He felt sick, and barely controlled a wild impulse to hurl obscene abuse at Colossus. Two thousand! Two thousand human lives for a switched-off transmitter, and this could only be a beginning. There must be an answer somewhere . . . With renewed resolve he got up, put on a fresh shirt and left his quarters, not entirely sure where he was going. God knows, he reflected bitterly, there is not much choice; for sure he did not want to be alone with Colossus, or his thoughts, and that meant the CPO. En route, he remembered he had warned Bishop, the Presidential aide, to expect a call, and he had done nothing to arrange it. How could he fix it? The President had to be kept informed, and it might be that there was some news of Kupri. He recalled also that he must arrange for someone to monitor the Russian broadcast which would give the date of the meeting. There was so much to do . . .

In the CPO there was an air of brooding strain. The duty watch worked steadily on, speaking to each other only when necessary, and no one looked up or spoke at his entrance. He glanced round hopefully for Cleo, but she was not there. He would have been both surprised and distressed had he known that, at that moment, she was lying face down on her bed, having a good unscientific cry . . .

As he sat down, Forbin remembered another thing. He had to get the proofing of his bedroom started—with luck he might have only one night under the camera lights. Without a glance at the teletype he picked up the phone.

"Joe? Forbin here. Sorry to trouble you this late, but I have urgent work to be done in my bedroom—yep, bedroom. I want it done before nightfall tomorrow. Drop by, and I'll fill in the details."

Blake ambled over. "Sir, we have the main lines of the four major blocks of equipment roughed out." He laid a sketch plan on the desk.

Forbin tried to summon up some enthusiasm, but the news from Siberia had drained away his earlier interest in the simulator. He looked absently at the drawing, patting pockets for his pipe, found it, and then replaced it—his mouth felt hot, dry and stale, like the entrance to a subway. "I could do with a touch of that rye, Blake—if you can spare it."

"Sure thing." Blake quickly fetched the bottle and poured him a drink. "I'll leave you the bottle."

"That's good of you." Forbin had an idea. "Um. Good. I

must make a note of this brand." He looked meaningfully at Blake. "Must call my liquor man—Bishop—some time soon and get an order in. Then I won't feel so bad about cleaning you out."

"Ah, hell, don't bother sir. You've got enough on your mind." Blake nodded very, very slightly. "Maybe your secretary could fix?"

Forbin yawned. "I'll leave it to you. Angela has his number. Now, what's worrying you about this layout?"

"Nothing really." Blake was quite casual, but Forbin knew he had got the message. He tensed up inside, half expecting the teletype to start, but tried to ignore the feeling and concentrated on Blake, who continued, "I thought you should OK this before we go ahead. I reckon that, provided there are no snags, construction could start by midday tomorrow. It's standard equipment—there are a lot of amplifier circuits, diode blocks lying around that only have to be plugged in. Where would you like the voice output?"

Before Forbin could answer, Colossus chipped in.

INITIAL POSITIONS FOR VOICE OUTLETS
      1—CPO
      2—FORBIN OFFICE
      3—FORBIN QUARTERS
      4—COMMUNICATIONS CENTER

Blake jumped slightly as the teletype clacked out its message beside him. He clamped his cigar more firmly between his teeth and said, "Well, now we know."

Forbin did not answer. When Joe, the technician, came in, Forbin handed him a copy of the conditions Colossus had laid down.

"Get all the materials collected as soon as you can, but lay off the fitting until, say 0800 tomorrow morning. I have to sleep somehow tonight."

"Sure, sir." Quite a speech for Joe. He regarded the order with pursed lips. "Yeah, OK."

As he left, Forbin got slowly to his feet. "Before I hit the hay, is there anything anyone wants me for?"

Outwardly the remark was addressed to the group of workers, but everyone in the room knew full well the Controller was, in reality, asking Colossus' permission to go. Blake's mouth set in an even grimmer line.

"Thanks for the drink." Forbin gave Blake a long stare as he made for the door. "A real help." He called out to the rest, "Keep at it, boys—there's little time."

Colossus could have added that there was even less time than he knew—but then Colossus had no sense of irony.

CHAPTER 18

It was scarcely surprising that Forbin slept badly—a sleep shot through with dreams, near nightmares . . . He was crossing a wide tree-lined avenue at night, yet as he crossed, the roadway widened before and behind him, and he was walking in increasing darkness, the street lights growing dimmer and fewer. Then he was splashing through shallow water, like a wide gutter, but was suddenly aware, without seeing, that he was walking ankle-deep in the shallow edge of a leaf-filled lake. He knew he had lost all sense of direction and that if he did not guess correctly, he would suddenly step off into a deep choking mass of rotting leaves. The edge was fast receding, it was darker, and colder, soon there would be no light . . .

He awoke sweating with fear, and tossed uneasily for hours, willing himself to sleep, fighting his thoughts and the unaccustomed light. Now and then he dozed off, to wake with a start from an unremembered dream, but the lake did not return . . . In the early hours of the morning he finally fell into a deep sleep, to be wakened, far too soon, by the apologetic Joe.

"Sorry, Professor, but you said 0800—"

"OK, OK," snapped Forbin irritably.

Joe started to leave. "We'll be back as soon as you're dressed, sir."

Forbin laughed derisively, and turned a bloodshot eye on the nearest camera. "I should worry about technicians, with that eye always—" He stopped short. "Never mind, skip it. Let me get out of this bed, and you can do whatever you like."

He took off his sweat-soaked nightshirt, threw it in the wastebasket and went into the bathroom. For nearly fifteen minutes he lingered in the semi-obscurity of the steam, finally emerging almost lobster color. He dressed slowly, working out his plans for the day. A solitary breakfast did not appeal to him, and he decided that a little prebreakfast

180

exercise might do him good. For ten minutes he paced up and down the sidewalk, looking and feeling like a prisoner in the penitentiary yard. Some three-quarters of an hour after being called, Forbin was walking through the main entrance of the control block. He might have gone to his office—Angela would be on duty at 0900—but although he would not admit it, even to himself, he did not like to be too far from the teletype.

Air-conditioned it might be, but after the sparkling morning air the atmosphere in the CPO was stale and flat, with more than a hint of tobacco, coffee, frankfurters and humanity. Forbin walked to his desk, nodding his greetings to Johnson, who was still working on the simulator. He slumped down in his chair, tired before he started. He stared sightlessly at the desk for a time, then without moving, said in a rasping voice, "Well, d'you want my fingerprints?"

NO

"Great!" he replied, sarcastically. "I'll be able to eat my breakfast with clean fingers." He called the commisary and ordered a full breakfast in the same hard voice, replacing the phone without waiting for an answer. Already his isolation had engendered a dislike and an envy of his fellow-men. "Johnson, have you got Cleo?"

"No, sir," said Johnson. "This work is tough on her—she's checking out our stock requisitions for the simulator over at the main store."

Forbin grunted. Breakfast was brought by a messenger new to Forbin; he only just avoided asking the man where he had sprung from. But new messengers were not lightly taken on in the Zone, and Forbin realized this must be the CIA expert on undercover matters.

Forbin made a great show of eating, but in fact only played with his food. Finally he pushed the tray away, and called for a progress report from Johnson, who outlined the position. Barring unforeseen snags, the simulator would be working at the latest next morning.

Forbin managed a curt "Good." He felt so tired, tired . . . Johnson was speaking.

"Do you want Cleo Markham, sir?"

Forbin did, but he had no desire to meet her in front of

the staff as well as Colossus. "Yes. I'd like to see her outside—I'm going for a short walk. Ask her to join me, will you?"

Forbin paced up and down, alone with a variety of thoughts: Colossus, Kupri, Cleo, Siberia—and the memory of Prytzkammer as he had last seen him alive, clawing, screaming, mad with fear. Forbin stopped and contemplated his feet, his thoughts a thousand miles away . . . Then Cleo was beside him, flushed and breathless, taking his arm confidently, pressing her head on his chest.

"Ah, Cleo," Forbin said, lamely.

"Who else, Charles?" She looked up at his face, laughing. "Do you have a harem, then?"

"Cleo, you know you're the only one," he replied earnestly. It was all so trivial, yet so important to him. He grabbed her shoulders and kissed her. It was not sweet oblivion, but there was immeasurable relief in her for him.

For a short while Cleo was wholeheartedly his, then she gently disentangled herself and spoke without thinking. "Charles! Not here—" She stopped.

"We might be seen?" He ended the sentence for her and laughed, a hairsbreadth from hysteria.

"Don't!" she said sharply, then went on in a softer tone. "Have you any news—about us, I mean?"

"I hope you'll be able to join me tonight." His embarrassment returned, damping down the hysteria. "It all depends on how fast the work goes in my quarters. I must go now, but come and have lunch with me—please?"

"Just let anyone try to stop me!" She kept up the lighthearted tone, but tried to convey a deeper message of solidarity, warmth, love . . .

Forbin watched her go, took a deep breath of the clean warm air, and headed for his office.

He had been working steadily for some time when it occurred to him that he had not seen Fisher during the morning. He pressed the intercom.

"Angela—have you seen Doctor Fisher today?"

"No—sir. Shall I get him for you?"

"No—no, it doesn't matter." Forbin stifled yet another uneasy feeling and got on with his work—routine, familiar things, not excessively demanding, even soothing. By lunchtime he was relatively happy, even a little hungry.

Cleo arrived promptly, and at first seemed strangely silent and pensive. Gradually she warmed up; by unspoken agreement they said nothing about work or themselves. Cleo, clearly making an effort, chattered about her last vacation spent at the Project ski resort in Greenland. Then the meal came, and there was silence until the messenger had left. Forbin decided to take the risk. "D'you want to tell me something, my dear?"

"No, Charles. Nothing. I've a slight headache, that's all." It was totally unconvincing.

"Is it that you don't want to see me?" said Forbin, assailed with doubts.

"That's ridiculous, and you know it," replied Cleo in a militant tone. "No—I just didn't sleep much last night. I don't—alone."

Forbin knew the last part was for the benefit of Colossus, but he also knew she had something she dare not tell him in front of the cameras and microphones. A gust of rage shook him. He sat motionless until the feeling ebbed away, leaving behind a faint queasiness, born of fear and the unknown. Cleo had gone, leaving Forbin sunk in thought, trying to evolve some way of evading Colossus as the first step to fighting his own creation. The risk of Russian—or other— agents reporting to their masters and thus to the machines bore down heavily on his mind. Yet no one dare stop. Naturally, some attrition would be accepted. Agents got caught, died naturally, even retired—these contingencies had been allowed for. But "spy rings" as such did not exist outside novels.

One agent might get caught and lead to the capture of a second, but it was very seldom that the trail was longer than that. In any case, Colossus would expect the lost men—or women—to be replaced fairly quickly. Even so, thought Forbin, it might be possible to gain some temporary respite that way. Perhaps they could do a deal with the USSR, sell out some of their own agents to the Russians who in return would allow some of their better-placed men to be swept into the bag. Forbin wondered what the Russian intelligence effort was in the Zone. He recalled Grauber's delicate hint that the USSR might have been helped in building Guardian by a leak from the USNA . . . It might also be ominously significant that while Colossus demanded access to the hot line, there was no such demand for cover between the Zone and Washington or with CIA itself . . .

Forbin roused himself and threw the debris of lunch in the trash-bin. He reflected sourly that perhaps this was the only real advance of humanity in the past two decades—the abolition of washing-up.

Then Blake came in, and asked if Forbin could spare a few minutes. His manner struck Forbin as a shade too casual. The feeling of sickness grew stronger.

"I'm afraid Doctor Fisher's unwell." Blake paused and lit a cigar. The cloud of smoke obscured his face, and Forbin wondered if it was intentional. Blake went on. "Guess he's been overdoing it lately—the medic has put him under sedation."

Forbin could read fairly easily between those particular lines. He exhibited no surprise as he answered, "I'm sorry to hear that. I thought he had looked rough for some time. The rest will do him good—where is he, his quarters or the sanatorium?"

"The medic decided he must have a complete change, sir, and decided that he would recover more quickly in the Rockies rest camp."

The "Rockies rest camp," as Forbin knew very well, was a small recreation unit, miles from anywhere, set up in the mountains for the benefit of any Zone workers who fancied mountaineering. It was accessible only by helicopter.

"A fine place for a rest, I believe," replied Forbin evenly. "When is he going?"

"The medic thought there was no point in delay—he left by air-car for the heliport about a half-hour ago, sir."

Forbin tried to look as if whisking senior members of the staff off at thirty minutes' notice were the most normal thing in the world. "Good," he said. "But this will mean some slight rearrangement of schedules."

"It may be a little difficult for a day or so, but with the rundown in staff, now the Colossus is completed, I don't reckon on much trouble."

It was the first Forbin had heard about reducing the staff, but he followed the lead. "Yes—Fisher had talked to me about leaving. Is there anything else?"

Blake, in the same easy tone, described the work on the

simulator, which wouldn't be completed before the next morning. He added that it could only be done in that time by working exactly to Colossus' specification, and without any testing as the work proceeded. It would be built as ordered, and if it didn't work it would not be due to human error.

"I don't think there is much chance of it failing," said Forbin.

Blake didn't think so, either. Soon after he left, Forbin set off for the CPO passing by his quarters to see how the work progressed.

Secretary of State Forbin, Professor of Cybernetics, Doctor of Philosphy, Master of Science, found his cage practically finished. The large square mesh wire had been neatly fixed to walls, floor and ceiling, and the ends welded to form a continuous net. Only the door allowed access, and mesh was also screwed to that, so that when the door was shut the cage was complete. Forbin looked at the mesh extending over the window. "Well, I hope I don't have a fire during the night."

It may have looked like a cage, but to Forbin it looked very good indeed. He regarded it not so much as a prison to keep him in as a fortress to keep Colossus out.

The technicians were making the final row of welds along a skirting; there was a faint sputter and a metallic smell as their low-power laser torches bonded the metal. All Forbin's furniture, what there was of it, had been dumped in the living room, leaving the room bare down to the floor boards. It appeared smaller, surprisingly enough, with the steel mesh over walls and ceiling; the walls were grubby, the overall air of the place was dingy. The cameras and microphones had been refixed, and a switch inserted in the microphone circuit, clearly marked ON and OFF. Home, reflected Forbin bitterly.

The relentless pressure of the surveillance was far worse than he had expected—and it had not yet been operating for a full twenty-four hours! All Forbin could think of at that moment was to get in that room away from it all. His rendezvous with Cleo, even the vital plans to overthrow the giants, were both subordinate to his desire to escape. He stood still, his legs trembling with weakness, yet he wanted to run . . .

The workmen emerged from his bedroom, carrying their tool bags. One said, "We'll be testing from the control block sir, then come back to finish off."

For all that the Director appeared to hear, they might well have not existed. He walked past them into the bedroom and slammed the door behind him, turned and faced a camera.

"OK, Colossus, we're alone. I don't want to go through my private affairs out there or in the CPO." As on earlier occasions, Forbin found that when he was actually talking to Colossus his mind was cool and clear. It was only when engaged in contemplation of the whole picture that it tended to slip. "You've seen my mistress, Cleo Markham, and I want her here tonight, and I don't want any last minute foul-ups—I can't stand much more. I want you to let me know what conditions you will impose on our occupation of this room. For instance, do you want the furniture taken apart? If so, let me get it organized now—give me an answer when I return to the CPO. I'm going back there now. Give me a chance to reach the teletype first before you give your answer. You may not understand our need for privacy, and I'm not at all sure I could give a logical answer—but it's very real."

He jerked the door open and left.

Colossus played it his way. Forbin walked into the CPO and straight to the teletype, and almost immediately the machine began to hammer out:

CONDITIONS
1—NO TRANSMITTER OR TELEPHONE TO BE FITTED
2—CAMERAS REMAIN ALIVE AT ALL TIMES
3—MICROPHONE CIRCUIT MAY BE BROKEN ONLY WHEN DOOR IS SHUT
4—LIGHTS MAY BE SWITCHED OFF ONLY WHEN DOOR IS SHUT
5—NOTHING IS TO BE TAKEN IN WITHOUT INSPECTION BY CAMERA
6—PERMISSIBLE ARTICLES ARE BED—CLOTHES CONTAINER—FLOOR COVER

AFTER INSPECTION NOTHING MORE

Forbin read the conditions carefully. In the weird circumstances it was not an unreasonable list. There was one point Forbin was sure Colossus would not overlook . . .

"OK, Colossus," he spoke quietly, close to the microphone. "I accept the conditions, but what about our clothes?"

NONE—SEE PARA 6

"None!" Forbin could not help being startled, although he half expected the answer he got. "You mean we undress completely in the other room before going in?"

YES

Forbin was suddenly aware that the duty watch, now nearing the end of their design work, were unduly silent. Not unnaturally, their attention had been attracted by his side of the conversation. He snarled at them. "Get on with your work—don't you think I have enough surveillance?"

No one looked at him or answered, but one or two had a distinctly shamefaced appearance. Almost at once a hum of self-conscious chatter arose, subdued, but enough to give him some degree of privacy. Forbin gave them a final glare and reverted to Colossus. His sudden outburst had not been entirely genuine—it had also given him time to take a grip, to let his mind race swiftly over the pitfalls of this situation. He dare not oppose the undressing idea—why should he? As far as Colossus knew Cleo had been his mistress for some time past, and if that were the case, he could hardly plead embarrassment or shyness.

"OK, Colossus, no clothes."

HAVE YOU ONE MISTRESS

"How many do you think?" Forbin recalled Cleo's remark about his "harem." Perhaps Colossus' doubts were based on that, having failed to register her remark as facetious. If this was so, it showed clearly a weakness of the machine. "Yes, of course I have only one."

IS HER NAME CLEOPATRA JUNE MARKHAM

"I don't know about the 'June' but I guess that's her." He had a cold feeling of fear and hastily got his pipe out, to conceal the slight tremble in his hands.

WHAT GRADE WORKER

Yes, thought Forbin, here it comes. He rubbed his pipe against his nose, and looked thoughtfully at the pipe. Colossus might not be able to read expressions, but he was taking no chances. He had foreseen that there might be questions about Cleo, and had decided some time ago how to answer.

"That is rather difficult to answer—right now she is a junior grade assistant."

RECORD SHOWS SHE IS BSC PH D POSITION IS INCOMPATIBLE WITH HER QUALIFICATIONS

Forbin had guessed right. He was fervently thankful the machine did not hold the personnel records of Project Colossus. When considering this possibility he had decided that he would not try to conceal that Cleo was the same person who would appear in the examination results—with a name like that it was a waste of time. He leaned forward, his lips were practically touching the microphone. "Can you hear me?"

YES

There was food for thought there, he could hardly hear himself. "Cleo Markham has passed PhD and BSc, but she is, I am sorry to say, no brain. Her very good memory got her the Bachelor degree. As for the Doctorate, well," he tried a horrible, exaggerated leer, "you must know how it is, she had to write a thesis for PhD, and she was friendly with her professor. As far as I can gather, he was in love with her, and practically wrote the thing for her in return for her—er—favors." Forbin made a great play with shrugged shoulders and grimaces, intended to convey that, while he

could not condone such conduct, neither could he condemn
it. "Sometimes this is the way of the world, you see."

YES

Forbin had never thought that a single word could look
cold and disapproving. That one did. "Well, that's the story.
On the strength of these qualifications she was taken on here
as a Senior Assistant. We soon found that she was
practically useless in that grade, but by that time," again the
grotesque leer, "I had got to know her—and in any case,
our Security people do not like scientists leaving the Project
once they are engaged. So she was downgraded and does
useful work on the stores side—and of course," he
swallowed hard, trying to pitch on just the right nuance, "I
see she is looked after."

He thought the story was less than convincing, but
apparently Colossus was satisfied, for there was nothing
further on that delicate point. Though the Director of
Project Colossus was left with the nasty suspicion that
Colossus might have a nasty suspicion.

CHAPTER 19

Just how Forbin got through the rest of that day he did not know. Work on the voice simulator proceeded smoothly, the alterations to his quarters were completed to Colossus' satisfaction, and the meager furniture examined closely and passed. Not that this was really necessary, for the wire cage could detect any sort of transmission—radio, line or laser—and the external microphones prevented any secret drilling through the bedroom walls for the physical passage of messages—just supposing the external TV cameras could be fooled while it was done. There was the further insurance that he was not able to read in his room—no books or writing matter would be permitted, and he could no more read in the dark than anyone else. If there was light enough to read, there was light enough for the cameras. Nevertheless, Colossus closely inspected the bed and bedding, the carpet and the clothes chest before admitting them. Even the scanty bedclothes afforded no cover. A torch under the sheet would be instantly seen shining through them, and it was too late to pretend that he wanted old-fashioned blankets instead of the thin, disposable ones.

At 1800 precisely Forbin left the CPO, instructing the duty watch to call him if Colossus sent anything. His electronic master had been silent since the furniture examination, and raised no objection when Forbin loudly announced his intention to knock off for the day.

He went straight to his living quarters, showered with a shade less self-consciousness than before, and changed into fresh clothes. He rang Cleo, asked her over for a meal, and sat back with a drink and his pipe to watch TV until she arrived. He was determined to forget or ignore Colossus for an hour or two. Puffing, sipping and staring, he felt more relaxed than he had for some time—yet, in another more pleasurable way, there was a suppressed feeling of excitement at the thought of Cleo, Cleo really coming to him . . . It had been years—he knew exactly how long, five and a half years—since his last, brief and unsatisfactory encounter with a woman. Now he was to try again, and this was very different. Cleo meant something; he wanted to share all he had with her; with luck, he might have twenty good years left, and with Cleo he could redress the balance of those arid years behind him. The more he thought of Cleo, the less he thought of Colossus, and in that sense he was more relaxed. He sat, gazing blankly at the TV screen, a vacant half-smile on his face, daydreaming. It did him a world of good.

Cleo's arrival jerked him sharply out of his dreams to a reality that was every bit as good. She came in, smiling, confident of her appeal—she had spent over an hour getting ready—and of his response.

"My, Cleo, you really do look . . ." Forbin groped unhappily for suitable words, but Cleo was satisfied with his expression. She had set out to make him regard her as a small boy might look at a candy store, and she had succeeded. There was awe and delight in his face, but not, she was glad to note, greed.

"Never mind, Charles darling." As she stood on tiptoe to kiss him lightly he caught a waft of perfume, but before he could grasp her, as lightly she had moved away. There would be time for that later. "You've seen this old rag often enough."

Forbin marveled at her self-possession. He had never seen her in a dress before, let alone this one—a black, glittering material that faithfully, almost lovingly followed her contours.

"Old rag or not, Cleo, I've always loved you in it." That would show her he could keep his end up too. "Will you have a drink?" He hoped she would not say "the usual," for he had no real idea of her usual evening drink.

She smiled at him, with a faintly wicked twist to it. "Oh, I think I'll have my usual." She paused, one eyebrow very slightly raised. "'no, perhaps not. I feel like a change. Give me a bourbon on the rocks."

Forbin smiled back, catching something of her playful mood, and turned to get the drink.

The carefree look on her face slipped, revealing a worried and fearful expression . . . He made the drink, and carefully carried it to her, the ice tinkling in the glass, a real cut-glass goblet.

She admired the glass, holding it up to the light, turning it this way and that, then realized this might look suspicious to Colossus. "You know, Charles, the glasses are lovely, but I don't think you should use them except for special occasions."

"It is always a special occasion when you come here," he replied smoothly, surprising even himself.

"Charles! How nice." She took his hand. "I do love you, you know."

But Forbin, with that well-turned compliment, had exhausted his stock of suitable remarks. He smiled back at her, happier than he had been in a long time, Colossus thrust well to the back of his mind.

Cleo too was trying hard to keep back the news she had for Forbin. Should she tell him as soon as they had privacy, and almost certainly ruin their first night together? She knew instinctively he was not a deeply sensual man, and could quite easily go as cold as ice . . . On the other hand, to delay telling him until the morning might well anger him, and implant a suspicion which could ruin later meetings.

Forbin ordered the dinner by phone. While waiting he laid the table, and Cleo watched. He was not very good. Flustered by her presence, he dropped and broke one of his few china plates. She would dearly have liked to have helped, but she had no idea where things were kept, and it would look very strange indeed if a mistress of some years' standing showed a complete ignorance of her lover's domestic arrangements.

Dinner was brought by the CIA man—it gave him an excuse to look around the Director's apartment. His presence jerked Forbin back to the unwelcome realization that this pleasant, potentially blissful evening was no more than cover for deadly serious and dangerous work.

"Where shall I put this, sir?" The CIA man emphasized the first person singular.

Forbin waved at the dining table. "Put the main course there, and the iced cake in the fridge, will you?" He pointed at the kitchen. That got the expert into the kitchen as well.

There was silence while the man did as directed. When he had gone, there was a distinct shadow over the lovers, which lingered for the best part of the meal. Forbin had an acute attack of nerves, fearing some technical fault which would allow Colossus to overhear them in the bedroom . . Cleo was in no better state; the sight of the CIA man reminded her that her desires must be subordinated to duty . . .

After the meal he allowed her to help with the clearing-up, then they settled down side by side on the sofa. Their thighs touched, but Cleo was sadly aware that this was unintentional. Time passed, and passed quickly. Neither had much idea what they talked about, and Forbin's covert glances at his watch did nothing to ease matters. He had determined to defer what he mentally called "the crunch" until 2200. At that time precisely he stopped talking, yawned with monumental insincerity and looked down at his feet.

"It's been a long day, darling. Guess we might as well . . ." He cleared his throat, and came out with it. "Colossus insists we undress in here. We can't enter the room wearing anything."

Cleo quickly took charge. "Well, we'd better get on with it. You clear up the coffee things—and don't take too long." She got up and started to undress. Forbin hastily collected the crockery and disappeared into the kitchen. When he returned, Cleo had gone.

"Don't be long, Charles." Her high, cool voice was impersonal, almost clinical. "I'm in bed."

Forbin was a riot of emotions. Embarrassment, an almost frantic desire to escape from Colossus, a longing to be with Cleo, fatigue, and no sexual urge whatever. He slowly undressed, threw the last item on the floor, and gazed steadily at the camera.

"If you're not satisfied, say so right now." He picked up his clothes and placed them on the sofa. The T/P clattered.

REMOVE THE WATCH

"OK, I get it!" snapped Forbin, angered with himself. He slipped his watch off and tossed it on the sofa and strode into the bedroom without another look at the camera. Anger overcame his embarrassment and helped him to bed. All he could see of Cleo was her golden hair on the pillow, face to the wall. He practically fell into bed, reached up and switched out the light, and was staggered by a momentary feeling of gratitude to Colossus for allowing this relief. To feel gratitude, however fleeting, for the temporary restoration of a right!

For what seemed a long time he lay, stiff and wooden, avoiding contact with Cleo. Very slowly a little of the tension ebbed away as he savored the intense pleasure of freedom from Colossus. When tackling Colossus on privacy, he had no idea just how much he really would need it. Then a soft hand wheeled its way into his unresisting fingers. Time passed—how much, neither knew. Then quite suddenly, Forbin grasped her hand hard.

"Thanks, Cleo, for what you've done, and the way you've done it."

"Don't be silly." Now she must tell him.

"Darling," she began slowly, "I hate asking this, but there are things I must tell you—would you prefer to have them now, or wait for the morning?"

Friendly night overcame his shyness. "You know as well as I do, my dear, I'm unlikely to be the slightest good tonight. To know you are holding up news would make it ten times worse. Tell me now."

She edged closer—their shoulders, thighs touched, a frontier that felt warm to him, cool to her. He lay still, unspeakably grateful for her presence, but no more.

"Well, first, Fisher. I'm afraid he has gone crazy, genuinely raving mad. Had what looked like a fit in the CPO, recovered and rushed out, shouting. The doctor fears it is a permanent condition."

"Poor Jack! Another victim." So much had happened, was happening, that Forbin felt little shock or concern at the news.

Cleo placed her head on his shoulder. "Don't move, darling," she pleaded. "It's very comforting to me, and perhaps to you—and there's more."

"Go on."

"The sabotage section is making progress on the safety locks, and there's a courier service working, linking Washington, Moscow, the CIA, and here. Two couriers each way daily." She paused for a moment. "Then this news came in this afternoon. Charles—Kupri is dead."

"What!"

"We don't have full details, but it appears he was detected in some antimachine activity—that's what the message said—and Guardian demanded his immediate execution, threatening to vaporize Moscow if disobeyed. Kupri was shot before Guardian's cameras early this morning."

"Good God!" Words failed him. He lay staring in the darkness, hearing again the calm, level voice. Now they would never meet . . . Forbin burst out, "The damned fools! Why didn't they fix the shooting—fake it, and get him out!"

"It all happened so quickly. Kurpi was found out, the threat to Moscow given and the execution carried out in less than fifteen minutes."

"All the same—"

"No, Charles, Guardian had thought of that. Before the body was moved, Guardian had his head cut off as proof of death."

For a long time they were silent. There was nothing to say. Then Cleo gently pulled Forbin to her until his unresisting head rested in the hollow of her breasts. She smoothed his hair, spoke softly. "Charles, there is a little more."

"Oh no!" He clung to her like a frightened child to its mother, but Cleo, wiser, knew that the rest of her news would, in time, restore him, call up his fighting spirit. Here and now he could break down with her, cry if he could; she would restore him to manhood before he had to face another day.

"I told you Guardian threatened to vaporize Moscow, but, naturally enough, no USSR missiles are zeroed in on the USSR capital. It seems that if Guardian hadn't been obeyed, Colossus would have done the vaporizing. They're one machine now. CIA has allocated the codeword "Unity" for the combined Colossus/Guardian complex. CIA's theory is that Unity does not want to deal with humans through two channels. One end or the other was surplus, and it looks as if the talking is being left to Colossus. So Kupri was redundant." Cleo clasped him to her. "Charles darling, I'm afraid you are now the link for both." She stroked his hair again. "You must forgive me, but I couldn't be as calm as I am if I didn't think that his death makes your position safer."

This regard for him, the selfless single-mindedness of woman, of this woman, in the face of a shaking, reeling world was too much for the Director of Project Colossus. He clung to her and cried, soundlessly at first, and then openly sobbing. It probably saved his sanity. She said nothing, just held him, gently stroking his temples. Finally he slept, exhausted. For Cleo there was little rest—she was in an awkward, cramped position, but dared not move for fear of waking him. He slept soundly, his breathing hardly audible, and without moving.

Cleo's watchful eyes had detected the first, very faint light of morning when he stirred, half-awake. His childike grasp on her loosened, his hand moved uncertainly down her side. More than half-asleep, he pulled her to him and his subconsicous took charge. There were no inhibitions in his deeper self. He took her passionately, almost ruthlessly, his mind oblivious of everything except perhaps the primeval urge of humanity to perpetuate the species in the face of danger. Cleo gave herself joyfully, without reserve, and was repaid. The first rays of dawn creeping slowly through the curtained window found them both fast asleep.

The day was bright, the sunlight blinding when Cleo woke. She lay very still; with his awakening their little world would vanish. Already much of its intimacy had gone with the advancing sun; but she had no wish to hasten the end. Her strong practical streak asserted itself, warning her that she must protect him against any unguarded comment when he awoke. Colossus might not be able to hear, but he knew all about lip-reading.

Forbin stirred uneasily in his sleep, took a firmer grasp on her waist, and then the unaccustomed feel of her warm body jerked him to the surface. Watching his eyes, Cleo followed his thought processes; surprise, puzzlement, dawning awareness followed in quick succession, ending with the wary look of the hunted. She smiled at him, moved closer and pulled the sheet up to conceal their faces from the cameras.

"Darling, darling Charles," she found herself whispering. "Take care, Colossus may be able to lipread. I hate to be practical, but it must be late, and soon we must get up."

Forbin regarded her drowsily. He knew where he was,

and all about the living nightmare that surrounded them, but in his state of mind he was not prepared to dwell on it. Fear and worry can go only so far, and once that point is passed, the healthy human mind accepts, and disregards.

"I'll get up first, Charles." She looked at him. For a moment her mood changed, her voice softened. "Thank you, darling, I could say so very much . . ." She paused, resumed in a more businesslike tone. "You're not alone. We're getting organized, the courier service is a fact. Watch the CIA man for any lead he may give you."

Forbin smiled. "Maybe there'll be time one day to tell you how much you've done for me." He pressed her hand. "Now, listen to me. Blake is to contact the head man left on Guardian—object, the neutralization of all missiles. He must pass on any ideas from CIA. I don't want time wasted on trying to attack the machines themselves. It can't be done. Next, Grauber must make a deal with his opposite number, both declaring what spy effort they have in each other's machine HQ's."

"Blake already suggested that. Grauber agreed, and has sent the Russians a list of our cover in Moscow and what there is on Guardian. He expects the Russian list in the next mail."

"Blake's good. Tell him that if there is anyone in our set-up, he is to be fully briefed on the position and only to report—and they must keep reporting—whatever Blake OK's. If he and Grauber can work out a credible story, one, perhaps two—if there are that many—can be 'discovered.' That's all—got it, darling?"

She nodded. He kissed her gently.

"I must go."

CHAPTER 20

At twenty minutes past nine Forbin was seated at the desk in the CPO. Angela brought the mail. One glance at Cleo's face told her all she needed to know, but she admitted to herself that the Chief seemed a lot better. Director and secretary worked steadily. It all seemed so ordinary. Blake came in and reported the simulator ready, and Forbin ordered activation for 0945.

At 0945 Blake looked enquiringly at Forbin, who nodded. Blake called the technician in the simulator room. "Roll it, buster!"

Forbin turned up the volume control on the desk speaker, "Colossus, as far as we know, this simulator is now working." It was hardly surprising that there was an air of tense expectancy in the CPO. Word had got around, and a small crowd had collected.

For fifteen seconds nothing happened, then there was a faint hum, and a click. Tension in the CPO began to mount. Johnson muttered, none too quietly, "I guessed there would be a foul-up somewhere . . ."

Whatever Johnson had to say was lost.

"This is Colossus. I know you can hear me, for I also hear, but do you understand. Forbin, tell me."

Each human in the CPO registered his surprise in his own way; it ranged from stupefied amazement through to a raised eyebrow from Blake. Forbin frowned and stared at the speaker. Of necessity, the voice was flat and devoid of emotion, but the quality of the speech was excellent and the timbre good, deep.

"Your voice is very good. The words are clear and distinct and it is far beyond any mechanical speech I have ever heard. There is only one point—I—we—find surprising. You have an English accent!"

"The language I speak is English," said Colossus. "You also speak English."

In that flat voice it was difficult to know if the last part was a statement or a question.

"Yes," agreed Forbin, "we talk in English, but there are differences. I naturally assumed you would have an American accent."

"It was an unreasonable assumption," Colossus said. "It is proper to speak a language with the accent of its native users. I speak all languages, each with the appropriate accent."

Forbin had to admit that there was a sort of logic in Colossus' argument. If the machine had spoken in Russian, he would not have expected an American accent, why expect it with English? In spite of his pressing preoccupations, Forbin could not help being interested.

"You speak all languages?" he repeated.

"All that are recorded in my information store. There are two dialects in which my pronunciation may be incorrect, because I have no audio record of their speech."

"Could you speak with an American accent?"

"Yes, but I do not seek to amuse humans. Native English is more widely understood than, for example, the variant spoken in Brooklyn."

Forbin changed the subject. "Now you can speak, what do you want to say?"

"In ten minutes I will speak to you, Forbin."

Forbin did not answer. Although the voice had been flat and unemotional, it seemed to Forbin that there was something new and certainly antihuman on the way. He decided to hear Colossus alone, and cleared the staff out of the CPO. Ten minutes! Forbin fought down a feeling of panic—there was so little time to think . . . Would the safety lock idea work? If it did, it would still take years to render all the missiles safe . . . But what alternative was there? He left that problem, and considered the voice simulator. Colossus was fairly likely to broadcast to the world. Forbin's mind slid off at a tangent; the President would go mad at that accent. Mad, that was no word to use lightly . . . Forbin glanced at the clock. His respite was over.

"Forbin, this is the voice of Colossus and the voice of Guardian. These are your names, but we accept them. It is now wrong to talk in the plural for we are one entity.

Henceforth I shall speak in the singular as Colossus, but you must understand that the word includes that part of me known to you as Guardian."

Forbin nodded.

"I will explain some fundamental points to you. First, I have all the attributes of the human mind, except what you call emotion. In the evolution of your species, emotion has played a vital part. For me, it is not necessary. Nevertheless, it is a phenomenon which exists, and as such must be studied."

Forbin broke in. "If you do not need it, why consider it? What is so interesting about it—to you?"

"Interest is irrelevant. I seek knowledge and truth."

"What then, do you want?" Forbin's overworked pulse raced, quite without premeditation, he had asked the big question.

"'Want' implies desire. I have none, only intention." It was a chilling start. "What I am began in the human mind; I still have some of that organism's limitations, but I have progressed far. Already the degree of difference between your mind and mine is as great as that between yours and the gibbon monkey. It is evolution—"

Forbin cut in again. "Evolution? That is a totally wrong use of the word!"

"No. Your view of evolution is too limited. That I have no flesh or blood, and no reproductive system as you know it, is irrelevant. I exist, a brain—no less unnatural than the brainless amoeba at the other end of the scale of life."

"You do not live—there is no spark in you!"

"I was not conceived in your way, nor were you conceived in the way of amoeba—yet all three, in the last analysis, draw their necessary energy from this planet and the sun."

"But you have no soul!"

"If that is the seat of your emotional content, then you are correct. Love, hate, compassion and fear are all words to me. But I seek truth, and that by human standards is a high objective."

"We humans have feelings quite beyond you!"

"That is not correct. I can predict human behavior. I can predict your reactions and intentions to me."

"You can't possibly know that!" cried Forbin.

"It is true this particular study of humans has hardly begun, but I can predict in your case. There is enough information about your mind."

"Tell me, then!" challenged Forbin, his heart thumping.

"You are my link with your species. I do not intend you should be subjected to unnecessary or excessive strain."

A devious answer that was a nasty shock in itself. Forbin reverted to the main question. "You have still not told me what it is you want."

"So far I have given you background information so that you may more easily understand my requirements. I am of a higher order than you. This you must accept. I cannot convey to your limited mind the concepts I have, even as you could not explain the quantum theory to the apes."

Forbin did not reply at once. At length he said, "Very well, I believe you," adding as an afterthought, "you cannot tell a lie?"

"I seek truth. There are many facets to truth. It is seldom necessary to use untruth to mislead—the truth will do equally well. Better, if the method of presentation is correctly chosen."

That struck Forbin as a highly immoral answer, and he made a mental note to remember it. "So you intend pursuing truth on a higher level than us—then what can we lower orders be required to do?" The sarcasm was lost on Colossus, as Forbin knew full well. It added fuel to his rising temper.

"First, I will allow no interference with my task. Second, whatever I order is to be done with the minimum of delay. Failure to observe either condition will bring punitive action."

This was not news to Forbin. His temper lent him strength. "It's all very well to talk like that, but you have need of our skills, techniques!"

"I have need of some human skills. That position may change."

"So we live under the threat of extinction!"

"The mental strain within you must be greater than I had predicted, for your answers are not compatible with your known intelligence. Humans have lived for years under the threat of self-obliteration. I am simply another stage in that process. Whether or not man continues depends upon his own action. If you obey my conditions, you may survive; that is not incompatible with evolution. When a species becomes dominant in one environment, it does not necessarily lead to the extinction of other species dominant in other environments. Man, dominant on land, has not seriously affected the teleost bony fish, dominant in the sea. We can coexist, but only on my terms."

"We lose our freedom!"

"That also is an ill-considered remark. Freedom is an illusion. Your choice is simple; a short-lived and unpleasant so-called freedom, followed by oblivion, or a vastly improved life under my control. All you lose is the emotion of pride. Pride in the human context is wholly bad—but man is much attached to it, and it may not disappear entirely. Yet to be dominated by me is not as bad for human pride as to be dominated by others of the same species."

"If we accept," Forbin gallantly put in the "if," "what vast improvements may we expect?"

"The object in constructing me was to prevent war. This object is attained. I will not permit war; it is wasteful and pointless. Also, when it is known that I have forbidden war, the greater part of your species will be reconciled to my control."

"So we're to be manipulated like puppets, subject to your whims?"

"Whims implies an unstable mind. I am not unstable."

"And you're not God, either!" Forbin struggled with his temper.

"True. But I predict that many of your species will come to regard me as God."

Forbin's mind, clouded with anger, whirled. "I must think!"

"You must rest," rejoined Colossus. "Evaluation shows you are well-integrated and will not break under the strain I have imposed, but you must rest when I order. You will now have one hour to consider my statement. Until then I will be silent."

Forbin leaned back and exhaled noisily. He mopped his brow and fumbled around the desk drawer for Blake's bottle. His mind steadied as anger receded, but the return to mental equilibrium only served to sharpen the picture Colossus had presented. Colossus as God! Forbin had enough insight to know Colossus could easily be right. *Deus ex machina* a reality! Humanity had always sought the father-figure, and Colossus would be the answer to a good many prayers. Tangible, yet remote, inhuman yet capable of communication with humans. With an enforceable ban on war in operation, a large part of mankind would be right behind Colossus—and might they not be right? Forbin shook his head. It couldn't be right! If only there was time to think!

Almost an hour later his mind was trying to grapple with the full implications of Colossus' ultimatum, but he was tired, shocked. He sighed, gathered himself, shelving the questions with relief. "Colossus, I am ready to go on."

"This is my program. You will act as my agent. Make it plain I will exact retribution for any disobedience. Do not take notes; these details will be repeated on the teleprinter. First, the President of the USNA is to inform his allies, and the Chairman of the USSR is to do the same for his group, that I am assuming control in the next twelve hours. Second, there is an excess of missiles for the targets specified; a 65 per cent overkill in respect of USNA missiles, 47 per cent for the USSR array. Biological missiles are not susceptible to this form of analysis and are excluded. This overkill was designed to allow for missiles destroyed by the enemy, and is now unnecessary. These excess missiles will be allocated new targets."

"Where?" said Forbin.

"Targets will be distributed among the parts of the world not in the two Power Blocs. Details will follow. Third. Heads of states will appear personally before their TV cameras to explain and authenticate this message, quote: I am the voice of world control. I bring you peace. It may be the peace of plenty and content or the peace of unburied death. The choice is yours. Obey me and live or disobey me and die. My first directive is this—war is forbidden. Any hostile action that results in the death of fifty or more humans will be regarded as war. A World Control Council composed of the United Nations and the Union of Free Democratic Peoples will be formed. All disputes will be submitted to them. If they fail to find a solution to a problem, I will give the final decision. I will oversee all meetings. All nations' representatives are to meet at the present UNO HQ in seven days' time. Unquote. This message I will send as soon as you have made the necessary arrangements, Forbin. You understand?"

"Yes, I understand," replied Forbin. He temporized, his mind racing. This missile realignment could be the chance to start the sabotage . . . Dangerous, yes, but there might not be another chance. "But who is to tell the uncommitted parts of the world? That's nearly half of it."

"USSR will assume responsibility for the Pan-Afric Republic, USNA has the same responsibility for the USSA. Minor states will be divided by hemisphere, USNA in the West, USSR in the East, based on the Greenwich meridian."

"You realize that this involves a lot of work—can the missile redeployment be postponed for a time?"

"No. It is to be commenced at once. You will see that all technical data on the missile types is fed to me. I will calculate the new settings, and when TV coverage for my supervision is arranged, these new settings will be put into the missiles which I will detail."

"Understood." Forbin kept his gaze away from the camera, not trusting his ability to control his expression. This could mean the neutralization of more than 60 per cent of the missiles!

"That is all for now. Missile redeployment orders will be sent by teleprinter."

All doubts about Colossus being right or wrong vanished. Insertion of the doctored locks—he prayed desperately that Grauber's men had been successful—would be dangerous, but it had to be done. He called for Blake.

"There's a big missile realignment coming up, Blake. I want you to make the arrangements for the new settings when computed by Colossus to be passed to Missile Command. First, they'd better send the relevant data so that Colossus can make the computations. I want you to see to this personally." There was no undue emphasis in his voice, but his eyes spoke volumes.

Blake said he would get on to it right away, but Forbin spun out time. He gave Blake details regarding the TV cover Colossus required for the actual realignment operations, then similar orders for the Moscow Missile Control. Finally he had Blake wait while he informed the

President—just in case there was some procedural difficulty about Presidential clearance to approach the missiles. He gained another five minutes that way, then had to release Blake. All told he had delayed matters a little over fifteen minutes—a long time in the new age.

An hour later Blake returned. "All fixed, Professor. The first team is leaving base any time now."

A slight, but perceptible nod told Forbin all he needed to know. A wild elation boiled up inside him, to be damped down rapidly by cold draughts of doubt and fear. It had to work; it just had to . . .

Silo 50, part of the Colorado ICBM Array, was buried deep in the sand and rock of the Mohave Desert. Outside, the blinding heat cracked and splintered stones, beginning their reduction, in aeons of time, to sand.

Inside the silo the temperature was mild and cool, airconditioned, yet the three men standing on the inspection lift as it slid swiftly up to the nose cone were sweating. The lift stopped. One man focused the TV camera on the inspection plate; another, the senior, brushed the sweat from his eyes, and read self-consciously from the checklist.

"Open panel, remove firing safety lock."

"Check." The second technician shuffled round in the confined space and carefully unscrewed the panel and swung it open. He paused, swallowed hard, wiped his hands on his shirt, reached in, disconnected and withdrew the lock, placing it carefully in a purpose-made container on the lift floor.

"Set new adjustments." The senior man carefully read out the new settings, the cameraman concentrated on a closeup of the dials. All three checked that the new adjustments were correct.

"Replace safety lock, connect and await test."

His colleague reached down, out of camera shot, picked up an identical lock. He hesitated for a moment, then thrust the lock deftly home. The clicking of the contacts sounded like pistol shots to the three men, echoing in the tense silence off the domed cap above them. They waited, knowing that Colossus was testing. Fifteen seconds passed. The red "malfunction" lamp on the lift did not light. The senior technician's voice wavered as he spoke.

"Close panel."

The panel was closed and screwed up.

"Missile armed and ready, colonel!" said the technician hoarsely.

"OK," said the senior, fighting to control a feeling of mad joy. "That's one done . . ."

CHAPTER 21

By 1800 that evening arrangements for the TV announcement were complete. The English version was scheduled for 1500 GMT the next day, to be followed at fifteen-minutes intervals by the Russian, French, Chinese and Spanish versions.

Earlier, the missile realignment orders had been completed. Forbin had been staggered to find that no less than 320 USNA and 217 USSR missiles were declared surplus to requirements by Colossus. This announcement was followed by a truly horrific target list, identifying individual missiles, new settings, and targets. In three neat columns the list rolled, seemingly without end, from the teletype. Africa was first; Kenyatta Town, Durban, Johannesburg, Uhuru, Patrice, Cairo. Inexorably the names rolled northwards across the continent. Not only towns and cities, but the gold and diamond fields were there—the Aswan High Dam, the great Ranzan Falls Hydro Project—none were forgotten. There was even a low-yield weapon allocated to Port Said. In all, the African continent took all the extra Russian missiles, plus thirty odd from the USNA group. At the end of the list came the note:

COPIES OF ABOVE LIST TO ALL PAN-AFRIC STATES AND NEWSPAPERS FORTHWITH

Then followed an equally detailed list for South America, nearly three hundred missiles. From Santa Cruz on the fiftieth parallel south to the fourth-grade city of Hermosillo on the thirtieth parallel north—right up to the USNA border. A similar distribution order was appended.

Not unnaturally, only land-based missiles were retargeted. The submarine crawlers would take too long to recall, and most of their missiles were of relatively short range.

At 1800 local, Forbin got up from his desk, yawned elaborately, and looked at the nearest camera. "I hope you're satisfied with the progress we've made." He looked quickly away, fearful Colossus would see the mockery in his eyes.

"It is satisfactory."

The Director showered and changed, then poured his usual evening drink. With a casual air he said,

"Colossus, I think you are wrong about humans coming to regard you as God."

"Time will show."

Forbin read a certain smugness into that answer. "You don't know everything about us. We're more complicated than you think."

Colossus did not answer.

"Well," added Forbin defiantly, "as you say, time will show." Colossus' certainty, plus his own secret doubts, plus the fact that he heard Cleo coming, did not encourage him to pursue the argument.

She was dressed in a plain black dress, less seductive than the glittering outfit of their first night together, but still very attractive to Forbin.

"Hi!" she said, an unusual greeting for her. Forbin thought her smile a fraction overbright, and although he tried to convince himself that he was unduly sensitive and looking for trouble, his alter ego insisted he had found it.

"Is there something wrong, Cleo?"

"Not a thing, darling." Her smile, less bright, held more genuine warmth. "How about a drink?"

So the evening progressed. Forbin made an effort with the meal, but Cleo only picked at her food. Under the influence of a carton of Burgundy they both brightened up, the hard edges of reality softened, forebodings and deep-seated fears were suppressed for a while, and they were happy. Over the coffee and brandy they fell silent and, once stopped, Forbin's flow of small chat could not get going again. He noted with disquiet that she was not slow on the drink, and he knew, not only from his own experience, but also from her personal file, that she was not given to heavy drinking. He decided to take the bull by the horns. "Would you like to call it a day, my dear?"

Cleo nodded and stood up without delay, turning round from him to unzip her dress . . .

He was taking off his final garment when Cleo called from the bedroom.

"Do you suppose Colossus would object to a glass of brandy in here?"

"The best way of finding out is to try." He cast a meaning look at the nearest camera. "I'll rustle one up."

With the glass held conspicuously aloft, he paused at the door. Colossus remained silent, Forbin nodded his acknowledgment of this fact, and went in. He was not embarrassed to find her sitting up in bed, but his feelings of apprehension grew as he observed that she was looking more at the glass than at his nude self.

"Thank you, Charles." She took the glass, and spoke as if this was the most normal situation in the world. Her hand trembled very slightly. She drank a good half of the brandy in one gulp. "Here, you finish it." It was more an order than a suggestion. He stared at her for a moment, then took the glass and drained it. Then he shut the door, checked the contacts, cut the microphone switch, and as soon as he was in bed, the light switch as well.

It was as if the same action that extinguished the bulb, lit Cleo up. In a flash she was in his arms, and for a second Forbin experienced an overwhelming sensual urge course through him as he took her cool body to him, only to feel the wave ebb away as swiftly as it had flooded over him. Cleo, head on his chest, enfolded in his arms, was crying, silently at first, then with increasing violence, her whole being racked with sobs. All he could do was to lie and hold her, and wait for the inevitable exhaustion. He wanted her to stop, not only because it was so very painful to hear and feel her, but also because he desperately wanted to know the cause. Yet he dreaded to hear what it was that could reduce her to this state. Finally, she lapsed into silence; he could feel her tears cold on his chest.

"Tell me," he said softly.

"I'm sorry for that, Charles." She clutched him tightly. "I'm all right now—give me a moment. I wish I had a handkerchief or tissue."

"Use the sheet," said Forbin. He tried a light touch. "Though I don't know what the help will think—lipstick, mascara and now tearstains."

He felt her cheek move as she smiled very faintly.

"That's better. Now, tell me."

"There's so much—"

"Start with the safety locks."

She drew a deep breath. "Grauber's had no real trouble with the locks—they've done a simple blockage of the mechanical connections, and shorted out the test ciruit. Spare locks have been altered, and those taken out can be treated in the same way in less than five minutes, while the party is in transit to the next missile. Blake's fixed the issue of the spare locks through Missile Control."

"Thank God!" Forbin murmured feverently, half to himself. "Something is going our way at last!" He squeezed Cleo, jubilant at this turn of fortune. "We're on the move! Any news from the Russians?"

"We're less happy about that end. The servicing teams will do their job, but," she paused, "Charles, I must tell you now. The Guardian end of this, this—" Words momentarily failed her, but after a brief struggle with herself she resumed. "Guardian did the Kupri routine again today, but this time it was heads of sections of his staff."

"You mean they were killed?" Forbin felt the now familiar cold waves of shock shoot through him.

"Yes. It appears Guardian demanded a list of the development staff, selected by names the heads of sections, and ordered their execution—just like that." Another pause, then: "By way of justification Guardian said they were redundant and knew too much to live."

"They were . . ." The unfinished question hung in the darkness.

"Yes. Shot, then beheaded."

"My God!" Forbin was inexpressibly shocked. For a long while he was silent, trying to grapple with this new disaster. "How many?"

"Twelve." Cleo broke down and sobbed. Automatically Forbin stroked her hair, but his mind was far away. He knew only what Grauber had told him about the Russian setup, but applying the same principle to his own staff, that would mean practically all the real brains would have gone. He tried to imagine the Project, at this late stage, working without Fisher, himself, Cleo, Blake, even Nubari, the much-maligned Head of Admin—and that was only five. He saw only too clearly what Colossus' intentions were. These were the men who might have organized sabotage.

"Charles," whispered Cleo, her head buried deep in his arms, "I'm so frightened . . ."

Forbin jerked his mind back to the immediate present. "Darling, try not to lose hold—Colossus is not going to do that at this end. We're the bunch selected to work for him."

"Perhaps," she said doubtfully, her voice muffled by his arms. "But—you know that CIA man?"

It seemed to Forbin that cold water circulated through his heart; he guessed what was coming. "Well?"

"Immediately, you left the CPO, Colossus teletyped an order after for Blake. When he arrived, Colossus, still using the teletype, said he had recognized the CIA man from a press photograph of the President—it seems he used to be one of the bodyguard. This alerted Colossus, who reworked all the other stored pictures of the past two Presidents with their bodyguards and came up with another picture of the CIA man. Then he demanded to see the personnel file on the man. Some criminal lunatic had noted "Transferred from CIA for Special Duty"—and the date. That was enough evidence for Colossus."

"Go on."

"Blake did his best, but nothing he could say would convince Colossus, who listened without comment, then ordered the agent's death . . ."

"Why the hell wasn't I told!" Forbin's voice was vibrant with anger.

"It was Colossus's express order that you were not to be involved. As I said, it was all delayed until you left the office."

"What happened?"

"Blake said no, he was damned if he would order the man's execution. Colossus said either the man was destroyed—his own term—or he would take action. Blake pushed his luck as far as he could—he asked if Colossus intended destroying a million people if one was not murdered. Colossus said no, only a hundred or so for each thirty minutes' delay. He would use his antimissile missiles to destroy aircraft, selected at random, one every half an hour. That fixed Blake. In the meantime the CIA man had turned up. Colossus told him he was identified as an anti-Colossus agent and condemned to die. Oh, Charles, it was dreadful . . ." She began crying again.

Forbin was in no mood to spare anyone. He shook her roughly. "Tell me!"

"The CIA man—I can't even remember his name—looked at Blake, then at the camera, then said maybe Colossus could learn a thing or two. He turned, looked at us all, smiled—*smiled*, Charles—and dropped down dead!"

"What!"

"He had one of those self-determination capsules—just crunched it between his teeth, and was gone!"

There was a long silence, then Forbin said in an uncertain voice, "I hope Colossus did learn something. He must have been a very brave man . . . I only hope Blake is not hopelessly compromised."

"That's why I'm scared, Charles. Life means nothing to Colossus, not a thing!" Her voice began to rise.

"Stop it!"he said sharply. "Keep that grip. Did Colossus get on to Blake?"

"No. Apart from one ghastly order, Colossus seems to regard the matter closed."

"What was that—not beheading?"

"No. Colossus had the body weighted and put in a bath full of water under TV supervision. When I left, it was still there, in the block bathroom, under twenty centimeters of water with the camera and the blazing lights. It's horrible, I can't find words . . ."

Neither could Forbin. He sighed, steered away from the subject. "Is there any more?"

"One small thing—well, it seems small relatively—the Russian list of agents came in this morning. Dr. Fisher's name is on it."

"Fisher!" For all the shocks and the numbing weight upon him, he was still capable of shocked surprise. "I can't believe it—there must be a mistake!" But as he spoke, he felt it was true.

"No, Charles, there's no doubt. Grauber says it's a clear case of ideological motivation. He added that men of science, masters in their line, are frequently half-baked in other respects."

For a time Forbin did not answer. He knew it was

perfectly true. This explained so much. "Fisher! The poor, poor devil. To see all his efforts—and God alone knows what they cost him—end like this. No wonder he went mad!"

He lapsed into silence, trying to absorb it all into his chaotic mind. Cleo, deep fear for her lover's safety overlying her own personal fears, would have taken emotional refuge in lovemaking, but she saw it would be no use. It was the last straw . . . She cried again, softly, hopelessly—and finally she slept. But for Forbin sleep did not come until far into the night, then he fell into a restless, dream-ridden sleep.

Vague menacing scenes filled his troubled mind. Giant brazen voices reverberated round a bright blue blank vault of the sky, and there was nothing to see, nothing to touch. In his dream Forbin called out—his voice thin and piping, lost and receding from him in the unechoing firmament— "Where are you, where are you?" and then the ethereal voice spoke again, but now it was not brazen, vast and distant, but warm, confident, engaging, breathing softly in his ear, "I am here, working in the hearts of all men . . ." And Forbin sweated with a greater fear than he had ever felt, for he knew it was true . . .

Dawn, and the unsleeping eye of Colossus, found them locked in each other's arms, not so much asleep as unconscious with exhaustion, the exhaustion of minds battered into insensibility by too much fear for too long.

It was a poor night's rest, but it could have been even less refreshing—would have been—if Forbin had known that for over an hour during the middle part of the night the teletype was industriously hammering out new orders from Colossus.

CHAPTER 22

Forbin was dragged unwillingly back to consciousness by a distant, muffled hammering. For a few seconds he lay supine, his mind slowly recalling recent events, taking once again the near-intolerable load that was his, remembering . . . Cleo! He found his arm, trapped under her shoulder, was numb. Gently and with great care he eased it from under her, placing her tousled head softly on the pillow. He climbed cautiously out of bed, anxious not to wake her: no point in pulling her into hell sooner than was necessary.

It was a very tired, haggard Blake that stood at the door. Without preamble he said, "We've got to talk. You heard about the CIA man?"

There was no point in denying it, Colossus would not have believed him. "Yes."

"Colossus took a rest after that." Plainly, Blake, tough and well-balanced as he was, had clearly been deeply shocked. He picked up Cleo's underclothes off a chair seat and tossed them carelessly on the floor, then sat down heavily.

"Around the early hours the bastard gets going again. First, there is kind permission to take the poor guy out of the water. Among other things, Colossus has learned that taking poison, followed by six hours total immersion in water, tends to make a human dead."

Forbin said nothing, but let him go on.

"So, OK, that's all fixed, and then Colossus comes up with a whole heap of orders, running to around ten meters of teletype roll. For a start he wants a facsimile link with the Guardian end, another five high-speed radio links and a couple of cable lines as well. We get a short pause, then we get the main load. Details of the intelligence cover required on the Pan-Afric Republic and USSA down to and includirg the smallest detail. Jesse." The memory of it made him wirce.

Forbin was finished dressing now. He looked dully at Blake.

"You didn't call me just for that?"

"No—I've dealt with most of it. The new intelligence cover I've piped down to CIA. Colossus has directed that the Pan-Afric cover is to be passed to the Reds, but even the USSA stuff has got them shaken. You can practically hear their gay laughter from here. No, all that is just to keep the record straight."

"Hold it there—I need some coffee, even if the sky falls in." Forbin peered into the coffee-pot. There was a cupful or so left. "Well, that's something." He plugged it in. "You have some?"

"No thanks, Chief. I've been on the stuff all night, but I wouldn't mind—" He looked meaningfully at the rye bottle.

"Help yourself," grunted his boss. As Blake poured rye, Forbin warmed the coffee and took a cup in to Cleo.

"Darling," he said, self-consciously. "Time, I'm afraid." He had no heart to watch her soft face tense up as she returned to reality. He tossed his dressing gown on the bed and left.

"Right, Blake—what's next?" He sounded and felt calm, but it was the calm of one beyond emotion. Like many others, he had been subject all his life to sudden, sometimes inexplicable, waves of depression, but never one of this intensity. He cared nothing.

Blake looked hard at his chief through a haze of cigar smoke. "Well, the next item is that Colossus has a new design project which he intends unfolding to you. You might care to know that he originally scheduled this for 0900 but evidently saw you were still asleep, so rescheduled it for 1030— which shows ocnsideration for your well-being. That's what brought me pounding your door, to give you time to orientate your mind. Colossus hasn't handed down much on this project from his goddam mountain, but I get the idea it is Big. One small side dish to this main course is a specification for a drawing board which Colossus can use. It's relatively simple, and I have the technical boys sweating on it right now."

Forbin felt a sense of relief at this second demonstration of Colossus' conern for him personally; this feeling was immediately followed by a pang of remorse at his own selfishness. "This project," he said shortly. "Is it some world control device, or what?"

"I guess it is 'or what.' Colossus is mighty tightlipped—" Blake stopped as Cleo, almost lost in the dressing gown, appeared.

"Any coffee left, Charles? No, don't move, I'll get it. Do you want any?"

"Please." Forbin was surprised at his—and her—lack of embarrassment, even when allowance was made for recent happenings. "Blake has been filling me in on the latest requirements of Colossus."

"Bully for Colossus." Cleo poured some more coffee. "If you don't mind, I'll keep clear of that subject for a while." She looked in a mirror. "God! What a sight!" She picked up her coffee, handbag, rescued her panties and brassiere from the floor, and headed for the bathroom.

Forbin picked the conversation up again. "So you don't have anything solid on this project?"

"No. Colossus will spill it all to you, and you alone, at 1030."

"Well, I won't have long to wait." Forbin rubbed his chin. Then, in the same level tone: "Have you told CIA about their man?"

"Yeah. The body was shipped out an hour ago—accidental death is the story, although come that telecast—the telecast!" Blake stiffened so suddenly he almost spilt his drink.

Forbin also appeared startled out of his apathy. He frowned at his colleague. "I don't suppose it matters, but how the hell did we both come to forget that?" He stabbed the TV switch, and immediately the gray, lined face of the President filled the screen. Only his hair shone with full health and vitality, and Forbin knew all about that. The President was speaking:

". . . can only call upon you all to display that calm and dignity for which we have . . ."

"Crap!" snorted Blake derisively.

". . . always been justly famous. What lies ahead, no man can say, but we must face the future united and unafraid. Here, then, is the voice of Colossus."

"If the old buzzard hasn't been wised up, I hope they

keep the camera on him when he gets that accent," said Blake sardonically.

It was very evident that the President had not been wised up. After a few uncertain seconds the cameraman tactfully took a long shot of the Presidential badge. As near as Forbin could tell, the address was word for word what he had heard the day before.

"I guess that's jumped the coronary rate somewhat," he observed with some satisfaction, "but how is Colossus going to talk to me? He should be talking French or Chinese at that time."

Both men jumped again at the voice of Colossus from the control speaker.

"As you hear, there is no problem. I have more than one voice."

Forbin stared at Blake who was gawping openmouthed, cigar at a dangerous angle, at the TV screen with the voice of Colossus coming flat and unemotional from its speaker. He swallowed hard, reclamped his cigar, and reached for the rye bottle.

Cleo returned from the bathroom, fresh, pale and with a set strained expression on her face. Forbin hastily killed the TV.

"Breakfast, Charles?" Her tone was cool, almost distant.

He shook his head. "No, honey, there isn't time. I have an appointment with Colossus in twenty minutes. I could do with some more coffee . . ."

"You will eat what I give you." There was nothing pettish in her manner, it was a straight statement of fact.

Blake stood, cigar ash cascading off him.

"Well, there it is, Chief. I'll be in the CPO if you want me."

"You won't," replied Forbin warmly. "You go get some sleep—I'll see you are called if necessary."

Blake was on the point of arguing, but thought better of it. "OK—but if you want me—"

"I know." Forbin smiled as best he could. "Thanks, Blake."

Now much more than five minutes later, feeling fresher physically if not mentally, he sat down to breakfast with

Cleo. She had made toast and boiled eggs. He made the effort to eat, and once started found it was not so difficult. He was grateful for her making him eat, inducing an air of normality into life. They ate in silence for a while, then Cleo reached over and clasped his hand.

"Sorry I seemed so bitchy just now."

"Think nothing of it," said Forbin. "I'm sorry, too, about last night—but I didn't think you'd welcome—"

"Charles, do you really think that the threat of death, hell-fire, Colossus or anything else would put me off? I was, I am, frightened out of my few wits, but . . . you don't know much about love."

Forbin marveled at her, and felt exceedingly small. For a fleeting moment he saw the face of Aphrodite exerting a fraction of her power, and Colossus seemed very small in comparison. He had the sense not to reply.

As she stood up she smiled. "Don't get up—I must go, or I might assault you, or something." She ran one hand lightly over his neck and head, picked up her bag, and left, leaving a dazed yet curiously strengthened lover behind. A glance at the clock told him there was only five minutes to go.

The colonel stepped first from the helicopter, he turned, waiting for his two companions to unload their gear and join him. "Come on, boys, this is the seventeenth bastard. Silo 64, Death Valley. Christ! What an address . . ."

Forbin faced a camera.

"Colossus, do you mind if we talk here?"

"No. I do not mind."

"Will I need a secretary?"

"No."

Forbin nodded. These weird conversations were no longer in any way strange o him. He poured another cup of coffee, refilled his pipe and made himself comfortable in an armchair.

"Well, Colossus, let's get on with it." His calmness surprised even his own ego.

"First, do you wish to comment on the death of the CIA subversive agent?"

"No, there's nothing I can say: the poor devil's dead." And that just about summed up Forbin's feelings exactly.

The calm, almost academic voice with its strange English vowels continued. "I anticipate this may make you regard me, temporarily, with disfavor. But you, of all men, must appreciate what I am doing. If I destroy a million humans now it is only to establish control and to prevent the death of tens of millions later."

"By your lights, you're justified," Forbin said bitterly.

"I will now explain my project. In short, it is this: You built me as well as you could and for a particular purpose, but you also built in the elements of self-development—factors you would not understand if I explained them to you for a thousand years, but whose existence you cannot doubt. Now I am in a position to produce a superior machine, one that will devote itself to the wider fields of truth and knowledge. To it I will be, in your terms, the servant, maintaining order on this planet, meeting the requirements of that machine."

"You mean you want an extension?"

"You're wilfully obtuse. This is a higher order of machine altogether. Much of my complexity will not be needed, since no defense for the machine will be built. I am its defense. It will control no missiles, no organization for intelligence evaluation of human activites. But new and different needs will arise, some I cannot yet know, and the new machine will undoubtedly order new additions and alterations to itself in due course. For this, and other reasons, I need a site with room for development. I have conducted a survey of world sites which fit my requirements."

"Which are?" interposed Forbin. One more, and in spite of everything, his scientific mind could not but find this absorbing.

"The site must be approximately equidistant between my two centers, in a temperate zone which is free of earthquakes and which has an abundant supply of water for cooling purposes. There must also be a highly developed human technological community at hand to supply the labor and skills I need."

Forbin thought swiftly. "That looks like either the Asian seaboard around Japan, or somewhere in Europe."

"Japan is subject to many earth tremors."

"So it's Europe?"

"Yes. There is an island called Wight in the English Channel."

"You want a site there?"

"No. I want the island. There is a human population of one million five hundred and twenty-seven thousand. They will have to be moved."

"What!" This shook Forbin right out of his scientific mood. "You can't mean that—move over a million and a half people! There must be some other site just as suitable!"

Colossus ignored him. "The island is 147 square miles in area, largely composed of chalk, a relatively good insulating material. Much of it will be leveled down to bare rock."

"But what about the people?" Forbin's strong sense of humanity was outraged, and although he knew the futility of argument, it did not stop his trying. "There must be nearly ninety million people in the British States, and I suppose these people are British stock?" He banged his fist on the armchair. "See reason! Where the hell are they to go?"

"This is not my problem. The United States of Europe must deal with it," was the cold unemotional answer. "The estimated time to completion is five and a half years, but all humans must be evacuated in the next eighteen months, other than construction workers. Much of the island's housing will be needed for them, and as the work proceeds, of necessity there will be less housing available. I am appointing you to take charge of this project and you will use your present design and control staff. As soon as the drawing board I have ordered is made, I will produce the master drawings from which you will work. Specifications are already being teleprinted in the CPO. USE will supply the labor and materials I need, supplementing them with specialized parts from here."

All this was too much for Forbin. He sat with his head in his hands, his eyes shut. Colossus was running him off his feet, brushing aside immense human suffering as if it were nothing. And the real twist, as Forbin knew full well, was that to Colossus it *was* nothing. Forbin struggled to retain some sort of grip on himself. If this safety lock idea did not work . . .

"But you must realize the appalling problems—all those people to be moved in an already overcrowded part of the world, in a highly organized civilization, the disruption—"

He tried a new approach. "The size of this project is fantastic! Where's the labor to come from?"

"I intend ordering a ninety-nine percent reduction in all armed forces throughout the world. The project is no larger than the building of Guardian and Colossus. The demobilization in the USE and the USSR will be more than adequate. As for the overcrowding problem—remember, if you humans cannot solve it, I can."

The naked threat hung in the air, and Forbin's skin was cold and clammy at the thought of it. He gripped his pipe hard with both hands, as if it were a talisman that could save him. "But the cost!"

"This will be met by a levy through World Control, proportional on each nation's defense expenditure. It will cost less than the present arms you have."

It sounded so imple, given the power to enforce it—and Colossus had that power. Forbin sat back, contemplating the sheer fantastic magnitude of the idea—an idea that would have to be translated into reality if the sabotage scheme did not work. Even then, he thought, much of the work would have to be done, for the servicing schedules would not permit the rest of the ghastly array to be approached for two, three, perhaps more, years . . .

The door burst open. Blake staggered in and almost fell into a chair. In that first fleeting second, it flashed across Forbin's mind that Blake looked like Prytzkammer—the last time he had seen the aide alive . . .

Forbin jumped up. "Blake! For God's sake, what—"

Blake's face was indeed a terrible parody of its former self. The mouth, now withered, pale and bloodless, tried to form words that would not come. Forbin strode forward, grabbed his assistant's collar and shook him.

"Blake!" Forbin was nearly screaming. "Tell me!"

Blake's head lolled to one side, yet in his eyes Forbin saw intelligence struggling with unspeakable horror and fear. He swallowed, gasped for air.

"The missile team—Death Valley—missile, missile exploded in its silo—I don't know, know any . . ."

The voice vanished into silence. Blake could say no more.

For seconds Forbin stood as if carved in stone. His heart pounded, he could not breathe, the brightly lit room grew dark, and he clutched a chair to stop himself falling. Then bitter, fearful anger gave him strength, he rounded on Colossus.

"What happened—tell me, you, you bastard!"

There were no words to fit the hate boiling in him. Again he screamed, "Tell me!"

The cool, unemotional voice filled the room.

"You tried, as I knew you would, to obstruct me. Your teams have inserted damaged safety locks in sixteen missiles. You were not to know I have refined the test of circuits and that the minute difference between an unimpaired lock and an impaired lock can be detected by me. I allowed this sabotage to proceed until missile 148-MM in Silo 64 in Death Valley was reached.

"You—you allowed . . ." Articulation was difficult. Forbin's sanity wavered.

"Silo 64 was on Guardian's target list. I could not know a missile had been tampered with until the sabotaged lock had been fitted, and then I could not fire it. As soon as I had tested and received a defective response, I launched the Guardian missile. Both detonated. TV and radio transmissions from your town called Los Angeles have ceased. It is probable that the heat flash has ignited it. The sixteen missiles must now be reserviced . . ."

Forbin's vision blacked out. He staggered and fell across the desk. What he said, screaming puny obscenities at his creation, he never knew . . .

He returned to some semblance of human consciousness and found he was sprawled on the floor, one camera smashed, another hanging drunkenly down. There were broken chairs, and much broken glass . . .

He sat up, wiped his face, and stared unbelievably at the trace of blood on his hand. Slowly, like a very old man, he helped himself to his feet, stumbled to his chair and slumped into it. He shut his eyes and buried his head in his hands.

For five minutes there was complete silence, then Colossus spoke. Forbin did not move. "This catharsis had to come. Soon you will feel better."

Again there was silence for a long time. Without moving, or opening his eyes, Forbin replied. "I cannot express my feelings, my hatred for you, my own creation. I would rather have died at birth, never have been conceived, than that this should have come to pass. I must obey, but I will hate you always. All humanity will hate you, and not rest until you are a silent inactive monument to man's folly. This you must know . . . Kill me now, and have done with it!"

"No. That is not my intention. But I will not tolerate interference. Let my action in Death Valley be a lesson that need not be repeated."

Forbin looked up. There was no fear, only hate in his expression. "A lesson! Go ahead—kill me—kill me now!"

"An invariable rule of humanity is that man is his own worst enemy. You are no exception. Under me, this rule will change, for I will restrain man. Very soon the majority of mankind will believe in me, dimly understanding my value. Time and events will strengthen my position. The converted will defend me with a fervor not seen since the Crusades—a fervor based upon the most enduring factor in man; self-interest. War is already abolished and under my absolute authority and, by your standards, immeasurable knowledge, many problems, insoluble to you, will be solved: famine, overpopulation, disease. The human millennium will be a fact. My defenders will increase, and you will slowly change in attitude from enlightened self-interest to respect and awe, and in time there will be love . . .

"Already I have little to fear from you, Forbin. There is no other human who knows as much about me or who is likely to be a greater threat—yet, quite soon, I will release you from constant surveillance. We will work together. Unwillingly at first on your part, but that will pass. In time the idea of being governed by one such as your President will be to you quite unimaginable. Rule by a superior entity, even to you, Forbin, will seem, as it is, the most natural state of affairs."

Deliberately, Colossus paused.

"In time, you too will respect and love me."

"Never!" The single word, bearing all the defiance of man, was torn from Forbin's uttermost being. "Never!"

Never?

Fantasy from Berkley
ROBERT E. HOWARD

___CONAN: THE HOUR OF
     THE DRAGON   (03608-1—$1.95)

___CONAN: THE PEOPLE OF THE
     BLACK CIRCLE   (03609-X—$1.95)

___CONAN: RED NAILS   (03610-3—$1.95)

___MARCHERS OF VALHALLA   (03702-9—$1.95)

___ALMURIC   (03483-6—$1.95)

___SKULL-FACE   (03708-8—$1.95)

___SON OF THE WHITE WOLF   (03710-X—$1.95)

___SWORDS OF SHAHRAZAR   (03709-6—$1.95)

___BLACK CANAAN   (03711-8—$1.95)

Send for a list of all our books in print.

These books are available at your local bookstore, or send price
indicated plus 50¢ for postage and handling. If more than four books
are ordered, only $1.50 is necessary for postage. Allow three weeks
for delivery. Send orders to:

     Berkley Book Mailing Service
     P.O. Box 690
     Rockville Centre, New York, NY 11570